MURDER ON A BUS TOUR

DAWN BROOKES

Storm
PUBLISHING

Ebook ISBN: 978-1-80508-947-6
Paperback ISBN: 978-1-80508-948-3

Cover design: Emily Courdelle
Cover images: Shutterstock

Published by Storm Publishing.
For further information, visit:
www.stormpublishing.co

ALSO BY DAWN BROOKES

Lady Marjorie Snellthorpe Mysteries

Murder at the Opera House

Murder in the Highlands

Murder at the Christmas Market

Murder at a Wimbledon Mansion

Murder in a Care Home

Murder at the Regatta

Murder on Holy Island

Death of a Blogger (prequel novella)

Rachel Prince Mysteries

A Cruise to Murder

Deadly Cruise

Killer Cruise

Dying to Cruise

A Christmas Cruise Murder

Murderous Cruise Habit

Honeymoon Cruise Murder

A Murder Mystery Cruise

Hazardous Cruise

Captain's Dinner Cruise Murder

Corporate Cruise Murder

Treacherous Cruise Flirtation

Toxic Cruise Cocktail

Cruise into Darkness

Carlos Jacobi PI

Body in the Woods

The Bradgate Park Murders

The Museum Murders

Memoirs

Hurry up Nurse: Memoirs of nurse training in the 1970s

Hurry up Nurse 2: London calling

Hurry up Nurse 3: More adventures in the life of a student nurse

ONE

Marjorie Snellthorpe jolted awake as the train lurched around a bend, her neck stiff from hours spent on a narrow bed. The rhythmic movement of wheels on tracks had lulled her into a fitful sleep. She blinked, momentarily disoriented by the unfamiliar landscape sliding past, before remembering with a small thrill of anticipation – she was on the overnight service from Paddington to Okehampton, the first leg of her journey to the coastal town of Bude, where the true holiday would begin.

She was thankful for the precious few hours of sleep she had caught. The knowledge that her friend and co-traveller, Frederick Mackworth, was in the room next door gave her a comforting sense of security.

Marjorie swung her legs over the side of the narrow bed, her feet finding the floor as she stood carefully, steadying herself to match the swaying of the train. After a refreshing wash, she dressed in the travel outfit she had put out the night before: a practical knee-length navy wool skirt, a crisp white blouse and dark navy cardigan. She slipped her feet into her flat-heeled walking shoes and brushed her hair. Feeling prepared for the day, she stepped into the corridor and negotiated the moving train's rhythm before knocking on Frederick's door. He answered immediately, already wearing one of his signature bold checked shirts and a clashing tie. His bald head shone as though he'd just added moisturiser.

The wrinkles around his light grey eyes crinkled. "Good morning, Marjorie. How did you sleep?"

"Considering we were rattling through the countryside at great speed, I'd say not bad, thank you. Obviously, it's never the same as sleeping in one's own bed, but it's not a bad way to travel and the bed was reasonably comfortable. How about you?"

"I hardly slept a wink, Marjorie, but I won't complain, I'm still glad we caught the train. I don't envy Horace driving Edna down yesterday, even if they were going to stop halfway."

Marjorie didn't envy Horace either, but it had nothing to do with driving. The idea of spending endless hours in a car with Edna would be enough to make her regret agreeing to the holiday. She had grown fond of her cousin-in-law and enjoyed being with her, just as long as it wasn't too often, and not too enclosed.

"Do we have time for breakfast?" Frederick drew her from her musings.

"Yes, I got ready to give us the opportunity to eat before the train stops."

"There are advantages to being in first class," said Frederick, with a wry smile.

Unlike Marjorie, Frederick normally travelled economy and bought the cheapest tickets available. She felt guilty about browbeating him into conceding that an overnight journey warranted a little more comfort, but he seemed happy enough. "Quite. Are you ready?"

"Yes," he said, stepping into the corridor.

Every seat in the dining car appeared to be occupied. The conductor greeted them with a courteous smile.

"Would you mind sharing?" he asked, gesturing to two vacant seats opposite a couple.

"Not at all," said Marjorie.

The couple appeared to be in their early fifties and steaming cups of coffee sat on the table in front of them. The place setting remained laid ready for food, suggesting they hadn't yet eaten breakfast.

"This is Mr and Mrs Carlisle," the guard said. "This is Lady Snellthorpe and Mr Mackworth."

There was a slight pause before the man raised two huge bushy eyebrows to look at them while the woman offered a reluctant nod, one hand wrapped around her cup.

"Please call me Marjorie," said Marjorie, shuffling in to the window seat.

"And Frederick," her companion added with a nod to the couple.

"I'll bring you some tea," said the conductor, leaving them.

Marjorie studied the couple opposite, noticing how they communicated through glances rather than words – a raised eyebrow from him, a slight shake of the head from her. Mr Carlisle's eyes were barely visible beneath the bushy eyebrows, and he sported an equally bushy, dyed brown moustache. It was almost as if the brows and moustache were compensating for his thinning hair. He wore a pale blue polo shirt beneath a V-neck jumper. Mrs Carlisle had dyed auburn hair and a beauty spot on her left cheek. She sat elegantly, drinking her coffee and perusing a fashion magazine, barely glancing at Marjorie or Frederick.

The friendly conductor brought them two pots of tea. Marjorie poured herself a cup of Earl Grey, and Frederick helped himself to standard breakfast tea. Marjorie put milk in the cup before pouring tea from a pot, whereas Frederick added his afterwards. She found it surprising she hadn't noticed this before, dismissing the notion that she might be less observant than she liked to think. Marjorie sipped her tea while looking out of the window reflecting on the many pots of tea she and her late husband Ralph had shared together. It never failed to amaze her how a simple task like drinking a cup of tea could trigger such memories: decades of happiness had ended so suddenly with Ralph's death. Sometimes these memories brought sadness, and at others it made her appreciate the marriage they'd had, and the new friendships she had formed.

The train raced through the countryside, and despite it being still dark, it wasn't difficult to imagine the beauty they were speeding past. She squinted to see if she could capture any details.

"I wish it were lighter," she said to no-one in particular.

"We were saying that earlier," Mr Carlisle's voice boomed over the clattering train. "Weren't we, Naomi?"

"Mm," said the woman named Naomi, with a noncommittal air.

The man opposite eyed them with dark grey eyes that peeked through the thickened brows. His eyes were dull compared to Frederick's light grey eyes that sparkled when he laughed. Being mid-October, the mornings were getting darker, although the forecast for today promised a bright, autumnal day once the sun broke through the ashen sky.

Her thoughts shifted from their breakfast companions and she let her mind wander to the Cornish coastline they would soon be exploring.

The conductor returned to take breakfast orders. Marjorie asked for a bowl of fresh fruit salad, while Frederick decided that toast and a pot of marmalade would be in order. The Carlisles ordered full English breakfasts with little attempt at politeness.

Following the conductor's departure, an awkward silence settled over them once more. Naomi returned to perusing her magazine, and the man focussed more on hiding behind his eyebrows and moustache than on acknowledging their presence.

A family at the next table engaged in an animated discussion of their holiday plans. Unlike the family, Marjorie and Frederick were going to spend the entire breakfast in stilted or non-existent conversation with the couple opposite. She watched Naomi flipping the magazine pages, barely spending enough time on any to take in the contents.

Frederick attempted to draw them into conversation. He looked at the man. "Have you been to Cornwall before? Sorry, I didn't catch your name."

The man once more lifted his eyebrows. "No, this is our first time. The name's Stan. We're taking a seven-day tour of the coast, starting in Bude."

"Oh, what a coincidence," said Marjorie. "That's what we're doing, isn't it, Frederick?" She hoped the unfriendly couple weren't joining the same tour, but something told her they were.

Naomi yawned. "I'll be glad to get started. I hate trains, we barely slept a wink."

Marjorie could believe it as Naomi must have needed an age to apply a full face of thick makeup on a moving train. When she lifted her eyes from the magazine, they were a striking green colour. She wore an autumnal ochre red dress that clung tight to some midriff bulges.

"At least we'll arrive at our destination soon," said Marjorie. "Are you joining the All Weathers tour?"

"Yes," said Stan, showing more interest. "You as well?"

"We are," said Frederick.

"Do you know any of the people on the tour?" Naomi's question came across clipped and accusatory.

"We're meeting two of our friends," said Frederick. "They drove down, and are bringing most of our luggage. At least we haven't had the hassle of trying to lug suitcases on and off British transport."

"Where are you from?" asked Stan, shooting his wife a warning glance as she opened her mouth, ready to fire another question.

"I live in London," said Marjorie, "Frederick lives in Bath. Edna, who we're meeting, hails from Harrogate and Horace... well, he has property everywhere. How about you?"

Naomi gave a sigh, as if relieved, but Marjorie had no idea why that should be.

"We live in Cambridge," Stan replied.

Breakfasts arrived, interrupting the brief conversation. Stan and Naomi began tucking into their fry-ups in perfect synchronicity that Marjorie thought spoke of deep intimacy. They no longer attempted to chat. Every so often, the couple exchanged glances as if sharing some quiet secret. Marjorie hoped they would be more friendly and relaxed once the official tour started.

The tour party was due to stay at a hotel in Bude overnight, giving them the day to explore the Cornish town. The official minibus journey would begin the next morning. Marjorie and her friends knew the tour leader, Faith Weathers from previous holidays: a capable guide who had set up her own tour company in partnership with an old friend. Marjorie suspected the man had become Faith's life partner, as well as her business partner. Their business had grown and offered tours all over the United Kingdom.

They hadn't seen Faith since she and her partner, Nick, had helped them deal with an awkward group of people Marjorie's son had asked her to host for the Christmas season a few years ago. Faith had stepped in and taken the group on tours of London.

When Stan finished his breakfast, he placed his knife and fork down on his plate. Naomi finished at the same time and looked up at Marjorie. Her eyelids were painted with a reddish colour, attempting to match the dress but not quite succeeding – a bit like Frederick's ties.

"So, you're a lady then?"

Marjorie sighed. It wasn't the first time her title had drawn unwanted attention. "Yes, that's quite correct. But I prefer to be called by my given name, Marjorie."

"Is this your husband?" Naomi asked bluntly. Why did her questioning sound more like an inquisition than a natural conversation? Marjorie found it mildly irritating that Naomi hadn't listened to the conductor when he introduced her and Frederick with different surnames, or when she had explained where they lived.

"Frederick and I are friends. My husband died some years back. I mentioned before that we're meeting two other friends who we often travel with."

"I suppose your husband was a lord."

Marjorie's patience was wearing thin, and she felt Frederick stiffen as he moved his plate to one side, making more noise than necessary.

"Yes, Ralph had a title." *Although it's none of your business,* she would have liked to have said.

Frederick appeared to have had enough of this line of conversation so addressed Stan. "What about you? Do you work?"

Naomi glared at Frederick, clearly not happy to be thrown off her unusual questioning style. Was there a hint of fear in her eyes?

Stan cleared his throat, giving the impression he was reluctant to answer but Naomi took over.

"We took early retirement." She and Stan exchanged another secretive glance.

Marjorie finished eating the remaining fruit, and recognising Frederick's tension, she placed her handbag on her lap.

"If you'll excuse us, we need to get ready for when the train stops. I expect we'll see you at the hotel."

"Hopefully not," Frederick said when they reached the corridor out of earshot of the eccentric couple. "Why do we always meet strange people? Weirdos, Edna will call them," he said.

"I doubt we'll see too much of them, and if we do, perhaps they'll be more relaxed. Let's assume they're tired. He didn't seem too bad once he got talking."

"Hmm." Frederick didn't sound convinced.

"Edna and Horace are good at bringing people out of themselves. I'm sure they'll be able to manage them," she added.

"Let's hope so, or this could be a miserable holiday before we even start."

Marjorie sighed. Unfortunately, Frederick, though a close friend, tended to see things through more negative lenses than the rest of them. He could be broody if left to his own devices. Most of the time, he was good company, and as soon as they were more rested and checked into the hotel, she felt certain his outlook would improve.

"Let's think positively. The group includes ten travellers, twelve with Faith and Nick. There's no reason we have to spend much time with Stan and Naomi Carlisle. Perhaps she's one of those people who doesn't cope well on little sleep."

"I wonder what they did for a living," Frederick said. "They were sheepish about that, secretive almost."

"Yes, that was rather odd. I wondered the same thing. Usually, people are in a hurry to tell you what they do, or did, for a living. It's a good way of opening up a conversation, but it clearly wasn't something they wanted to discuss. I bet Horace gets it out of them. And if he doesn't, Edna will," said Marjorie. "And in Edna, I think Mrs Naomi Carlisle will meet her match," she added, chuckling.

Frederick's smile widened. "You're right, if anyone can put that woman in her place, it'll be Edna."

Marjorie hoped there wouldn't be any conflict during their tour of Cornwall. She had been looking forward to it since they'd separated after the Henley Regatta. This trip was Edna's idea, something to tick off her bucket list.

"I understand autumn is one of the best times to tour the Cornwall coast," said Marjorie.

"Yes, I heard that too, and because it's off-season, fewer tourists, which is a bonus, apparently the summer months are horrendous in the best spots. I bought a guidebook, and I've been reading all about Cornwall and its history. We're visiting some amazing places. The views along the rugged coastline will be second to none."

Pleased to be on safer ground, Marjorie nodded. "I just need to pop the last few items into my overnight bag. I'll join you when the train stops in Okehampton."

As if reading her mind, an announcement came over the intercom: the train would arrive at their last station in five minutes.

"Those changing for Bude, please be advised it's a fifteen-minute walk," the announcer continued. The next part of the journey would mean taking a bus. Marjorie and Frederick had already agreed to take a taxi to the bus stop. Had the Carlisles been more pleasant, she would have offered to share the fare.

"I wonder what this week has in store?" Marjorie mused out loud as she gathered her belongings. *Hopefully, not murder*, an inner voice replied.

TWO

Frederick's stride slowed until he came to a dead stop right in front of Marjorie. She assumed the weight of their overnight bags, which he had gallantly insisted on carrying, was causing him problems. He wasn't as fit as their athletic friend Horace, but his pride wouldn't let him admit it, so Marjorie had accepted the chivalrous offer.

"Would you like me to take my bag?" she offered, noting his reddening face.

"What? Oh, no. It's not that," he replied, his voice difficult to hear over the cacophony of train announcements echoing around the station. He leaned closer. "It's them." He nodded his head in a forward direction.

Marjorie's eyes followed his gaze, until they landed on Stan and Naomi Carlisle, standing on the opposite side of the ticket barrier, locked in a serious conversation. She also noticed a ticket collector eyeing her and Frederick with a furrowed brow and a hint of suspicion.

"We should keep moving, Frederick. Standing here makes us look suspicious. If we're not careful, that man is going to have us searched by the transport police."

Frederick's jaw dropped. "You can't be serious?"

"One can't be too careful these days, and he looks like he means business. Anyway, the Carlisles are moving on. Are you sure you wouldn't like me to carry my bag?"

"Absolutely not. I've got it. Come on." Marjorie sometimes marvelled at the male ego. Frederick's blood pressure was clearly rising from the way his face became redder with every step, yet he ploughed forward.

"At least extend the handle and use the wheels," she suggested.

"Oh? I forgot these modern bags have wheels." His shoulders relaxed, and a faint smile appeared on his lips as he followed her advice. After taking a deep breath, his steps became lighter and more assured. Frederick picked up the pace, and they passed through the barriers without issue. The guard who had been watching them was preoccupied, dealing with someone who didn't appear to have the correct ticket. Perhaps the man had thought, like she did, that Frederick was just struggling with their luggage. Though Marjorie shared Frederick's eagerness to avoid running into Stan and Naomi again, she was keen to reach Bude. If the couple decided to travel to the bus stop by taxi, they would just have to accept it.

At that moment, Marjorie heard a familiar voice.

"Over here, Marge!"

Both she and Frederick turned towards the clarion call. Marjorie saw Edna and Horace hurrying across the concourse. Never had Marjorie felt so pleased to see her cousin-in-law, who emerged just as trouble might be brewing. The whirlwind that was Edna Parkinton could be unnerving at times, but on this occasion the uncontainable spirit propelling forward was comical, and a delight to behold. So much so, that, had Marjorie been the hugging kind, she would have wrapped her arms around her. Instead, she watched in horror as Edna closed in with alarming speed. It seemed she had no such misgivings about public displays of affection, ploughing into Marjorie with all the subtlety of a locomotive.

"Thank goodness we found you!" Edna said, pulling Marjorie into what might have been a warm embrace had the whole thing not felt so awkward.

Marjorie cast a desperate glance at Horace, who stopped just short of them. Hoping she would be released soon, she stood stiffly. Edna took the hint and let her go.

"Hello, Marjorie." Horace leaned down and kissed her on the cheek, a much preferable greeting. "It's good to see you."

"We thought we'd missed you. Horace hadn't considered how busy the roads are from Bude to here."

"Well, we couldn't be happier to see you two," said Frederick, shaking Horace's hand enthusiastically and giving Edna a smile.

Edna caught on, her brown eyes twinkling with mischief beneath the false lashes. "That's very welcoming coming from you, Fred. Was the train not cosy with your—"

"Don't spoil it," Marjorie interrupted, sensing Edna could be about to suggest something unwelcome like 'your Marge'. She had a knack of dropping hints with the subtlety of a bulldozer ploughing through rubble. "This is a wonderful surprise, though. You've spared us from another hour of public transport. The last part of a journey always seems to be the longest."

"I know what you mean," said Edna. "It was such a long drive from north to south yesterday."

"I thought you were breaking your journey in the West Country?" Frederick said.

"We were," explained Horace, "but Edna wanted to spend a night in Bude, which is why we could collect you this morning."

Frederick's grey eyes sparkled with delight. "Very lucky for us."

"Do you need a hot drink before we leave?" Horace asked, stroking his neatly groomed moustache.

"We've not long had breakfast, but if you would like something, we're happy to oblige," Marjorie replied.

"Good," said Edna, "because I'm parched, not to mention I want to know why you're both overjoyed to see us. You don't fool me, Fred." She gave Frederick a knowing look.

OVER CUPS of tea and coffee, Edna's interrogation began while wolfing down an enormous toasted teacake slathered with jam and butter. "Come on then. Out with it."

Marjorie spoke for Frederick, who was prone to fumbling for words under Edna's scrutinising gaze. She made him nervous. "If you must know – as well as being delighted to see you both – we are rather keen to avoid bumping into a couple we met over breakfast."

"Too lovey-dovey, eh?" said Horace, winking.

"Get your mind out of the gutter, Horace Tyler, or you'll be going back to Bude on your own."

Marjorie didn't point out how ludicrous that sounded when Horace was the one with the transport, so she continued. "I don't mean to sound mean-spirited but they were odd."

"Odd how?" Edna quizzed.

"I've been trying to think how to describe them. Sneaky – that's it, they appeared sneaky."

"And the woman, Naomi, was downright rude and impertinent about Marjorie's title," Frederick added.

Edna raised an eyebrow. "You don't mention your title unless you need to."

Sometimes Marjorie's title came in handy when required to disarm people. "I'm afraid the conductor did it for me."

"What makes you think you would see them again, anyway?" Horace asked. "Anyone would think they're coming on our tour."

"I hate to inform you, but Stan and Naomi Carlisle – that's their names – are doing just that," said Frederick.

"Doing what?" asked Edna, finishing up her last mouthful of teacake, then washing it down with strong coffee.

Not for the first time, Marjorie wished Edna would pay more attention. "The Carlisles are booked on the same tour we are," said Marjorie.

"Bloomin' great! Why can't you meet nice people when you're travelling? You always have to bring the dregs of society."

"It's hardly Marjorie and Fred's fault if they met these people on the train," said Horace. "They would be on our tour irrespective."

Edna wiped her mouth with a napkin, reapplying lipstick with the aid of a compact mirror. Like Naomi, she wore a full face of makeup, but unlike Naomi, she had an array of hairstyles and colours to choose from via wigs. Edna had suffered permanent alopecia following chemotherapy some years before. Today, she wore one of her favourites, a blonde wig, usually signifying she was in a good mood. Edna's wig choice varied according to her mood, and sometimes to match her clothes. Marjorie gave a low chuckle.

"What's so funny, Marge?"

"Nothing. And I don't believe we're being fair to Stan and Naomi Carlisle. As I mentioned to Frederick, it could be they were tired after the overnight journey. Even first-class train compartments aren't as luxurious these days. Speaking of beds, what's the hotel like?"

"It's amazing," said Edna. "You'll like it, Marge. I got the receptionist to swap rooms around so we are next door to each other."

Any pleasure Marjorie had derived from the unexpected arrival of her two friends dissipated at the thought of being in the room next door to Edna. Usually, she asked Faith to keep them as far apart as possible. Not that she didn't enjoy spending time with her, but she did like to feel she had privacy when in her own room. Being next door would result in numerous knocks on the wall, and on the door.

Horace shot Marjorie an apologetic look, while Frederick had an annoying grin on his face.

"I also managed to get Fred and Horace adjoining rooms," said Edna, smugly.

Frederick frowned, and Marjorie couldn't help laughing. "We'll have a wonderful time. Now tell us more about the hotel?"

Edna spent the next twenty minutes regaling them with how welcoming and accommodating the staff at the Falcon Hotel had been since they arrived the day before. Marjorie half-listened to the stories about every person they had met, and the meals she had eaten since arrival. One would have thought they'd been there for weeks rather than one night.

Marjorie was happy to be with her three friends for a week of adventure. Even Frederick seemed happy as they chatted. He had shrugged away his earlier melancholy. The Carlisles would present no problem to them and wouldn't be allowed to shatter her enthusiasm for the tour ahead.

"The hotel overlooks Bude Canal," said Horace, "as do our rooms. I had an amazing night's sleep."

"Me too," said Edna, "so we can chat all night if you like, Marge."

"That won't be necessary, thank you. My night, though comfortable, wasn't as luxurious."

"Fine," said Edna, crossing her arms. "We've got all day, anyway."

"Did you meet anyone from our tour?" Frederick asked.

Edna's brows furrowed and her lips turned downward as she frowned. Her previously bright and excited expression flicked into annoyance. Her eyes narrowed as she looked at her companions as if a dark cloud had passed over. "Not really."

"What about that charming woman?"

Ah-ha, thought Marjorie.

"What about her?" Edna snapped.

Oblivious to Edna's change in mood, Horace pushed on. "Miriam Butterfield. Mim, she likes to be called. She's a local artist and is joining our tour to scout out new subjects."

"What does she paint?" Frederick asked, equally oblivious to Edna's downturn.

"I'm not sure, but whatever she does, I'm sure she's very talented. A fine-looking woman too."

"You're so obvious, Horace Tyler. Anyone with a pretty face and you're putty in their hands," said Edna. "She's nothing special and I've never heard of her, so she can't be that good."

Like a lamb to the slaughter, Frederick didn't hold back on the thought that Marjorie had but would not have said. "Since when have you been an expert on art?"

"What would you know?" Edna snapped.

Marjorie had no idea why she always felt the need to protect Frederick from Edna, even when he started digging his own grave, but before he got himself into a bigger hole, she intervened. "If you don't mind, I'd like to get to the hotel. What are our plans for today?"

"We got a welcome letter from Faith when we checked in. She and Nick are arriving early this afternoon. She's arranged for us to meet the rest of our travelling companions in the bar for after-dinner drinks. Although it's optional," Horace said. "The rest of the day is ours to do with as we wish."

"We thought a walk along the beach and maybe an afternoon drive if you two are up to it," said Edna, clearly happy to end the artist conversation.

Marjorie wasn't concerned about this Mim Butterfield, and neither should Edna be. Horace liked to charm women if he could because, in his head, he remained younger than his eighty-odd years. Besides, his flirtations were usually one-sided and not grounded in reality. It was always possible he might one day attract a gold digger, but Marjorie hoped that day would never come. He was an integral part of the awesome foursome, as Faith Weathers herself had named the quartet, and she would hate to lose touch. As he strolled ahead with Edna in cheerful conversation, Marjorie felt certain he was too fond of her cousin-in-law to have his head turned. Horace, as always, wore a tailored suit which he might need to change if they were going for a walk on the beach. Frederick now carried just his own bag as Horace pulled Marjorie's more modern piece of luggage, along with no protestation from her.

"I like to do a bit of painting myself," Frederick said with an optimistic jauntiness. "I wonder if this Mim Butterfield would be open to giving me tips?"

Now it was Marjorie's turn to frown. This would not do.

THREE

After unpacking the suitcase that Horace and Edna had kindly brought with them, a sudden, sharp rap on the door startled Marjorie, followed by a shout.

"Are you coming, Marge?"

I might have known, Marjorie inwardly groaned, grateful they were only staying the one night. She removed her woollen coat from the back of the door and exited into the corridor.

"How do you like your room?"

"From the little I've seen, it seems very comfortable," Marjorie replied, glancing back at the cosy interior with its plush bedding and furnishings. "What's the hurry? I thought we weren't leaving for another hour."

"Horace has ordered a tray of tea and coffee because they've opened the secret garden – the weather being so good and all," explained Edna, her heavily painted eyelids moving up and down with excitement.

"I expect this will become self-explanatory when we get there," said Marjorie.

"It's lovely, and has amazing views," Edna said, taking her arm. "They rarely open it in the autumn, but Horace convinced the manager we wouldn't blow away. It's unseasonably warm, I don't think you'll need that." Edna pointed to the coat hanging over Marjorie's arm.

"I'll bring it along just in case," she said. Edna might be right about it being warm indoors. Bright sunlight had greeted their arrival at the hotel, its white façade making it feel even warmer, but she would still need a coat if they were going to sit outdoors. The south of England was warmer than other parts of the country, but it could equally attract harsh weather from the Atlantic. Best not to take any chances.

"Whatever you say, Marge."

When they moved outside, it must have been around 10am. Marjorie had left her watch in the bathroom when changing and forgotten to put it back on again, so she couldn't be certain. Horace had changed out of the suit he wore to meet them at the station and still looked dapper, though dressed more casually than usual in cream flannel trousers, a crisp white polo shirt and a cream jacket. The dyed toupee he wore to hide a bald patch that Marjorie had never seen was neatly attached. He and Frederick were chatting to a tall, distinguished-looking man in his late fifties. He had silver-grey hair, and sported a casual, though fitted, navy suit. A worn notebook stuck out of the left pocket of his jacket. All three men stood as the women arrived.

"These are the friends we mentioned. Lady Marjorie Snellthorpe and Edna Parkinton," said Horace. "This is Professor Bodwin Miller, he's the expert on history Faith mentioned in her email."

Professor Miller shook their hands before they all settled. He didn't have the look of a stereotypical scruffy boffin often portrayed in television programmes. Behind his warm greeting, Marjorie thought his blue eyes seemed troubled.

"Are you based in Cornwall, Professor?" Marjorie asked. She hadn't read the email Horace mentioned. It must have arrived after they started their journey.

"No, but it's my area of interest. Cambridge is where I lecture, mostly. I have a house in the city. These days I'm more of a peripatetic lecturer, although I supervise PhD students in Cambridge. I spend a lot of time in Cornwall. My specialism is ancient settlements."

Horace poured Marjorie tea and Edna coffee while the professor explained more about his specialism. The professor had a half-empty glass of whisky in front of him, which was more stereotypical.

Edna yawned. Ancient history wouldn't be her favourite topic, and certainly not one she would discuss at this hour. Generally a night owl, theatre and music were Edna's passions.

"Bodwin's talking on our tour," Frederick said with enthusiasm. Frederick's interest in history was genuine. He turned to the professor before the others had time to respond. "What can you tell us about Tintagel Castle?"

Marjorie hoped Frederick's enthusiasm wouldn't be too arduous on the professor, but the latter appeared keen to regale them with snippets of history surrounding the place they would visit the next day. Every so often, Horace chipped in with a question or a comment. Horace didn't have a particular interest in history, but he found it easy to converse with most people and always found common ground. Frederick, on the other hand, was usually more withdrawn. It pleased Marjorie to see him so animated.

Edna sipped her coffee, the glazed expression revealing a zoning out. Her eyes were on the views. Marjorie gave her an encouraging smile.

"You were right, Edna. It's warm enough here to manage without my coat."

"Told you. You should listen to me sometimes. Being a northerner, I'm usually right about the weather."

Marjorie couldn't link the two. She couldn't see how living in the north made one a weather expert, even if it was colder up there. Still, Edna had been kind enough to collect her and Frederick from the station at an hour when she would prefer to be in bed, so Marjorie would not challenge her generalisation. Not yet anyway.

The men continued discussing Cornish settlements, and soon the professor shifted the conversation to the intriguing topic of smuggling, which captured Marjorie's attention. Even Edna, who had been refilling her cup from the coffeepot on the table, showed a flicker of interest.

"Smuggling," Professor Miller's eyes lit up as he took another sip of whisky. "Now that's where Cornwall's history is fascinating. The rugged coastline here is tailor-made for clandestine activities, with its countless hidden coves, mysterious caves, and isolated beaches. The local population back then considered it a legitimate trade, rather than a crime."

"Was it really that prevalent?" Marjorie leaned forward, her curiosity engaged. She had gleaned some knowledge from Winston Graham's *Poldark* novels but couldn't be sure how much of it was grounded in historical reality.

"Oh yes, Lady Snellthorpe," the professor assured her.

"Please call me Marjorie," said Marjorie.

"Okay, Marjorie. By the eighteenth century, it's estimated that half of Britain's brandy funnelled through Cornwall's covert channels. The locals had a charming way of referring to it as 'free trading' rather than smuggling – a clever euphemism, wouldn't you agree?"

"Sounds quite romantic to me. And fair play to them. Most people were poor back then," Edna said, her voice carrying a mix of nostalgia and bitterness. Edna had grown up in a home where money was tight and could be sensitive on the subject, but Marjorie had never imagined she would condone crime.

"Hardly romantic, Mrs Parkinton," the professor said, his tone serious. "While we might imagine dashing smugglers in the moonlight, the reality was far more brutal. The revenue men and smugglers frequently engaged in bloody battles. Some of the local families involved were quite ruthless."

"Mm," said Edna. "And please call me Edna, I can't abide being called Mrs Parkinton."

Ignoring Edna, Frederick spoke up. "Any notorious families?"

"The Carter family of Prussia Cove was among the most notorious," Professor Miller replied. "Though interestingly, they had their own peculiar code of honour. They employed locals and helped them earn a decent living."

Horace chuckled. "A Robin Hood of Cornwall, philanthropic thieves?"

"Something like that, although as I said, they were violent with the customs men, who had to be protected by the military," the professor said. "My personal theory – and mind you, this is just speculation – is that the smuggling trade was far more organised than most historians acknowledge. I've written several papers on the subject. The local gentry were often involved, providing storage in their cellars and financing rogue operations, all the while pretending to be legit."

"Like organised criminals today," Marjorie observed.

"Precisely! The parallels are quite striking. Though I must say" – he lowered his voice conspiratorially – "some of the old smuggling routes were still being used well into the twentieth century. During my research, I've found evidence suggesting—"

A sharp gust of wind rattled the teacups as a door opened behind Marjorie, who pulled her coat over her shoulders, glad she'd brought it after all. The professor's troubled expression returned.

"You were saying, Professor?" she prompted.

"Oh, yes." He seemed to collect himself while Marjorie turned to see who had entered and saw the Carlisles. Stan gave her a nod, but Naomi ignored her, yet pointedly took the next table, turning her back on them.

"I was going to say that some of these historical networks have modern applications, but perhaps that's a discussion for another time. I need to go, I have something else booked." The professor rose, leaving his half-empty whisky glass behind.

"What an odd man," said Edna. "One minute, he's droning on for hours, and the next, he ups and leaves."

"I think we should do the same," said Marjorie, adjusting her head as a warning to Edna not to say anything further. She needn't have bothered. Naomi Carlisle pushed her chair backwards, scraping it on the floor, and the couple left as quickly as they had arrived.

"Perhaps I'll stay and finish this pot of tea after all." Marjorie sat back down in her seat.

Horace's eyes gleamed as he shot her a look. "I take it that was them?"

"Yes, they startled the professor, didn't they? I wonder if he knows them... They mentioned they were from Cambridge."

Edna huffed loudly. "Is somebody going to tell me what's going on? Because I've got no idea what you're talking about."

"That was the Carlisles, Edna. The couple that Marjorie and Fred met on the train this morning. They came and went. Marjorie's suggesting they were the reason for Bodwin's hasty departure," said Horace.

"Why didn't you say so in the first place?"

"I couldn't, when they were right behind us," said Marjorie.

"They had a bizarre effect on Bodwin," said Frederick.

"It could have been a coincidence," said Marjorie. "Although, if our first impressions are right, and he knows them of old, perhaps he didn't want to get bogged down in a conversation with them."

"They weren't making conversation," said Frederick.

"No, but did you notice how they sat within hearing distance? I think they had every intention of listening in to our conversation. And the professor wasn't staying while they were here. They scarpered almost as soon as he left. Very odd behaviour."

"He's an interesting man, though," said Frederick. "I could have listened to him all day if that troublesome couple hadn't arrived."

Edna fake-yawned, putting her hand over her mouth. "Maybe you could have, but all that historical claptrap bored me. And what does he know about ancient settlements? It's not as if he was there, is it?"

"You seemed interested in the smuggling topic," said Marjorie.

"Yeah, well, it was different, and something I could relate to."

"Be careful, Edna, or we'll be thinking you have a sideline in organised crime," said Horace.

Marjorie chuckled.

"You know what I mean, it's more contemporary. Smuggling still goes on today, doesn't it? It wouldn't surprise me if it still happens along the Cornish coast," said Edna.

"People smuggling, maybe," said Frederick, "but I don't think they bring contraband over the waters anymore."

"Don't you believe it," said Horace. "What about all these ferry crossings to and from France? Don't people come back with boots and lorries full of booze and cigarettes not declared and sold on? Plus, people still smuggle drugs in."

"If you don't mind," said Edna, "I've had enough of this conversation. What about getting on with the fact that we're on holiday and somebody promised to take me to the beach?" She gave Horace a pleading look.

"And that someone will keep his promise," said Horace. "When we're ready, I'm very happy to wander around Bude and take a walk along the fine sandy beach."

"I'd like that too," said Marjorie. "Although I might stick to the path. It's a gorgeous day, although a little on the chilly side since the wind's got up."

"I think Mim said she's got a gallery somewhere in Bude," said Horace. "Perhaps we should—"

"No," said Edna. "We are not going to any art gallery belonging to your new fancy woman."

"She's not my fancy woman, Edna. Why do you mistake my intentions?" Horace winked.

Edna grinned. "I say we forget about historical settlements, smuggling gangs, caves, coves, and art galleries for the rest of the day. I want a walk by the sea, some candyfloss, and maybe an ice cream. And to be honest, fish and chips on the beach this evening."

"I'll go along with the ice cream," said Marjorie. "But fish and chips on the beach? Certainly not. If you want fish and chips on the beach, you're on your own in the dark. You can have fish and chips for dinner at the hotel. I for one will eat dinner that comes as part of our package."

"Whatever you say, Marge," said Edna. "I don't mind as long as we get out."

"You're the one who wanted to come up here in the first place," said Horace. "You coerced me into asking the manager to open, especially for you."

"And much appreciated it was until we met Mr Boring, who likes the sound of his own voice."

Marjorie knew someone else like that but held her peace.

"As most academics do, Edna," said Horace. "It doesn't make him any less interesting. He had a lot of knowledge, and I was happy to hear it."

"Yeah, well, that's as may be, but I'd had enough. Thank goodness for the Carlisle weirdos."

"You've made that clear," said Frederick. "But I would have been interested to hear more. I look forward to chatting with him again because he knows a lot about Tintagel Castle. I don't think we ever finished that conversation."

Edna shot Frederick a scornful look.

"He might be interesting, but I never trust a man who drinks whisky in the morning. Now, can we finish these drinks and make a move?"

"Anything you say," said Horace.

Marjorie was still wondering why the professor reacted to the Carlisles in the way he did. Had their paths crossed before? Did he too find them rude, or could there be more to it?

One thing was certain, the Carlisles were trouble and Frederick's first impressions were right. They should avoid them as much as possible. Professor Miller's hasty departure spoke volumes. He didn't strike her as a man who would react like that without good reason.

As they moved back to the door leading inside, hidden by a large palm, Marjorie noticed a man with a full head of wavy brown hair, a trimmed beard, and wearing vintage white spectacles, hunched over a table writing copious notes in a thick book. He didn't look up from his writing. How long had he been there?

FOUR

The four friends enjoyed a stroll along the seafront. The salty breeze blew on Marjorie's face while they chatted, catching up with the latest news. Though they regularly spoke over the telephone, nothing compared to the warmth of face-to-face conversations to grasp a proper sense of what was happening in each other's lives.

Edna and Horace saw each other regularly as he was a frequent traveller who liked to check on Edna since her hospitalisation with pneumonia. Despite carrying excess weight, Marjorie thought Edna looked well. Her mind went back to the last time they were all together at the Henley Regatta in the summer. "Lovely, apart from the murder."

"Did you say something, Marjorie?" Horace asked.

"Sorry. I must have been thinking out loud. I was recalling our holiday in Henley."

"Ah, say no more," said Horace, with a knowing wink, his green eyes twinkling. He turned to Edna. "Do you still fancy a drive?"

"Not if you're too tired. You did a lot of driving yesterday. We could find a place for lunch and then go shopping."

Frederick sighed. Edna, on a shopping spree, wasn't what any of them needed. "Lunch would be nice, I'm feeling peckish. It must be all this sea air," he said.

They entered a busy café, the air filled with the rich aroma of ground coffee, fresh fish, and pleasant chatter. After ordering light lunches, they found a table in a cosy corner. Once they acclimatised to the hum of conversation and the clattering of cutlery, they fell into a comfortable silence.

Edna's enthusiasm for afternoon shopping waned as they ate. "You know what?" she said, her voice sounding tired. "I think I'd like to go back to the hotel for an afternoon nap. I've not been sleeping well recently."

Marjorie chose not to remind her that earlier, she had boasted of a wonderful night's sleep. She understood the elusive nature of rest, pondering whether one could ever catch up on lost sleep.

"I'll walk you back," said Horace. "To be honest, I wouldn't mind a kip myself. I'm not used to driving such long distances without a layover these days."

"Sorry," said Edna.

"Don't be," he replied with a reassuring smile. "It meant we helped these two escape the Carlisles. It's a pleasure to be together again. I've been thinking recently about how nice it would be if we all lived closer to each other. Maybe one of those luxury retirement communities."

"You really do need a sleep," said Edna, laughing. Horace joined in, but Marjorie sensed he wasn't joking. At least not about the idea of living closer to each other, she doubted he was serious about the retirement complex. They weren't getting any younger, but the challenge for each of them was being comfortable in their own homes. Marjorie's mansion, as Edna liked to call it, was too big for her now. Yet, with her son Jeremy frequently using it as a free conference centre, and enlisting her to host his business associates, she found herself busy enough.

Perhaps it might be time to pass it on to him and move into something smaller. But she had friends in Hampstead and regular social gatherings that filled her days. That said, it was a dwindling group as some had passed away and others were less mobile than they once were. She sighed heavily.

"What would you like to do after lunch, Marjorie?" Frederick asked, drawing her from her thoughts.

"Anything, except shopping. I'm happy to explore Bude some more."

"We'll see you for dinner then," said Horace, pulling Edna's chair out as she stood up. The two of them left the small café like an old married couple. Marjorie wondered if that's what Horace needed – a wife.

"Are you ready?" Frederick asked, a strange look on his face. Could he be thinking the same thing?

"I am," she replied.

Having determined not to go shopping, Marjorie and Frederick ended up doing just that, meandering through side streets, and in and out of shops catering to the whims of eager tourists.

Frederick paused longer at a pottery shop where they watched a skilful potter hand-paint a delicate vase. On exiting, Marjorie's eyes were drawn to a standout sign on the other side of the road. A vivid yellow background with bold black lettering read: MIM'S ART GALLERY.

Frederick, noting the same sign, couldn't contain his excitement. "Oh, that must be the art gallery belonging to Mim, the artist Horace mentioned."

"Would you like to go inside?" Marjorie was a keen art fan herself, and the allure of the gallery tugged. Although, she reminded herself, she really mustn't buy anything. The walls of her home were already adorned with a lifetime of precious acquisitions, including some rather expensive pieces. It was a love that she and Ralph had shared and she cherished the memories of the hours they had spent choosing the pieces for their home, followed by the discussions over where to hang them. Yet, she thought with a sigh, there was no space to add to her collection. As it was, the lack of space forced her to rotate paintings, storing some away for months, and then bringing them out again.

There were the favourites – original pieces that she kept on display, those she would never hide away. Especially those she and Ralph had chosen together: tangible reminders of their love. But what if she downsized? Would she pass them to Jeremy? The thought unsettled her, knowing his interest in art lay in its monetary value, rather than its beauty. The larger canvases came to mind, knowing they wouldn't fit into a smaller home. And the idea of selling them would feel like a betrayal. She knew that Jeremy and his avaricious wife would do just that once she was gone. But she consoled herself with the thought that, by then, it would no longer be her burden to bear.

Marjorie was happy to be pulled from such weighty thoughts by Frederick's enthusiasm.

"I'd love to check it out, if you don't mind," he said, already crossing the road.

An old-fashioned bell sounded as they entered the shop, letting the person know potential customers had arrived. A young girl, no older than twenty, emerged from a back room and took a seat behind the counter. She had a bright smile.

"Do you mind if we have a look around?" asked Frederick.

"Please do," she said.

Marjorie and Frederick separated, each admiring different paintings. Frederick studied a few closely, looking at the descriptions under each painting.

"Are these originals or prints?" asked Marjorie.

"We stock a few originals, but most are limited edition prints. You'll see on the card. If it says one of thirty – the artist doesn't print over thirty of each work – it means it's a print. The oil paintings are originals."

"Are they all by the same artist?"

"Not all," said the girl, "most of them are by Mim. That's Miriam Butterfield. She signs her full name on the paintings but prefers Mim. We also sell and display works by local artists, with a few from further afield. The gallery hosts displays every so often on a particular theme."

"Thank you. That's interesting." Marjorie spent much of her time admiring landscapes. Landscapes were her favourite style of art. And who wouldn't love to own an oil painting showing rugged Cornwall in all its glory?

The bell sounded again, and a family of four entered. One of the children, aged under five, was being carried by her father. A boy aged around ten accompanied them, making it clear he was reluctant to be there by sighing continually.

A few minutes later, they left. A middle-aged couple entered and were far more enthusiastic, and didn't frown at the prices.

The bell pinged yet again, but Marjorie didn't look up this time until she heard a woman say, "Thanks for holding the fort, Ginny. I'll take over now."

"This is the artist herself, Mim Butterfield," said the girl named Ginny.

"Hello," said Marjorie, studying the woman who had grabbed Horace's attention the night before. She looked around late forties, stood at around five and a half feet and wore a floral headscarf completely covering her hair and paint-splattered, flowery dungarees over a long-sleeved red jumper.

Mim nodded a greeting but left them and the couple to their browsing while she took over the seat that Ginny left. The couple bought a small print before leaving.

Frederick was gushing. "Did you paint these?" he asked, pointing to a set of miniature oil paintings in rustic frames.

Mim joined him. "Yes, they're mine. Do you like art?"

"I like this kind of thing," said Frederick.

Marjorie would happily buy him the painting he admired, knowing Frederick kept a tight rein on his purse strings. But he would be offended if she dared suggest it.

While Mim and Frederick chatted, a painting captured Marjorie's attention. She looked at the title underneath: *Tintagel Castle at Dusk.*

"This is interesting," she said.

"That's an original," said Mim. "I try to capture the local scenery in all its moods and weathers." Marjorie studied it and felt it had a sombre darkness that other works in the gallery didn't. She had heard of mood artists and wondered if Mim Butterfield was one.

The moody landscape drew her focus to other paintings. Marjorie moved to another collection stacked against a wall. She bent down to examine them and noticed they shared a similar darkness to the Tintagel Castle piece.

"I don't display those. They're just for my interest," said Mim, appearing behind Marjorie. "Occasionally, I bring them out for a Dark Art exhibition. There's a lot of that in Cornwall."

"I see," said Marjorie. Is that past, or present?"

"Both," said Mim, before returning to the counter.

Frederick continued browsing bright and lighter landscapes more in keeping with his taste.

Mim's attention settled on her computer screen, her brow furrowed as she concentrated.

Marjorie was about to suggest she and Frederick leave when the bell clanged again.

A tall, slim woman with bleached blonde hair in her sixties stormed in, almost toppling a potted plant. She cast it a disdainful glance, as if it shouldn't have been in her way.

Mim looked up from her computer, her mouth tightening into a thin line. "Geraldine," she said coldly.

The woman fixed a glare on Marjorie and then Frederick. If she meant to scare them away, it wasn't working. Marjorie, while uncomfortable, refused to be intimidated, and Frederick continued browsing with a resolute calm.

"What can I do for you?" Mim's smile did nothing to remove the ice from her eyes.

This wasn't the charming Mim Horace had praised. She was more akin to the creator of the dark paintings lurking in the corner.

"We need to talk," Geraldine said, a demanding edge to her voice.

"As you can see, I'm busy," Mim snapped.

"I'd hardly call two people browsing and not buying, busy," Geraldine countered with biting sarcasm.

Frederick shot an uneasy glance towards Marjorie.

She moved next to him. "Time to leave?" she spoke in a hushed tone.

"I think we'd better," he said.

The dinging bell sounded their exit and as soon as they left, Marjorie turned to see Geraldine leaning over the counter, snarling, clearly not holding back on whatever disagreement they were having.

"What do you think that's all about?" asked Frederick as they paused outside the gallery. Marjorie chose a spot where they could discreetly look inside.

"I don't know, but let's stay a moment. I'd hate their argument to develop into physical violence. They look so angry with each other."

"Maybe it's a business deal gone wrong," said Frederick. "Perhaps the woman bought a painting, and the gallery won't take it back."

"That's a possibility," said Marjorie. "These things happen."

They lingered outside, pretending to peruse a map Frederick produced from his pocket. All the time they could hear raised voices coming from inside, but nothing to suggest it would turn violent. The two women eventually left the counter and retreated into the back room to finish their disagreement.

"Did you want to buy anything?" Marjorie asked Frederick.

"Not really," he said. "My place is too small for any more."

"There's a limit to how many things one can accumulate in a lifetime. One has to decide when to stop. I only buy art as gifts these days, but I saw nothing that my housekeeper or house-maid would like."

"And Johnson would be more interested in a new Rolls." Frederick gave her a cheeky grin.

"Indeed," said Marjorie, smiling. "Shall we leave the two ladies to their argument and move on? Without going inside, we won't know what it's about and it's really none of our business."

"Very unprofessional of that woman to storm in like that with customers in the shop."

Marjorie felt Mim's reaction was unprofessional too, but perhaps she had been provoked. "Gone are the days where the customer was always right," she murmured. "Would you like afternoon tea out, or back at the hotel?"

"If you're not too tired I'd like to try that tea shop we saw on the seafront earlier," said Frederick.

"I'm not too tired, but I'd like a rest before dinner if that's okay with you?" said Marjorie.

"My thoughts exactly," said Frederick.

As they strolled away from the gallery, Marjorie heard the loud ring of the bell once more. She turned just in time to see Geraldine marching out uttering frustrated curses into thin air. The door quivered under her forceful exit but the tension from a spring mechanism prevented it from crashing shut. If Mim had this kind of effect on people, it might suggest she shared a similar temperament to the Carlisles. In which case, their holiday might lack the tranquillity she had hoped for.

FIVE

Horace sat perched at the bar with a younger woman, her back to Marjorie, cosying up to him. The woman leaned in as if no-one else existed, which Marjorie found odd. Onlookers might have assumed they were a couple, given the woman's familiarity as she placed a confident hand on his knee.

From where she stood, Marjorie could see the woman had brown hair, a cascade of wild waves, accented with streaks of red. The bohemian style of her brightly coloured dress was nothing compared to the vibrant scarf hanging loosely over her shoulders. Horace's eyes were fixated on her.

The pair held drinks and laughed loudly as though they had known each other for years. Marjorie cleared her throat.

"Good evening, Marjorie. Please allow me to introduce you to Mim, she's a famous artist in these parts." As Horace spoke, his eyes shone and the woman swivelled around to face Marjorie. She immediately recognised her as the artist, Mim.

"We visited your gallery earlier but didn't meet properly. How do you do?" said Marjorie extending a hand.

"I'm well, thank you. Horace has been telling me all about

you and your friends." Mim's tone suggested she was less pleased by the interruption than her words implied.

Marjorie didn't reply, unsure what Horace might have shared with Mim and what her interest in him was. She hoped he hadn't mentioned anything about their sleuthing escapades.

Considering Marjorie and Frederick had witnessed an unpleasant argument between Mim and an unknown woman in the gallery earlier, Mim showed no sign of embarrassment. She had what Marjorie would describe as an open face, round brown eyes, and didn't appear to go in for a lot of makeup. Her fingernails were cut short and when they shook hands Marjorie noticed paint stains. She wore a heavy brutalist chain, at odds with her otherwise flowery style. Multicoloured earrings dangled to her shoulders, settling on the scarf.

There was no time for further conversation as Edna entered the bar wearing a thick layer of freshly applied makeup and a change of hair colour and style. She had opted to be a brunette this evening. Marjorie admired the way Edna dealt with her alopecia through her multitude of different coloured wigs and styles. The smile left Edna's face when she saw Mim.

Horace leaped up, offering Edna his stool. "Can I get you ladies pre-dinner drinks?"

"White wine for me," said Edna, not taking the stool, her tone sullen.

"I'll have a sparkling mineral water, please, and save the wine for dinner," said Marjorie.

"We're just waiting for Fred, and then we can go through. Faith stopped by and said she'd introduce us to the others after dinner, although we've met a few already." Horace turned to the bartender and ordered their drinks, paying on his card.

An awkward silence descended before Mim broke it.

"Hello again," she said to Edna.

Edna's eyes narrowed, ignoring the greeting. "Don't you live in Bude? I didn't think you were staying at the hotel."

Marjorie had to admire Mim's temerity for not taking the bait. "I'm not, but I often pop in here for a drink, that's why I was here yesterday. The hotel displays some of my work. I've booked dinner tonight so I can meet the rest of our tour party."

"Why don't you join us?" Horace offered.

Edna's eyes bulged, threatening to pop. Her brow furrowed into a deep frown as her cheeks flushed bright red, visible despite the heavy layer of rouge. She gripped her drink so tightly, Marjorie feared the glass might break.

"That's kind of you, Horace," Mim replied, her fingers tapping the side of her glass in time with the music travelling through the bar, "but I'm eating with someone I met earlier. Casey visited the gallery, and we got chatting. She's also in the same party."

Mim seemed friendly enough, but something about her niggled Marjorie. Perhaps it was the feeling that Mim was weaving a well-practised sales pitch, or that her cosying up to Horace might not be genuine. More likely, it was the uncomfortable memory of the altercation she and Frederick had witnessed in the gallery. Horace was easy prey for a pretty face. And therefore, a gold digger, but why did he seem so besotted? Marjorie had met his granddaughter who was about the same age.

"Here's Casey now." Mim seemed relieved.

"Sorry I'm late," said the newcomer, an energetic woman in her late twenties with black hair pulled into a neat ponytail revealing multiple earrings in each ear. Slides in both sides of her hair kept any straggles in place. She wore blue jeans and an oversized jumper and black-framed spectacles. Marjorie's eyes moved to the nose ring. Most fashions she could accept, but nose rings were something she couldn't get used to. It must be an age thing. "I had a problem with the lock on the bathroom door but the manager's going to have it fixed while we eat."

Casey stopped for a breath as if just noticing them. "I see you've made friends already."

"Horace Tyler at your service," said Horace, flashing the newcomer a warm smile. "This is Marjorie, Edna, oh, and here comes our fourth member, Fred."

"Frederick," Marjorie muttered under her breath.

"A pleasure to meet you. I'm Casey, Casey Sims."

"I was just telling Horace and his friends you're a member of our tour party," said Mim.

Casey nodded but appeared distracted. "We'd better head in," she said, "I'm not sure how strict they are on times and we're five minutes late."

"We'll see you after dinner then," said Marjorie.

"You will," said Mim, winking at Horace who flushed red. She and her new friend Casey headed into the dining room.

Edna exhaled a sigh of relief as she drank some wine. Marjorie wished Edna didn't make her jealousy so obvious and would accept that Horace was friendly to everyone he met. He could be a flirt but it wasn't in any way serious. Mim however... His eyes followed her in a distant, longing way. Marjorie wondered if she reminded him of someone from his past.

"Drink, Fred?" Horace asked.

"Thanks, but I'll get tap water with dinner," said Frederick.

"That was Mim, the artist I mentioned," said Horace to Frederick.

"We met her when we visited her gallery this afternoon," Frederick said, giving Marjorie a knowing glance. "Beware, Horace."

Marjorie jumped in, not wanting to discuss the unpleasant argument and shatter Horace's illusions when he seemed so happy. "We know very little about the other one, Casey," she said. "She'd just arrived. Apparently they also met at Mim's gallery."

"Yeah, and she had problems with the lock on her bathroom door. As if we needed to know about that," said Edna.

"Sometimes, Edna Parkinton, I despair at your manners," said Horace.

"What did I do?"

"Never mind. Drink up, old girl, and let's get some food. I saw that strange couple go in about fifteen minutes ago," said Horace to Marjorie.

"You never complain about Marge's manners," Edna said. "Why is it always me?"

"Because my manners are impeccable, even when I don't like someone," said Marjorie.

"If you say so, Marge, but you're not perfect."

"I said nothing about being perfect, but we should try to get along with the people we're going to spend the next week with."

"She has a point," said Horace, who had a special ability to curb Edna's moods and make her see the bright side. Their friendship was a reason, if not a justification, for Edna's rudeness towards Mim.

"Okay. I'll be on my best behaviour from now on," Edna said.

"In that case, shall we?" Horace knocked back the remains of his whisky and held his arm out for Edna. Edna took it, carrying her wine through to the dining room.

"Why didn't I think of that?" said Marjorie.

"What?" Frederick asked.

"Nothing important," she said, leaving her half-drunk mineral water on the bar.

The restaurant bustled with the chatter of other guests. It appeared the hotel was fully booked. Aromas wafting from the kitchen teased Marjorie's senses, adding to her hunger. A waiter led them to a spacious table for six, overlooking a well-lit patio. No sooner had they settled into their seats than Edna shot a sharp disapproving glare at Horace.

"So you booked a table for six, did you? You were expecting your new artist friend to accept your invitation, I suppose. You're so predictable, Horace Tyler."

"Never was a man more misunderstood," said Horace, a mischievous grin spreading across his face as another couple appeared at their table.

Edna's anger evaporated fast when she saw them. "Faith! It's great to see you. And Nick too."

"Likewise," said Faith, taking a seat next to Marjorie. "I hope you don't mind my sneaking us in at your table. I checked with Horace and he assured me it would be a pleasant surprise."

"And so it is," said Marjorie.

"Understatement of the year," added Edna. "Certainly better than the company he's been keeping since we got here."

Faith raised a quizzical eyebrow but Marjorie moved the conversation away from Edna's new rival. "You look well." Faith looked radiant, her partner Nick's eyes were sparkling.

"You've changed your hair," said Edna. "Trying to keep up with me, are you?"

"I wouldn't presume to do that, but thank you for noticing," Faith replied with a twinkle in her eye. Not only had she changed her hair colour from brown to red, but the new style also framed her face perfectly.

"It's a bob, Marge," Edna pointed out, with the authority of a hair connoisseur, which of course, she was. Marjorie noticed Edna patting her wig, recognising that style and colour bolstered her confidence and sometimes helped cover the insecurity Edna felt about her permanent alopecia.

"I knew that, Edna, but thank you for the reminder," Marjorie said, keeping a dignified tone. In truth, the name of the style had slipped her mind for a moment but admitting it would unleash a torrent of teasing from Edna about memory lapses and suchlike.

"Are you all settled in?" Faith asked.

"Very well settled, thank you," said Marjorie.

"How are you, Frederick?" Nick asked.

Frederick looked up from studying the menu. "Very good, thanks. Looking forward to sleeping in a proper bed tonight." Marjorie was pleased he didn't mention travelling down with her again, or Edna wouldn't be able to resist childish innuendos. "This hotel's a fantastic choice, by the way."

"We've used it before and had excellent feedback, so when we were planning the itinerary for this tour, we agreed it would be the best place to begin. The north Cornwall coast is full of hidden treasures. Have you met anyone from the tour party yet?"

"A few," said Marjorie.

Before the conversation went any further, they ordered drinks and meals. While they waited for dinner, she was pleased to see Nick continuing to engage Frederick in conversation. Horace and Edna chatted to each other and Marjorie returned to the conversation with Faith, explaining she and Frederick had met Stan and Naomi Carlisle but had had little opportunity to get to know them. "Just before dinner we met the two ladies dining over there." Marjorie motioned to a table across the room, not mentioning the visit to the gallery.

"Ah yes. Mim's a local artist and Casey's a PhD student, I've only communicated with the latter via email. She was a last-minute booking."

"We also met the professor you mentioned in your email," said Frederick, joining their conversation. "An interesting chap."

"Bodwin Miller," said Faith. "He offered to give us talks at various intervals during our travels and we couldn't say no. It's rare you get an expert giving their time for free."

Marjorie noticed Edna still engrossed in conversation with Horace, otherwise her promise of being on her best behaviour might have met its first bump in the road. "He was telling us all about smugglers this morning," said Marjorie.

"Yes. His specialism is ancient settlements but Nick says his obsession is with smuggling, past and present."

"I preferred the parts on ancient settlements," said Frederick. "He promised to tell us more about Tintagel Castle tomorrow."

"It seems the only person you haven't met then is Arthur Denton," said Nick. "He's more on my wavelength. A historical crime writer."

"How interesting," said Marjorie.

"I thought you'd find him interesting," said Faith, "but please, don't turn this into a true crime holiday."

"I don't know what you mean," said Marjorie, with a smirk. "Horace and Edna haven't met the Carlisles yet."

Faith didn't tease Marjorie any further, and Marjorie was pleased because the moment crime had been mentioned, Frederick's face had switched from happy to tense.

Perhaps it might be better if they didn't spend too much time with Arthur Denton, although she would be interested to discover how he constructed his crime stories. She supposed the historical aspect involved a lot of research and wondered if this was a research trip for him. He might have to visit the places he uses in his novels, although these days one could take virtual tours on the internet. Not to mention, enough bloggers detailed their travels to provide intricate details.

Marjorie presumed the author would be on the front row when it came to picking the professor's brains on the history of Cornwall. *That's if he intends to use Cornwall as a setting for one of his novels at all*, she thought. *He might just be on holiday.* She hoped so for Frederick's sake. His wish was most likely to stay away from Arthur Denton, no matter how good a writer, or how interesting.

Marjorie, on the other hand... well.

SIX

The next morning the tour party, along with Faith and Nick, boarded the minibus. Horace had arranged for someone to drive his car from Bude to their final destination. Having witnessed Horace's generosity frequently, Marjorie didn't find it surprising that he had so many contacts willing to help him out when he needed them.

Nobody in the tour party had met the elusive Arthur Denton as he didn't attend the post-dinner get-to-know-you drink session the night before. Marjorie spotted the man she assumed was him, sitting on the back seat with a briefcase covering the other to ward off any uninvited person from joining him. She recognised him as he scribbled in the same notebook she'd seen him writing in the day before when they were chatting with Professor Miller. Perhaps he preferred eavesdropping as a research method, rather than bothering to speak to people. It would explain his standoffish behaviour.

"Now the real holiday starts," said Edna, nudging Marjorie as she took the aisle seat next to her.

Frederick and Horace settled into seats on the opposite side of the aisle and Mim climbed aboard and had a chat with Faith before sitting next to Casey.

Faith took a few moments to explain how the seat belts worked, and to request that everybody kept them fastened while travelling. "The Cornish roads wind, and if others try to overtake, it can be dangerous. It will be much safer and a legal requirement for you to keep seat belts fastened at all times," she said.

As soon as everyone had done as she requested, Faith continued. "I hope you don't mind but we've been asked to make a slight detour on our way to Tintagel Castle. We're going to stop off at Boscastle, but rest assured we have plenty of time." Faith waited to hear if anyone raised objections. When they didn't, she said, "In case you didn't read my email, Professor Miller has kindly offered to give talks at various locations throughout the week, beginning at Tintagel Castle."

Frederick murmured appreciatively, but otherwise the announcement was greeted with silence. Faith took her seat and Nick started the engine. As soon as the minibus sprung into life, they were on their way.

Marjorie peered out of the window, promising herself she might come back and spend more time at the Falcon Hotel.

"You know, I had the best night's sleep I've had in a long time," she said to Edna as the hotel disappeared in the distance.

"Yeah, me too. That's two nights in a row. I rarely sleep, as you know, Marge."

That was something Marjorie didn't know because whenever they shared a room, or were forced to share a room, Edna's snoring kept her awake the entire night. How Edna imagined she didn't sleep remained a mystery. Marjorie was used to broken nights, often interrupted for no reason at all. She chose to sit up in bed and read or go downstairs and make herself a mug of hot chocolate before returning to bed. She found she could survive on less sleep than had been the case in her youth when she needed a lot more. Many people her age suffered the same thing.

Marjorie moved her gaze away from the outside, seeing Horace happily chatting to Frederick, keeping him entertained.

Nick steered the minibus out of Bude and onto the main roads, although Marjorie wouldn't describe the one they were travelling along as a main road as it only allowed for single-lane traffic. The first thirty minutes of the journey were all stop-start.

"Can you remember how long it's going to take to get to Tintagel Castle, Marge? I don't think I heard when Faith explained everything last night. I was tired."

Tired and concentrating on a whisky glass, thought Marjorie, but her excuse for not listening a few moments ago was another mystery. "It would have taken about half an hour with clear roads but Faith has just informed us we are detouring to a place called Boscastle first."

"I didn't hear anything."

"Have you had your hearing tested recently?" Marjorie asked.

"Of course I have. The thing is, they've given me some fiddly digital hearing aids, but I can't get on with them."

Marjorie now understood. It wasn't about wearing fiddly hearing aids, it was about acknowledging the vulnerability of the ageing process. For someone strong like Edna, it was diffi-cult to acknowledge weakness. Marjorie hated using her walking cane for the same reason. "That would explain why you didn't hear Faith's announcement," she said. "You might want to keep them out when we get to Tintagel Castle because Professor Miller is going to enlighten us with a brief history of the place before we roam free."

"Blimey, how did I miss that bit?" said Edna. "Professor Boring is going to enlighten—"

"Edna, keep your voice down! He'll hear you." Professor Miller sat just a few rows ahead but was thankfully engaged in conversation with Faith. Most likely discussing their plans, and how long he would have to give the talk. As they continued the journey, Marjorie scanned ahead, studying their travel companions. She couldn't see Arthur Denton because he was sitting at the back. But their seating afforded them a view of the rest. Casey and Mim seemed to have plenty to talk about. The Carlisles sat across the aisle from the professor, who every so often surreptitiously glanced their way. "Something's going on between those three," said Marjorie.

"What three?" asked Edna.

"Oh, I'm sorry. Did I say that out loud? I was just thinking."

"Well, don't think out loud unless you want me to hear what you're saying, my hearing's not that bad," said Edna. "If you're talking about the weirdo couple you met yesterday and Professor Boring, I agree. There's something odd about them. I suppose you've noticed how they hang around the professor but never speak to him." This time Edna lowered her voice so that only she could hear it.

"And vice versa. Not that he hangs around them. In fact, I get the distinct impression he's uncomfortable with their presence. I wonder if he knew before they came that they would be among the party?" Marjorie said.

Two rows in front of them were unoccupied as the minibus could seat sixteen. Faith had explained over dinner she wanted to keep the numbers down to ten, plus the two of them so that it wouldn't be too uncomfortable for those travelling. And if anybody preferred to sit on their own like Arthur Denton behind them, they could choose to do so.

"I forgot to tell you, Marge. After you went to bed last night, me and Horace saw that Casey girl having a set-to with Professor Boring."

"Arguing with the professor. What about?"

"We couldn't hear everything, but she told him she was going to write an article about unethical practices in academia.

He said something like, what's that got to do with him? And she said, you'll soon find out, won't you? It was all a bit weird if you ask me. Anyway, we didn't hear the end of it because they moved off into a quieter part of the bar and continued their heated discussion out of earshot. It wouldn't surprise me if that strange couple were somewhere in the vicinity. Probably hiding behind plants," Edna said, giggling.

Marjorie wondered if somebody else might have been listening as well. "Have you spoken to the writer yet?"

"What writer?"

"Oh, Edna, do you never listen? Faith told us over dinner. The man in the seat at the back," Marjorie whispered. "Arthur Denton is a historical crime writer. I noticed him as we were leaving the garden room yesterday writing in that book of his, but I don't know how long he'd been there. I got the feeling he might have been listening to our conversation."

"Can't say I noticed him then, but now you mention it, I saw him mooching around after dinner."

"After dinner? But he didn't join us for drinks."

"No, he skulked around in the background. I thought he must be waiting for someone or been another guest in the hotel. Which he was, I suppose."

"I missed that, Faith said he hadn't turned up."

"To some extent, he hadn't because he hung around just outside of the bar. Like I said, I didn't think he was one of our party, although Horace might have mentioned something about him being an author because he spent the whole time scribbling notes in his book."

"How odd. Why wouldn't he join us?"

"Authors can be introverts, you know, a bit like me."

Marjorie pushed down a laugh. "I can't say I've noticed that."

Edna guffawed. "It's all right, Marge, I was joking. Perhaps the author bloke's writing a book about people getting knocked off on a bus tour in the 1920s or something."

"As long as it remains in the 1920s," said Marjorie, slightly concerned. "If he chooses to be aloof, I suppose we'll have to accept it, but it's odd that a man would join a bus tour when he doesn't wish to socialise with anyone on it. Perhaps he's working to a deadline or something."

"Yeah, I'm sure you're right, Marge. That's probably what it is. You know what publishers are like, always putting authors under pressure."

"I wouldn't know," said Marjorie. "And I'm surprised you do."

"You'd be surprised at some of the stuff I know, Marge. Remember, I used to sing in clubs. I met all sorts of people during my career, and some of them were writers and would-be writers."

"Did you meet anyone famous?"

"How would I know? I don't read much. I prefer magazines, but if I pick up a book, it's a rom-com. Those authors didn't hang about in the clubs where I sang. A few I spoke to wrote about celebrities. One woman said she was writing a book about pop culture, and someone offered to write my biography."

"Really? That would have been interesting. I take it you said no."

"Too right I did. You know the saying, Marge, don't air your dirty washing in public. I'm not letting the world know the ins and outs of my life. You never know what might come of it."

"I hardly think you have anything to hide, Edna." *Or anything people might want to read about in a book,* went unsaid.

"As you've said in the past, Marge, we've all got something to hide. If not hide, things we'd rather people didn't know about us. Anyway, I might come across as brash, but underneath it all I'm a private person. I'd rather keep it that way."

"I remember you had a television interview about your career, or was it how you dealt with cancer?"

"A bit of both, really. It was a northern programme. Remember, they aired it in the middle of the night and you got stroppy, thinking it was going to give us away when we were trying to investigate a murder."

"Shush, Edna. We don't want everybody on the bus to hear things like that. Plus, I never get stroppy."

"Whatever you say, Marge. But it's only the truth. We're quite good sleuths when it comes down to it. Not that I take as much pleasure in it as you and Horace seem to. I'm with Fred on that one, I'd rather wine and dine than chase murderers around."

"On that occasion, I seem to remember it was you pressing us to investigate a murder, or murders."

"Yeah, right, Marge. Anyway, I've had enough of this subject, and in answer to your original question, I can try to talk to the author later, if you like. Turn on my charm and all."

"Er, perhaps we could save that for the right occasion. I'm looking forward to hearing Professor Boring, as you call him, talk when we get to Tintagel Castle. I agree with Frederick, he's interesting, and clearly very knowledgeable."

"If I were you, I'd reserve judgement on that one, he's attracted a few people who aren't as fond of him as you are."

"You mean Casey?"

"And the weirdos."

"Oh, yes, and them. I haven't quite decided whether they are also people who prefer to listen in, because they certainly weren't talkative over breakfast on the train, or whether they are people who like to make others feel uncomfortable."

"I'm inclined to go with the latter. I don't know why these sorts of people come on communal holidays."

"You're right, Edna. It's hard to understand. They are certainly making the professor feel uncomfortable. Each time I look down the bus, he's avoiding eye contact with them, while watching what they're up to."

"Mr and Mrs Crazy then," said Edna, who was always good at alternative names for people.

"Indeed," said Marjorie. "I expect when we get to know each other we'll all laugh about our first impressions."

Edna moved on to other subjects for the next thirty minutes, alternating between speaking to Marjorie and shouting across the aisle to Horace, despite him being a short distance away. Marjorie wondered if it was Edna's hearing problem causing her to shout, but then, she'd done it for years so it seemed unlikely. Still, she would have a word with Horace and ask if he could exert his influence to persuade Edna to wear at least one of her hearing aids.

Frederick, Marjorie noticed, had an ear pod in his right ear and was most likely listening to music or an audiobook. He wasn't the best traveller and didn't always enjoy listening to Horace. Marjorie found Horace interesting but his proneness to bragging made Frederick feel inferior.

Travelling with friends was very different to travelling with a husband. If Ralph were here, he would be absorbed in a book, rather than looking out of the window. Cornwall was another of those places they had always meant to visit but never did.

Shaking away unbidden thoughts, Marjorie gazed out of the window, trying to people-watch from her vantage point. Her small stature of only five feet half an inch made it difficult. She accepted the challenge, pleased that the seatbacks weren't too high. She could observe, if not hear, people interacting. Observation could often be more useful than listening.

SEVEN

Nick stopped after around an hour's driving and parked in a public carpark. Faith announced from the front that they would stay for forty-five minutes.

"Professor Miller informs me that Boscastle has one of Cornwall's most picturesque harbours, and the village has a fascinating history encompassing witchcraft and maritime heritage. The Museum of Witchcraft and Magic is a five-minute walk if you wish to pay it a visit, otherwise, have a wander."

Once the passengers disembarked, they gathered in a group, some stretching their legs. Marjorie noticed Arthur Denton slip his notebook inside his briefcase and hurry away from the bus before anyone could dare approach him. *Anyone would think we have an infectious disease*, thought Marjorie.

The Carlisles also moved with an unusual urgency, walking behind Professor Miller, appearing calculated enough to keep him in sight without being obvious in their pursuit. The professor wore the same suit as the day before but had donned a striped scarf which he wrapped tight around his neck while he walked.

Marjorie shook her head. It was all very strange.

Casey and Mim left the group telling Faith they were going to the museum. Casey barely took her eyes off her phone screen while walking.

"I'm amazed these young people don't have more accidents," remarked Marjorie.

"What are you on about now, Marge?"

"Nothing. Just ignore me." Given the heated exchange Edna had witnessed between Casey and Bodwin Miller, Marjorie wondered if Professor Miller was to be the target of the young woman's article. And if so, what had he done to deserve her wrath?

"Can't say I'm into the dark arts. Does anyone fancy a cuppa?" Horace asked, joining Marjorie and Edna after chatting to Faith. "Faith says there's a café next to the harbour that does speciality coffees."

"That would be perfect, as long as they also serve tea," Marjorie replied.

Frederick had already wandered in that direction saying he wanted to photograph the ancient harbour walls.

"We'll catch up with Fred and let him know where we're going."

As the trio settled at a table in the café, Marjorie observed Frederick from the window, speaking to Professor Miller. The professor said something, but then walked away, taking a solitary stance by the harbour wall. She watched as he consulted his notebook, removing what appeared to be old documents. The Carlisles lurked nearby, pretending to admire the view while clearly monitoring the professor's every move.

Frederick joined them inside, a sullen look on his face. Marjorie suspected he'd been rebuffed.

"Over here, Fred," called Horace. "Your coffee's on the way."

Frederick took a seat, remaining quiet. "Did you get some good snapshots?" Marjorie asked.

"Yes. Would you like to see them?" Frederick immediately perked up.

Ignoring Edna's eye roll, Marjorie said she would very much like to see them. Perusing the photos via the small screen on Frederick's camera took all her concentration.

"You should put your reading glasses on, Marge," said Edna.

And you should wear your hearing aids, came the inward retort. Relief came along with her tea, the coffees, all accompanied by plates of freshly baked scones, clotted cream, jam and butter. At least Marjorie's efforts had cheered Frederick up and he was buttering a scone with enthusiasm.

Marjorie looked from the scone in front of her, to Horace. "I don't remember asking for these."

He shrugged. "When in Rome and all that. I know that traditionally you have Cornish cream tea in the afternoon, but I couldn't resist the smell of fresh baking. Reminded me of my childhood. My mother made amazing scones."

"I thought your mother was Romanian?" Edna said.

"And so she was, but she embraced baking, and some English traditions are worth learning. At least, that's what she told me."

Marjorie added butter, jam and cream to her fruit scone and took a bite, feeling it crumbling in her mouth. "Oh, it's delicious, and still warm. Thank you, Horace."

"My pleasure."

They all tucked into their unexpected treat while drinking tea, in her case, and coffees in theirs. "I believe that a cream tea should be accompanied by tea," she said with a chuckle.

"Ah well. We don't want to be too predictable, do we?" Horace said before lowering his voice. "After Edna and I witnessed the fracas between our Professor Miller and that Casey girl last night—"

"What fracas?" asked Frederick.

"We saw the two of them arguing," said Edna.

Frederick frowned, Marjorie suspected he felt left out.

"I only found out myself on the bus," said Marjorie.

"Well, I did a little digging while Fred was listening to his music on the bus" – *and in between Edna shouting*, thought Marjorie – "and there was a scandal at his former university, about five years ago – something about complaints from students. Nothing was proven, but three students left the university rather abruptly."

"Let me guess," Edna said, "one of them was Casey Sims?"

"Got it in one," Horace confirmed. "Though I couldn't find out the details. The university dismissed it as bitter under-achievers. The professor stepped down soon afterwards and has worked, as he told us, peripatetically ever since. His reputation, as far as I can tell, remains intact, and he's considered one of the leading voices of Cornish settlement history."

Marjorie pondered, while watching Arthur Denton, who had positioned himself at a corner table inside the café with a clear view of the harbour, the professor, and the Carlisles. His pen moved rapidly across his notebook, and occasionally he snapped discreet photos on his phone.

Marjorie found the dynamics within the tour party increasingly intriguing. What had started as a simple tour was shifting into something more complex. Were they really a group of strangers happening on a holiday, or players in an unknown game of chess?

Faith entered, nodding at Arthur Denton before joining them, a concerned look on her face. "Has anyone seen the Carlisles? We need to leave in five minutes, and I can't find them."

"They're just..." Marjorie began, but looking out the window where the trio had been five minutes before, she realised the mysterious couple and Professor Miller had disappeared from view.

"Maybe they've gone back to the carpark," said Edna, wiping crumbs from her blouse.

A moment later, Marjorie spotted them emerging from behind a building. Professor Miller seemed rattled, while the Carlisles maintained their usual impassive expressions.

"There they are," said Faith.

After a pleasant stroll back to the carpark, they re-boarded the minibus and Marjorie noticed Casey typing furiously into her phone. Mim flopped into the seat behind her, folding her arms across her chest. Casey turned around and whispered something but Mim glared through the window. Perhaps the museum hadn't been all they thought it would be.

Arthur Denton returned to his solitary position at the back, no longer writing, his attention focussed on Professor Miller and the Carlisles as they took their seats.

The atmosphere on the bus had shifted subtly but distinctly. As the minibus pulled away from Boscastle, Edna leaned over and whispered, "I've got a bad feeling about this lot, Marge. Remember our Scottish Highlands holiday? This is feeling awfully similar."

Marjorie shook her head. "Let's not think like that. Clearly some of these people have crossed paths in the past, but I'm sure it's coincidence they are on the same tour."

"I hope so, Marge because I'm telling you, I've got a nasty feeling about this."

THE MINIBUS WOUND its way along the coastal road, eventually pulling up close to the entrance for Tintagel Castle. They all got out while Nick turned the vehicle around to park in the village.

The magnificent headland rose before them with the ruins

of the ancient castle perched dramatically on its cliff edge. The October winds whipped around them, carrying the cry of seabirds and the distant crash of waves. Despite the gale, the sun appeared, dispelling the cloud forming over Marjorie.

"Gather round, please," Faith said. "We'll take the bridge across to the island. If any of you have difficulty walking, let me know. Nick's hired a couple of wheelchairs if required."

Edna nudged Marjorie. "You might need one of them, Marge."

"I will not," Marjorie protested.

"Well, you'd better use your stick then," said Edna.

Marjorie always carried, but rarely used, a fold-up walking cane, but felt on this occasion she might need it to make the crossing. Edna's breathless symptoms would make it more likely she would be the one needing a wheelchair, but Marjorie resisted mentioning it. Faith offered Marjorie a reassuring smile before continuing.

"As I mentioned earlier, Professor Miller has kindly offered to give us a brief talk with some historical context once we reach the upper courtyard. It's optional, of course, but when you do go it alone, please stick to the marked paths and be mindful of the edges – they can be treacherous, especially in the wind."

With the walk underway, Marjorie enjoyed surveying the landscape. Frederick was already taking photos. Wild thrift and sea campion dotted the cliffsides, their hardy flowers showing hints of pink and white despite the change of season. Ravens cawed as they circled overhead competing with seagulls. Marjorie didn't claim to be an expert on gulls but noted a few varieties hovering overhead and out to sea. As they crossed the modern footbridge that spanned the chasm between the mainland and the island, Marjorie noticed how the Carlisles continued to position themselves directly behind Professor Miller, while Casey and Mim brought up their rear, speaking in urgent, hushed tones.

Arthur Denton had actually joined the group this time, though he maintained a careful distance, his notebook clutched against his chest, protecting it from the strong crosswinds. White-capped waves crashing against the dark rocks below punctuated the spectacular views across the Atlantic.

"The geology here is quite remarkable," Professor Miller began soon after they reached the upper courtyard. "These slate and granite formations have withstood centuries of..." He paused, glancing nervously at the Carlisles, who moved closer to him.

"Perhaps we should go nearer the edge," Naomi Carlisle suggested, her voice just audible above the wind. "The view of the cave formations is better from there."

"That's not advisable," said the professor, "but if you wish to take the risk, madam?" He held out his arm. Stan whispered something to Naomi, and they stepped back.

"My wife was joking," he said. "Do carry on."

Professor Miller continued his talk and gave a brief history of a legend from the Dark Ages. One where King Uther lusted after a Baron of Cornwall's wife, Igraine. When the baron hid her at Tintagel, Uther got help from Merlin the magician and took a potion that changed his form into that of Igraine's husband. "Legend has it that Igraine slept with Uther" – the professor shot a derisory look towards the Carlisles – "thinking he was the baron, and King Arthur was born from the union. It's a myth, of course," Professor Miller continued, "but many things occurred in these parts that leave one to question the world we know. Smuggling, too—"

"Thank you, Professor," said Faith. "That was very interesting, I never knew that part of the story."

Professor Miller didn't seem too happy at being cut off in his prime.

"Now, you can all take some free time to explore. Please eat when you wish and we'll meet back at the bus in two hours."

"Thank the Lord for Faith," said Edna as the group dispersed. "I thought he was going to drone on forever."

"I'm surprised you could hear what he was saying above the noise of the wind," said Marjorie.

"I heard enough, Marge. Trust me."

Frederick left them, following the professor.

"I don't think our Fred agrees with you, Edna. He's gone to bend the professor's ear," said Horace.

"Well, good luck to him. Let's go for a walk."

"You go ahead, I'll wait for Frederick," said Marjorie. As the pair moved out of sight, Marjorie turned around. She'd forgotten to use the restroom before crossing the bridge and, although it meant repeating the journey, she didn't want Edna chiding her over it.

On arriving back at the spot where the professor had given his talk, nobody from her group was in sight. Suddenly, Marjorie heard the most terrifying cry, followed by a series of thuds – first a sharp crack, then the horrible tumbling sound of something bouncing off the rocky outcrop before the unmistakable sound of something hitting rock. Marjorie, along with a few others, moved closer to the edge to see what had happened. On the rocks below, she recognised the striped scarf Professor Miller had been wearing. He lay still, and the body contorted in such a way as to make it clear he was dead.

Chaos ensued as people appeared from every direction, all determined to peer over, despite the risk. Shouts of "What happened?" and "Oh my God!" echoed across the headland as tourists abandoned their sightseeing to rush towards the commotion. A woman screamed when she saw the body on the rocks below, while her friend pulled out her phone to film the grisly scene. Children cried as their parents hurriedly dragged them away.

"Please move back from the edge!" Nick shouted, his voice difficult to hear over the growing commotion. He and Faith had appeared a few moments after Marjorie. Nick had his back to the edge, frantically waving his arms as more tourists surged forward. "Get back – it's dangerous!" A teenager with a selfie stick pushed past him, trying to get a photo.

Faith stood frozen for a moment, her face pale, before frantically tapping keys on her phone with shaking hands.

"Does anyone have a signal?" Faith shouted over the din of voices and crying. Nobody appeared to. "I'll run back to the visitor centre and call the emergency services," she called out, already running. "Nick, keep people away from the edge."

Casey came from behind a rock, her tote bag blowing in the wind. She ignored Nick's instructions, and peered over the edge, phone in hand, taking photos. She wasn't the only one. Despite the tragedy, phones appeared to be everywhere. Nick was doing his best but struggled to keep the gawpers back.

"Have some respect!" an elderly man shouted at a group of young people posing for photos and selfies with the cliff edge in the background. A tour guide from another group tried to herd her charges away, but they kept craning their necks for a better view.

Marjorie didn't understand why the younger generation – and older, if she was honest – felt the necessity to take macabre photos of tragedy.

The Carlisles stood motionless amid the growing chaos, their faces not quite as impassive as before. While tourists pushed and jostled around them, snapping photos and asking questions, they remained still. Marjorie couldn't interpret the look shared between them – was it shock, or relief? Perhaps something else entirely. Marjorie was in no doubt the couple had known the professor before the tour started.

Arthur Denton scribbled in his notebook, keeping it pressed close to his chest between notes. When he wrote he angled the pages away from any potential observers, his eyes darting around as if checking who was watching.

"Please listen to me before anyone else goes over. Keep back from the edge!" Nick commanded. "The emergency services will be here soon."

Marjorie stared at the spot where Professor Miller had stood a short time before, her mind racing. The wind was strong, but not strong enough to throw a grown man over the side.

Behind her, Edna and Horace arrived, followed by Frederick. His mortified look told her how upsetting this would be for him.

"Thank God you're all right, Marge," said Edna.

The sound of approaching sirens echoed across the headland, cutting through the babble of voices and crying children. As the first paramedics appeared below, people started spreading on the rocks as security personnel from the castle arrived, blowing whistles and forming a human barrier to push people back from the dangerous edge. Above them, the ravens continued their circular flight, their harsh calls now seeming more like omens than natural sounds. Mim trained her phone camera on them. The wind carried fragments of conversation from the dispersing crowd: "Did you see him fall?" "Did he do it on purpose?" "Get that on video." The beautiful autumn day had transformed the tourist destination into a scene of tragedy and vulgar curiosity.

The tragic incident at Tintagel Castle would remain engraved on Marjorie's mind for a long time. Especially the piercing cry of a man falling to his death.

EIGHT

"Marge, where did you go? We looked everywhere for you and Fred before any of this happened," said Edna. She had barely said a word as they took their time getting to the bridge, pausing every so often to catch her breath. The exertion, along with the tragedy, seemed to take their toll and Horace looked worried about her.

"You're exaggerating, Edna. We occasionally looked out for them," said Horace.

Edna huffed, but that seemed to be all she had the breath for.

"Let's get back across the footbridge, my legs feel a little weak," said Marjorie, more for Edna and Frederick's sake than her own.

"You go on," said Horace. "Edna and I will be along soon."

Frederick took Marjorie's arm, and they crossed the bridge in silence, which was more than could be said for most people overtaking them. The accident was at the centre of every conversation. Once on the other side, they found a comfortable bench on the terrace of the café.

"Let's just sit here for a while." Marjorie watched as most

people queued to get inside the café. She was struggling to come to terms with what had happened.

When she looked up, she saw Horace and Edna. Edna joined them on the bench, which overlooked the sea, gasping for breath.

"The police have arrived," said Horace. "The paramedics are attending to him. Faith's down there too, she must have headed that way after calling for help."

"How does one get to him?" Marjorie asked.

"Nick told me there's access to the cove via Merlin's cave. He's certain it's the professor, and that he's dead."

"It is the professor," said Marjorie. "I recognised his scarf. And he's quite dead."

"What do you think happened, Marge?" Edna was recovering her breath now that she was sitting.

Before she got the opportunity to reply, Frederick appeared carrying a tray with tea for her and coffees for the others. She hadn't even noticed him leave but was grateful for the warm liquid. "They serve light lunches, but I don't feel very hungry," he said.

"Thanks, Fred." Horace tested the coffee for heat, before taking a gulp. "I can't believe what's happened. We were just saying it's the professor down there and he's dead."

"How can you be sure?" asked Frederick, placing the empty tray on a nearby table and rejoining them.

"Marge recognised his scarf, and Nick's convinced it's him." Edna took a large gulp of coffee before nudging Marjorie. "Go on then, Marge. What do you think happened?"

"I don't know, Edna. I'm as confused as everybody else. Did any of you see what happened?" She struggled to get the image of the crumpled body out of her mind.

"The last I saw, you were with him, weren't you, Fred? What happened?" Horace asked.

"I don't know. I tried to talk to him after Faith interrupted his talk," said Frederick. "But he seemed distracted, and troubled."

"That's not surprising after the stupid Carlisle woman tried to goad him to go close to the edge," said Edna.

"Which is why I'm surprised he did," said Frederick. "He should have heeded his own warning, but I was a bit put out, actually. I regret it now..."

Marjorie shook her head at Edna, pleading with her cousin-in-law not to be unkind. Edna took the hint and closed her mouth over whatever she had been about to say.

"... I couldn't find any of you, so I tagged onto the end of another group who had a guide. The guide expanded on the legend of King Arthur. Retelling the Uther and Merlin story that the professor had touched on, but he said there were other versions as well. We'd turned a corner so I wasn't anywhere near to what happened. The wind was howling a gale from where we were, and I couldn't hear anything other than gulls until I heard the man's cry. Where were you?" His eyes locked on Marjorie's.

"Taking a stroll," she said, still not wishing to reveal her reason for her diversion. "What about you two?"

"Me and Horace went for a walk because he was interested in – can you believe it – the wild flowers?" Edna shot Horace a derisory look.

"I'm interested in that sort of thing," said Horace. "I can take history to a point, but didn't we come to see the wild Cornish coast's scenery and rugged hills? Fred likes his nature too."

"Well, I don't disagree with you," said Edna, "about the overdose of history. I had just about had it up to my neck by the time we left."

"Bodwin Miller seemed very troubled," said Frederick.

"Are you suggesting he threw himself off the cliff?" Marjorie quizzed.

"I don't know what I'm suggesting, Marjorie, but something wasn't right."

"Especially with all his hangers-on, particularly that Carlisle couple. I wonder where they were when he went over, they probably tormented him into doing it," said Edna. "You heard what Naomi said," Edna added.

"I also heard his response, and he was having none of it," said Marjorie. "I can't imagine their opinions influencing him at all. Like Edna, I'd like to know where they were when he fell because if anyone saw anything, it would be them. They've been snapping at his heels ever since we arrived in Cornwall."

"Yes, snapping is about right," said Edna. "I wouldn't liken them to a faithful dog following the master, though. It's more malicious with those two."

"Did anybody see where Casey was?" asked Horace.

"Not me," said Frederick. "I expect she was with Mim somewhere."

"None of them were near us," said Horace. "I assume the same as Fred. Mim and Casey were most likely together as they seem to be joined at the hip."

Was that a slight hint of resentment in Horace's voice?

"Let's not presume anything for now," said Marjorie.

"What about you, Marge? Didn't you see anything? You're being secretive about where you were."

"If you must know, I needed a comfort break and missed everything. I was on my way back to find you all when I heard him cry out." A cry that she couldn't get out of her head.

"You should have heard the crack as he hit the rocks," said Edna.

"I heard quite enough, thank you."

"So Fred thinks he did himself in, but I suspect he got over-interested in his historical pursuits and toppled over."

"Both are feasible," said Horace. "It will be interesting to hear what Faith has to say. I don't know where she was when it happened."

"Oh, I can tell you that," said Marjorie. "She and Nick were turning a bend carrying a flask of coffee."

"I hope this doesn't put an end to our tour," said Frederick. "The professor was interesting, but we still have a lot more to see."

"Why would it affect us?" said Edna.

"Because of another possibility," said Marjorie.

She watched Edna and Frederick's jaws drop in unison. "Don't go there, Marge. I'm warning you, don't you dare," said Edna, putting her empty cup on the tray.

"Well, we have to face the fact that people on this tour aren't all they seem to be," Marjorie countered.

"You can't really believe someone pushed him off?" said Horace.

"Actually," said Marjorie, "until proven otherwise, that's exactly what I'm suggesting happened."

"I can't believe you, Marge. Someone dies, and here you go again," said Edna, "Miss Marple imagining foul play. Again. Not possible, Marge. Lightning doesn't strike everywhere we go."

Frederick's brow furrowed as he removed his hat, scratching his head anxiously before checking behind to see if anyone else was listening to their conversation. "I'm with Edna. It's not likely," he said. "How many times can the same group of people come across dead bodies and murder?"

Frederick was correct and often showed wisdom as well as anxiety. If they did need to investigate, they would need his unique skills. "Well, the police come across both all the time," said Marjorie, weakly.

"Yes, but as I've pointed out before – frequently – we're not the police, Marge," snapped Edna. "And I don't want to be the police. And I certainly don't want to be involved in another investigation. This is my bucket-list treat and I will not have it ruined by you and your murder theories. I'm determined to enjoy every minute. I'll be blowed if the death of some boring professor interferes with that enjoyment."

"Oh, that's rather harsh," said Horace. "Even for you, Edna. Whether or not you find it inconvenient, a man has died. The least we can do is find out what happened."

"Here you go, always siding with Miss Marple. May I point out something? You are not detectives in some amateur dramatic society. And let me tell you for nothing: murder is dangerous, and so far, we've been lucky muddling through investigations. Just remember I've been attacked. Fred's been attacked. Marge has been threatened with death. In fact, the only one who's come out totally unscathed is you, Horace Tyler."

"Steady on, don't be tempting fate, Edna. Besides, nobody's going to be harmed. All we need to do if necessary is a little investigating."

"Well, you can do it on your own."

"I'm sure Faith will be game enough to help us," said Horace, scratching his chin.

Edna was going redder and redder. Marjorie could only hope Horace would row back a little before she blew a gasket.

"That's the trouble with you and Marge, isn't it? This sort of thing is all a game. It's not a game to me, it's not a game to Fred, and it's certainly not a game to Professor Bor— erm... Miller. And as for Faith, take one look at her. She's horrified. Her business could go down the pan. Especially if it turns out to be a murder."

"Oh, I don't know," said Horace. "I think the saying goes: any publicity is good publicity. She'll have people queuing up to join her tours."

Marjorie studied Edna and Frederick's faces, both of which were bordering on panic. Edna might be coming across as uncaring but the reality was, she looked shaken. Bluster was how Edna coped with stress, so it wouldn't pay to continue arguing at present. "Let's assume for now that the professor's death was a tragic accident. Or that the man was troubled enough to throw himself off a cliff."

"But you said—" Horace began.

"I know. We will keep in mind that there have been some strange goings-on among certain people. In fact, I would say all of them behaved peculiarly around the professor apart from Mim, the artist."

"And the author," said Horace.

"I'm not so sure about him, He's often been around the professor."

"Doing book research, I expect, Marge," said Edna.

"Somebody must have seen something," said Marjorie.

"Yes. The person who shoved him over the edge," said Horace.

"Oh, will you stop it, Horace Tyler."

"We can always hope that if something untoward caused his death the police show more interest than we've experienced in the past," said Marjorie, remembering several annoying incidences where their theories had been ignored – even ridiculed.

"Anyway, button up, here's the rest of them," said Edna.

Marjorie saw Nick and Faith corralling the remainder of their party into the café. This could only mean one thing. The police would be coming to speak to them soon.

NINE

Faith's eyebrows furrowed, her lips pressed together and her eyes flickered with worry, as she joined Marjorie and friends.

"I'm really sorry about what's happened. The police have asked us to stay until they decide we're free to go." She nervously tucked a loose strand of hair behind her ear. "They want to interview everyone who was in the vicinity at the time of death."

"It's true then, Professor Miller is dead?" Horace questioned.

Faith checked over her shoulder, making sure the gathering crowds weren't within earshot. "I'm afraid so. From what I gather, the emergency services believe he fell: a tragic accident."

Marjorie picked up on the tremor in Faith's voice as she continued, "One witness told the police they saw Bodwin... the professor... leave the marked path and head towards the edge. I'm surprised, but someone from the police will be along soon, and others might have witnessed the fall. Why he left the path is a mystery to me having warned Nick and I to emphasise the importance of keeping to the marked paths."

"Perhaps he felt he knew the area well enough to veer off," said Horace.

Faith nodded slowly, rubbing her forehead with her right hand. One of her gel nails had snapped in two. "That could explain it. One paramedic I spoke to said they have had an unusual amount of wet weather, which is causing the entire area to destabilise." She sighed. "It's a shame our visit to the ruined castle has been brought to an abrupt end, but as soon as we're allowed to move on, we can check in at the hotel where we're staying for the next two nights."

"That's fine by me," said Edna, with a hint of impatience. "I'm not a fan of ruined castles anyway, but the views are incredible." She glanced around at the distant landscape.

"I'll be glad to leave," said Frederick, a shudder in his voice. "It must have been terrifying for him, I hope he died quickly."

"One thing we can be sure of," said Horace in a matter-of-fact tone, "is that his death would have been quick when he hit the bottom. How long it took him to get there is another matter."

"Quite," said Marjorie, noting the look of horror on Frederick's face, "but we don't need to think about that, do we?"

Faith eyed Marjorie, opening her mouth as if to say something, but then closing it again before addressing them all. "Hopefully we won't be here for too much longer, but you might want to grab some lunch." Faith walked away, shaking her head and muttering to herself. Marjorie watched their attractive guide retreat inside the café to join Nick and the others. As a cloud fittingly blocked out the sun, Marjorie's thoughts were well and truly occupied with the events that preceded the four of them sitting on the bench.

"I understand the professor fell over the cliff?"

Marjorie gave a start, though she wasn't entirely surprised to hear the man's gruff voice begin with no preamble. It was the first time Arthur Denton had acknowledged them, and the first words she'd heard him speak since the start of the tour. "Did any of you see what happened?" he demanded.

The man towering over their seat was taller than six feet with hunched shoulders. Brown hair protruded from his peaked cap and she noticed pale blue eyes behind his round-framed spectacles.

"Sad business, but no, we saw nothing," said Horace, shaking his head.

Denton appeared to tut, and impatiently said, "I asked that lot in the café, but nobody seems to be in the mood to tell me anything." He gestured towards the inside café. "They just ignored me."

Perhaps because you've been doing the same since you arrived, thought Marjorie. She pulled her collar up against the cool wind, reflecting on how some people seemed to have no insight into their own behaviour but were often the first to judge others. Denton struck her as one such person.

"We were just discussing it with Faith," said Horace, always willing to be friendly, even to those who didn't deserve it. "It's a mystery, none of us saw where the professor went after the talk. Fred here was the last to speak to him."

Denton's eyes shot towards Frederick with a suddenness that caused him to shrink back. His bald head immediately betraying embarrassment and surprise, it flushed even before his cheeks did. He put his hat back on as if aware of the sequence.

"He wasn't in the mood for talking," said Frederick. "I asked him a question after his talk, thinking he might have wanted to say a lot more before he was cut off." Frederick had clearly been annoyed at Faith's ending the professor's presentation, but she had been right to do so. People were getting cold in the wind and were showing signs of boredom. Frederick continued. "He seemed distracted. I expect others might have spoken to him after me."

"How about you, Mr Denton?" asked Marjorie. "Where were you when events unfolded."

Close up, the man looked older than he did from a distance. His face was weathered: early fifties she guessed. He removed his cap. "You know my name?"

"Faith mentioned it yesterday," Marjorie replied, her eyes urging him to answer her question. Ordinarily she wouldn't have been so direct, and there would have been a polite exchange of introductions. However, the man's brusque approach didn't warrant such consideration.

"I was sitting on a ledge... a safe one," he added, "taking notes. I'm a writer." His voice carried a hint of pride.

"Yeah, we heard that. A crime writer," said Edna. "This'll make an intriguing scene for one of your books, won't it?"

Arthur Denton's lips thinned, twisting into a semblance of a condescending smile that struggled to reach his eyes. "Not really. I write historical crime fiction, not contemporary. And as far as I'm aware, no crime has been committed."

"I thought that was the idea of fiction," said Edna, always a dog with a bone when confronting the unpleasantness of humanity.

"What makes you so certain a crime hasn't been committed?" asked Marjorie.

Denton studied her with his cold eyes. "Because I'm a crime writer, I get a feel for these things. The silly man shouldn't have strayed away from the safety of the paths. He was warned. We all were."

"That sounds rather unfeeling," said Horace.

"Maybe so, but true. The professor should have kept to the paths. It's as simple as that. The edges around here are treacherous."

"You know the area then? Have you visited before?" asked Marjorie.

"Many times. I have a cottage in a small village in south

Cornwall. My books are based in the county. The plots revolve around historical smuggling, and there was a lot of it."

"If you live in Cornwall, why are you on our tour?" asked Frederick.

"Cornwall has many advantages, but its roads aren't one of them. Driving is tedious, as you must have realised leaving Bude this morning."

Marjorie had been pleasantly surprised that the journey had been better than expected, but she didn't want to detract from the conversation, so she remained quiet on the subject.

"I'm considering setting my next novel in historical Boscastle. With its witchcraft history, it would make an interesting plot. Tintagel Castle is my second choice, but after today I'll probably go with the former. Tintagel could feature as part of the story, or at a later date. I'm hoping other places on the tour might inspire me. Setting is important."

"Boscastle wasn't on the itinerary until we got on the bus," said Marjorie.

Denton cleared his throat. "No, but having visited, I'm keen to use it."

"If all your novels are set in Cornwall," said Frederick, "you could include each place in a book."

"I only focus on one book at a time, although I make notes that might feature in the future. Smuggling is familiar to my readers, which is why I thought the witchcraft part might spice it up a bit. Another alternative is to go off topic altogether and write an earlier historical novel, perhaps a retelling of the Uther-Merlin conspiracy to get Igraine to bear a child. The magical element adds something different."

"Sounds like either would make an interesting plot," said Horace. "I'm Horace Tyler, by the way, this is Lady Marjorie Snellthorpe, Edna Parkinton and Fred Mackworth."

"Frederick," said Frederick.

"Arthur," said Denton, somewhat reluctantly.

He gave little impression of being interested in getting to know them, as Edna had clearly noticed, saying in her usual blunt fashion, "I don't think he wants to be best mates, Horace."

Her comment, far from giving offence, resulted in a genuine, though brief, grin as Arthur eyed her.

"Do you write under your own name?" Horace remained undeterred.

"No, I use a pen name. As Edna here has noticed, I'm a loner. I don't want strangers recognising me in the street. Most people in my village know what I do, but they respect my privacy. I hoped nobody on the tour would know what I did."

"Even if we hadn't been informed, your scribbling in the notebook rather gives the game away," said Marjorie.

"And good luck with that privacy bit now. I would imagine rumours spread fast around here, and the press will hound us for the rest of our trip," said Edna.

"Accidents such as this one aren't big news around here," countered Denton.

"Are you suggesting people fly off cliffs all the time?" said Edna, incredulous.

The smile reappeared. It seemed Edna was getting through to their reluctant companion. "Not often, but not a rarity, either. We have rugged and treacherous terrain. Visitors sometimes misjudge the dangers."

"I take it protecting your privacy means you're not going to give us any titles of your books," said Horace.

"I don't mind giving you a title. Since you already know what I do, my secret's already out."

It's your other secrets I'm more interested in, thought Marjorie. "Did you notice anything unusual while sitting on your ledge, Arthur?" she asked, keen to bring the conversation back to the late Professor Bodwin Miller.

"Nothing. When I'm writing, I see nothing but what's on

the page or in my head, which is immersed in the plot. Sometimes, I don't look up for hours."

That's not quite true, thought Marjorie, having noticed him looking up frequently to see where the Carlisles and Professor Miller were throughout the morning.

"You still think the professor guy fell then?" said Edna.

"What else could have happened? I've already said, I've got a nose for these things. If I thought something sinister had occurred, I'd be the first to tell the police."

Marjorie didn't quite believe a crime-writing author would be so quick to reach the accident conclusion under the circumstances, particularly one plotting his next novel. Whether or not he wrote contemporary, it seemed an ideal plot point. Pushing someone over a cliff edge didn't confine itself to the now. Especially a cliff steeped in centuries of history.

"Did you see anybody else pass by?" asked Horace.

"No, that's why I was asking if you saw anything. I was writing notes from the visit to Boscastle this morning. I went to the same museum as those two women."

"Casey Sims and Miriam... Mim Butterfield," said Marjorie. "I'm surprised you haven't met Mim, she has a gallery in Bude."

"I might have seen her, but I don't make friends easily."

"You're telling me!" said Edna, chuckling. "You have to speak to people to make friends."

Once more, Arthur Denton reacted well to Edna's direct bluntness. "Okay. Maybe I'm not looking for friends."

"Why were you in the museum?" asked Marjorie.

"As we were there, I thought I'd brush up on my witchcraft," said Arthur.

"It must be hard to switch off," said Horace, clearly enthralled by the man and his profession. "If you let me have a list of your books, I'll pick one up. I like a bit of crime fiction myself, although I usually read modern detective stuff. Edna showed an interest in smuggling yesterday when the professor was regaling us with some of its history. I might buy her a copy."

"Don't bother," Marjorie heard Edna mutter under her breath.

"Edna prefers romcoms. She told me so on the bus," said Marjorie.

"I'll read it myself then," said Horace. "I might even pass it on to you, Fred, seeing as you like history so much."

"I've gone off it after this," said Frederick, his tone sullen. "And I don't read fiction."

"I don't know about you lot, but I'm starving. If we've got to hang around here, we might as well have lunch like Faith suggested," said Edna.

Arthur Denton took the hint. "I might do a bit more writing."

They rose from the bench, and Denton took their place. Marjorie turned around. "Just one more thing, Mr Denton. You say you live in Cornwall, but you're not from here, are you? Cambridge, is it?"

Arthur Denton's face clouded. He didn't reply.

"How did you work that out, Marge?" Edna asked, when they went indoors carrying their empty mugs.

"A hunch."

"Cambridge is becoming a theme, isn't it?" said Horace.

"Indeed, it is," said Marjorie, deep in thought.

TEN

Following the police interviews and the aftermath of Professor Miller's demise, Marjorie and the rest of their tour party checked into an inn at Trebarwith Strand, as planned. Although the police were treating the professor's death as accidental, the officer she had raised concerns with told Marjorie there might be follow-up questions. From his attitude, she suspected he had said it to humour her rather than meaning it.

Feeling tired after the overnight travel, the long day previously, and the shocking events of the morning Marjorie was delighted to have a room with a view of the sea. The inn's ambience struck her as refreshing, like discovering water in a desert, and from what she had observed, checking in had seemed to calm everyone in the group.

Marjorie's room was tastefully decorated in a modern style, and the bed boasted a memory-foam mattress. She had recently invested in a new mattress to ease the aches that often greeted her on waking.

From next door, she could hear banging and laughter, and recognised Edna's and Horace's voices. When checking in, Edna had charmed the manager into switching her to a room next to Marjorie. Again. A few well-practised flutters of her false eyelashes and the brazen patting of her brunette wig had done the trick. Either that, or the man decided it was the best way to deal with the force that was Edna Parkinton.

Marjorie no longer minded Edna being next door, as long as she didn't suggest one of her late-night 'girlie' talks that to date had never materialised, therefore what Edna meant by the term remained a mystery.

Not long after dressing for dinner, Marjorie heard a knock on her door. She opened it to find a black-haired Edna wearing a black-and-white knee-length dress with long sleeves, a white chiffon scarf draped around her neck, and carrying a matching white handbag. As always, Edna's high-heeled shoes made a statement. Tonight's were closed-toe black patent. Marjorie had changed into a cream dress along with a black cardigan for warmth. Her shoes had a small heel. It had been decades since she'd attempted to wear heels to look taller; she accepted the stark height difference between the much taller Edna made even greater by her cousin-in-law's ability to wear heels and not trip over.

"I see you're ready, Marge. The boys are going to wait for us in the bar."

Marjorie chuckled at the reference to Horace and Frederick as boys. After retrieving her handbag from the chair, she replied, "Let's not keep them waiting."

At dinner Marjorie observed different members of the tour party settling at tables. The Carlisles sat with Casey, Faith and Nick. Mim walked straight past them and sat alone in the glass-covered balcony, despite the autumnal weather outside. Arthur Denton didn't show. Marjorie guessed he might dine later or perhaps had requested room service.

The sound of waves crashing against rocks outside evoked memories of the dramatic scene earlier.

When checking in, Faith had promised them the food at the

inn would suit every palate. According to online reviews, dishes on offer could be basic or a tastebud extravaganza, she'd informed them. Judging by the beautifully presented fresh lobster tails on her plate, Marjorie needed no further convincing. Edna and Horace had ordered steaks that looked cooked to perfection, and Frederick's crab was almost a work of art. Marjorie had been torn between the crab and the lobster, but as she tucked into her choice, she was thrilled with it.

Every table was occupied in the small restaurant, which buzzed with cheerful chatter, accompanied by the clatter of cutlery. Marjorie focussed on the food in front of her, pleased the waiter had offered to crack and tail the meat for her.

As far as Marjorie could tell, nobody from their tour party seemed upset by the professor's death. Edna had told them over drinks, she was keen to dismiss the whole thing and accept the police's working theory. Marjorie understood her cousin-in-law's desire to accept the accident conclusion but suspected her motive was more about them continuing her dream coastal tour.

Since the shocking turn of events, Frederick's mood had dropped. Marjorie understood him well enough to recognise he seemed to be suffering a quiet mental trauma. She empathised; Frederick appeared to be in the minority who had liked the dead man. Like Edna, Frederick expressed a wish to put the accident behind them.

Marjorie studied the Carlisles while she ate. They had appeared suspiciously buoyed by the professor's death. Judging by the cheery conversation coming from where they were sitting, they remained so. The wine flowed freely at their table, its effects clear in the raucous laughter between the Carlisles and Casey Sims. Faith and Nick were a little more circumspect.

Mim, Marjorie noticed, was keeping her distance, dining in the conservatory with her back to them all. Every time Marjorie caught a glimpse of her, she seemed preoccupied, barely acknowledging the friendly smiles of the waiting staff. Her behaviour led Marjorie to conclude that the professor's death had affected Mim in a manner similar to Frederick.

When Edna finished her last bite of steak and set down her cutlery, a fresh burst of laughter erupted from the nearby table. "Those two have had personality transplants, if you ask me," she said. "At this rate, they'll be offering to buy drinks, and if they do, I'm accepting."

"Despite your wishful thinking, Edna, the transformation is interesting," said Marjorie. "It was obvious they didn't like the professor, though it doesn't explain their curt behaviour to Frederick and me at breakfast yesterday."

"Okay, I see where you're going with this. Just because they didn't like him, doesn't mean they knocked him off, Marge."

Marjorie studied the Carlisles again, "It doesn't, Edna, you're quite right, but—"

"But nothing," Edna snapped. "Why do you always see murderers under every table, or every bush?"

Edna was the queen of misquotes but Marjorie had long since given up trying to correct her. "I'm sorry, but I just cannot accept the accident theory."

"Why not?" Edna asked. "You weren't around because you snuck off to the loo, remember? The wind was howling a gale. Maybe it snagged his scarf."

"Perhaps, but Professor Miller knew his way around Tintagel Castle, he mentioned how many times he'd visited the place – six, if my memory serves me right."

Edna's meticulously tinted eyebrows shot up, almost meeting her wig's hairline. "So what?"

"If that was the case, don't you find it strange how he wandered off the main path and ended up taking a dangerous route? And even if he did, I can't see how he would have allowed himself to fall over the edge."

"Perhaps overconfidence got the better of him," said Horace. "These academic types can be so knowledgeable they sometimes believe they're invincible. Maybe his confidence led him to make an error of judgement, and it killed him."

"I don't doubt his confidence," said Marjorie, "but was it his knowledge of Tintagel Castle, or something else happening within this party that led to his error? I put it to you it may be the latter."

"Okay, Marge, you win. You're obviously convinced there's foul play here, and much as I hate to admit it, your instincts in the past have been right. What do you want us to do about it?"

Marjorie eyed Frederick, who was picking at the remaining morsels of crab. She needed his support. They all waited for him to finish the last mouthful. He finally lifted his head.

"I've been thinking about it ever since we arrived here. All I can say is that Professor Miller was troubled – I even feel guilty for leaving him and wonder if I should have tried to find out what was bothering him, but I can't do anything about that now. It's hard to imagine him falling unless he was so worried about something else, he wandered astray. I've done that before when I've had things on my mind."

"Moody people can do that," said Edna.

Frederick ignored Edna's dig, lowering his voice, though there was no need as the raucous noise from the neighbouring table made it unnecessary. "The people that were directly responsible for his mood change. My hunch is the Carlisles know more about what happened than anybody else. I'm not much of a sleuth, but I'll help if I can."

"That's where you're wrong, Fred," said Horace. "You're an excellent researcher. That's a good place to start. I vote we find out what the Carlisles have to hide, and what it was they disliked most about Bodwin Miller. Why wouldn't they leave the man alone, even though they didn't speak to him? Now they've opened up a bit, me and Edna could ply them with drinks and see what we can get out of them while you do your brilliant internet stuff."

Frederick's mood visibly lifted, a sparkle returning to his grey eyes. He had a lovely smile, made all the better by the fact it wasn't as common as Marjorie would like to see. His chest swelled with confidence following Horace's compliment. "I can do that. I'll get onto it as soon as I get back to my room. I'll let you know in the morning what I find."

"Yeah, and while you're at it, I think you need to have a look at that Casey Sims woman as well," said Edna. "There's still the row she had with Professor Boring last night. And the veiled accusation about academic misconduct. I'd like to know what that meant. It might have something to do with what Horace said earlier. The thing that resulted in her leaving – or more likely being thrown off a course at – Cambridge."

"Yes, I've been pondering that one too," said Marjorie. "I could try to speak to Casey while you distract the Carlisles."

"Mim seems very upset by it all," said Horace, his eyes drifting towards the conservatory. "I don't know what's going on with her. I do hope she'll be all right. She seems such a sensitive soul, just like someone I once knew."

Edna sighed. "Don't be fooled by her. You know what these artistic types are like: up one minute, down the next. I'd hate to live with their moods."

Marjorie clamped her mouth closed to keep her from saying something she might later regret. Edna had showed repeatedly that she had an unpredictable variety of moods, often swinging back and forth like a pendulum. When she trusted herself to speak again, all she could manage was, "Quite." She made a mental note to ask Horace what had triggered this new infatuation in case his vulnerability was being exploited.

Frederick's crinkled eyes met Marjorie's, and in that subtle glance she felt they were on the same wavelength. Gathering her thoughts, she added. "Frederick, I also think we should consider Arthur Denton. He might be from Cambridge or at least have spent time there. He showed an unhealthy interest in the professor, albeit more subtly than the Carlisles. It wouldn't hurt to find out more background on his life before he became a writer. As for the pen name hiding his identity, I imagine one only has to do an internet search these days to discover who the writer behind the pen really is. It's not like in the days of George Eliot, is it? And we know she had a lot to hide."

"Wasn't that because she was a woman and it was a man's world?" Edna remarked.

"Partly, but partly to avoid the scandal of an unmarried woman living with a married man," said Horace, winking.

"I thought the same thing," said Frederick. "Not about George Eliot. That man Denton's not who he says he is, not to mention he's got ice in his veins. I didn't take to him at all. If Horace hadn't introduced us, he wouldn't have cared. Not once did he ask who we were, or where we came from. Plus, he lives in Cornwall so what's he doing on this tour if he's such a loner? I'm not convinced by his story. All he seemed interested in was who saw what. It makes you wonder if he was fishing for, or hiding, information."

"And the biggest question of all is why did the professor move from the safety of the paths?" said Marjorie, sighing. "Is it, as Horace suggests, that he was overconfident? Was he under-taking research for one of his academic papers – he mentioned writing papers on ancient smuggling and so forth? Or..." All eyes were on her as she racked her brains for what she was trying to say.

"Go on, Marge. Tell us."

"Or," she continued, "Was he lured away from the path under a pretence, and pushed?"

"That makes more sense to me than anything we've heard so far," said Horace. "What did you make of the police? They seemed in a hurry to close the books on the case, didn't they?"

"I had a word with the sergeant in charge of the case and explained there had been some unusual behaviour from certain members of the tour party, but he didn't pay much attention to me," said Marjorie, recalling an occasion where a belligerent detective inspector had barged into her home, almost arresting her housekeeper because he wouldn't listen.

"Unforgivable," said Horace.

"I think he assumed I was an interfering old biddy with too much time on my hands."

"Yeah, well, he needs to go back and read his Miss Marple books, doesn't he, because that's what the officials thought of her. I've said it before, and I'll say it again: Marge, you've got one of the sharpest minds when it comes to crime."

"Thank you, Edna."

"Even though you get muddled sometimes, I'm sure that's why you don't always use your stick. You're forgetful."

Marjorie let out a heavy sigh. *And then you have to go and ruin it,* she thought. "I don't forget, I choose not to use it." *Especially when you're around,* went unsaid.

"It's satisfying to know that the awesome foursome is back in action," said Horace.

Whether Marjorie was right about the professor being pushed over the cliff edge or not, she felt they had a duty to find out. And if the police would not investigate, then the awesome foursome would.

ELEVEN

Faith and Nick left the merry trio of Carlisles and Casey, arriving at Marjorie and friends' table.

"We just wanted to check how you are all feeling following our curtailed day out? As I said earlier, I'm sorry it cut our visit to Tintagel Castle short, and for what happened," said Faith.

"It's hardly your fault, is it?" said Edna. "Unless you pushed him off the cliff," she added, cackling. Edna's cackle resulted in one of hers and Horace's joint snorting sessions. This was a habit that was hard to break, and trying would make it last longer. Marjorie had learned one had to allow it to finish its course.

"The police and paramedics reassured me – although that might not be the right word – that Professor Miller must have stumbled and fallen, and I'm inclined to believe them." Faith's face flushed, noticeable even beneath the makeup.

"Why don't you join us for coffee?" Horace offered.

Faith and Nick sat down while Horace ordered after-dinner coffees all round. Marjorie would have preferred tea, but as it wasn't listed on the dinner menu, she went along without comment, not wanting to put anyone to any trouble.

Faith's eyes narrowed as she studied them. "Please don't tell me you believe otherwise?"

"Judging by their faces, I believe our sleuths think there's more at play here." Nick squeezed Faith's upper arm affectionately. The four had first met Nick when he had driven them around London while they were investigating a suspicious death. Marjorie had hoped that Faith would find happiness through their relationship and it seemed she had.

Once hot drinks were on the table Marjorie answered, checking first that people at other tables were not listening to their conversation. "We can't say for sure, but we are keen to find out."

"Some of us are," said Edna, brow furrowed.

"We observed some oddities, let's put it that way, that we'd like to look into," said Marjorie.

"Oh dear," said Faith. "Should I be worried?"

"Not at all," said Horace. "Everything's under control. We'll do what we do best and play the innocent, nosey old parkers. Nobody will suspect us, and we'll have the answers to our questions before you know it."

Marjorie hoped it would be as simple as Horace stated but doubted it would be that straightforward. She added cream to her coffee before taking a sip of the hot liquid. It was bitter, but the cream helped soften it.

"I hope so," said Faith. "And I also hope you're wrong because I don't want our business to be adversely affected. We're just taking off, aren't we, Nick?"

"Yep, it's been a busy time," he said, patting Faith's hand. "Can't complain."

Marjorie felt certain Nick was good for Faith, who had a poor history with men, often choosing the wrong type. On this occasion, she'd got it just right. She and Nick made an ideal couple, and more importantly, he respected her. Faith had told Horace how Nick supported her with her mother who could be demanding and overbearing. That, in Marjorie's opinion, deserved bonus points.

"Horace reckons it'll do your business good, either way," said Edna glumly.

"Really?" asked Faith.

"Oh, yes," said Horace. "Things like this are on trend these days."

"You make murder and mayhem sound like a fashion accessory," said Faith.

"Not quite, but I mean, why do you think people go on ghost walks and murder mystery weekends? If they can get on a tour where an actual murder took place, or even a fatal accident – not related to your safety measures of course – they're drawn by that sort of thing. As I said to the others, I don't think you have to worry about your business. Plus, you know I'll always put business your way."

"I'm grateful for everything you've done, Horace, and how you've supported us since we launched All Weather Tours. It wouldn't be the same without you, and it wouldn't be where it is today without your support."

"Think nothing of it," said Horace. "Your company is the best we've had. When my sons are entertaining overseas visitors, you're the first person they think of these days."

"I've got to know them well and we get a lot of off-season work from them. In fact, we've got a whole series of London tours next month. It's excellent having work in November. In December, we're planning a trip to Northumberland."

"You see. This tragedy won't affect your business at all."

"I've been trying to tell her that," said Nick, "but she's a born worrier. It was a risk going it alone with Faith having worked for Queen Cruises and Travel for so long, but I think she's made the right decision, don't you?"

"Absolutely," said Marjorie, "you're thriving on it, dear. In fact, I've never seen you look more radiant."

Nick grinned again, stroking Faith's cheek. "Me neither."

"Did you enjoy the food?" Faith asked, blushing again.

"Delicious, just as you described," Marjorie said, noticing Edna pouting into her coffee cup. *What's got into her?*

Faith picked up on the look too, it seemed. "Was your dinner okay, Edna? If not, I can have a word."

"It was delicious. It's not that."

"What is it, old girl?" Horace asked.

"I would have liked the option of dessert, but you took it upon yourself to shake your head on our behalf. Typical bossy bloke."

"Oh dear, I'm in the doghouse. I'll make it up to you and buy you an extra glass of whisky when we're done here."

Edna grinned. Marjorie marvelled again at Horace's ability to curb Edna's moods before they came to anything. That reminded her, she hadn't yet spoken to him about Edna's hearing aids.

"You should tell them," said Nick, breaking through Marjorie's musings.

"Tell us what?" Edna asked.

"I had the impression you wanted to say something when we were at the castle, but you stopped yourself," said Marjorie. "What's on your mind?"

"It might be nothing," said Faith.

"And it might be something," said Nick.

Seeing Edna open her mouth, Marjorie raised a warning hand to prevent her snapping at Faith. Her cousin-in-law was already stressed about the possibility a murder had taken place, and obviously over missing dessert. A stressed Edna was a doubly impatient Edna.

Horace too, appeared to have noticed Edna's body language, and the potential for an explosion; he laid a comforting hand on her forearm before looking at Faith. "Why don't you tell us what's bothering you. You know what they say: a problem shared and all that."

Faith checked behind but the Carlisles and Casey had moved on to desserts and were chatting happily. "I can't be certain, but someone might have taken Bodwin's notebook."

"And someone definitely took his briefcase," added Nick.

Marjorie felt this was a significant development. "Why don't you start from the beginning and tell us what happened."

"As you know, I made my way down to the rocks where... where... you know..." Faith fiddled with a gold chain hanging around her neck before continuing. "Anyway, I explained to the officer in charge who I was and told him I recognised the man as Professor Miller. He asked me a few questions, also requesting the name of his next of kin. I gave him the name of Bodwin's cousin – that's who he'd put down on his emergency contact form – as you know we take names and contact details, just in case."

Edna drummed her fingers on the table. Anyone but Faith would have felt the full force of an Edna 'get on with it' tirade, but Marjorie was grateful she settled for taking her frustration out on the table.

"He asked me if, before they contacted someone living hundreds of miles away, I'd have a brief look at the body."

Nick put his arm around her shoulder. "I should have been with you."

"Nick couldn't be in two places at once, he was busy with the police officer who had stayed up at the castle."

Heavier finger-drumming, now accompanied by a knee bouncing up and down hitting the table from underneath. Marjorie followed Faith's worried eyes as they looked at Edna, who forced a tight smile.

"That must have been awful," said Frederick, drawing a glare from Edna, who might tolerate Faith's ramblings, but not his deterring her from getting to the point.

"It was, but that's when I noticed Bodwin's notebook was missing. He carried it everywhere and jotted things down, not as obsessively as the author, but it was always with him."

"I noticed it in his jacket pocket when we first met him yesterday, and saw him looking at it in Boscastle," said Marjorie.

"Maybe he left it on the bus, or it landed on the rocks when he fell," said Edna, rolling her eyes. "It was a long way down you know."

"It wasn't on the bus, but that's what the police sergeant said when I told him, and it made sense at the time until..."

Before Edna lost control, Marjorie intervened. "Until you realised his briefcase had been stolen."

"Yes," said Nick. "Once everyone checked in this afternoon, I labelled the professor's suitcase and realised the briefcase was missing—"

"Hang on a minute. How on earth did you know it had been stolen, Marge?"

Marjorie sighed, wishing Edna would pay more attention... or wear her hearing aids.

"Nick told us about five minutes ago, Edna," said Horace, gently.

"More like half an hour ago. How am I supposed to remember everything when people take forever..." Edna hesitated, realising Faith was visibly upset. Instead, she looked at Nick. "And you're sure it was there in the first place?"

"Positive, I loaded it myself. I loaded everyone's luggage, and he asked if I'd mind storing it away from prying eyes. He removed the notebook and put it in his pocket."

"Interesting," said Marjorie. "This makes our foul play theory more plausible. But what was in the notebook that was so important?"

"It could just as easily be an opportunistic theft, or even someone taking the briefcase by mistake," said Frederick. "And maybe the notebook wasn't taken at all and, as Edna suggested, fell on the rocks and floated out to sea by now."

"I agree about the notebook, but I don't believe the briefcase thing is a mistake," said Nick. "It was the only one. Arthur Denton was carrying his with him."

"I'm glad we've told you," said Faith.

"Have you mentioned the briefcase theft to the police?" Horace asked.

"I'll do it in the morning. I think they've got enough on their hands for now. And I wanted to give whoever took it the chance to bring it back," said Nick.

Having finished her coffee, Faith stood up, her eyes puffy. "If you don't mind, we'll say good night. Who's joining us on the *Doc Martin* set tour tomorrow?"

"We intend to," said Horace. "Edna's a fan."

Marjorie felt a moment of confusion, but then remembered Edna and Horace were talking about a village where they could visit settings where scenes were shot for a television programme they both watched.

"I'll enjoy a free day, if you don't mind," said Marjorie.

"Me too," said Frederick. "I'm sure Marjorie and I will find enough to keep us entertained around here. We could take a walk."

"Indeed," she agreed.

"So we'll see you two first thing then." Faith looked at Horace and Edna. "Goodnight all."

Nick took Faith's arm, and they left the restaurant. Once they were out of earshot, Edna raised an eyebrow. "Come on then, Mr Benefactor, tell us, what was that all about?"

"What?" asked Horace, looking confused.

"You know what. All that 'thank you for helping us set up our business' talk."

"Oh that. You already know I sent a few clients or asked my sons to send a few clients Faith's way when she and Nick started out. She's such an excellent tour guide, she now gets regular work from Tyler Avionics. It's as simple as that. Although she thanks me for what I did, and still do, all I do is point people her way if any of my old contacts ask me for names when they need to entertain people from overseas. Which they still do ad nauseam, as if I'm their social secretary. Everyone I've sent their way gives them repeat work. I haven't heard a bad thing, so it's a win-win situation."

"Quite right," said Marjorie. "She's a marvellous woman. And Nick's given her more confidence. I'm pleased to see her so happy."

"Yeah, did you know they are in the same room, Marge?" Edna said, winking.

"That's none of our business, Edna. Now, I suggest we park the notebook and briefcase issues for now and move into the bar as our fellow travellers have done. It's time to circulate, we have work to do."

"I'll go up to my room and start the internet researching," said Frederick.

Horace tapped his nose. "Come on then, gang. Time the awesome foursome went to work."

"You and Edna leave first and collar the Carlisles. I'll finish my coffee and follow," said Marjorie.

Frederick waited until Horace and Edna retreated into the bar before saying, "You will be careful, won't you?"

"I promise."

"In that case, I'll head upstairs."

Marjorie sat for a few minutes but didn't finish the coffee. She really wasn't a coffee drinker, but it allowed Horace and Edna enough time to do what they did best. She noticed Mim exiting the balcony and, worried she was heading for the bar to speak to Casey, Marjorie got up quickly and followed.

TWELVE

It couldn't have worked out better for Edna and Horace. Casey had plonked herself in a comfortable armchair at the far end of the bar with a drink on her table, tapping frantically on her phone. The Carlisles were sitting on a large, leather settee in front of a wood-burning fire, which was set against a feature wall. The low ceiling featured exposed beams. Edna nudged Horace, motioning to the couple.

"I see them," he said in a low voice.

"I'll make myself comfortable near the fire," Edna said in a voice loud enough to be heard.

"What can I get you to drink?" he asked.

"The usual." Edna trotted over to where the Carlisles sat. They looked up cheerfully, so she took her opportunity. "Do you mind if we join you?"

"Feel free," said Stan.

Edna settled in an armchair at one end of the sofa. "We haven't been properly introduced," she said. "I'm Edna Parkinton, a friend of Marjorie Snellthorpe and Frederick Mackworth. I understand you met them on the train yesterday."

"We did," said Naomi. Although friendly enough, neither

seemed keen to engage in conversation. Edna hoped Horace would hurry because they were making moves as if they were about to retire for the night, and their glasses were almost empty. On cue, Horace appeared, placing a whisky in front of Edna before moving to the chair at the opposite end of the large coffee table and placing his drink down. The measures were generous, which made her grin. "I'm reliably informed this is a top-notch local whisky called No.9," Horace said.

Before he could sit down, Edna motioned with her head to the glasses in front of the couple.

Always game for subterfuge, he grinned. "It's a pleasure to meet you at last," he said, offering his hand to Stan, who shook it, and then to Naomi. "I'm Horace Tyler. I take it Edna's introduced herself?"

"She has. I'm Stan and this is my wife, Naomi." Something about the affectionate way Stan introduced his wife stood out to Edna.

"Can I buy you a drink?" Horace offered. The couple looked at each other and nodded in unison.

"If that's all right, yes please, I'll have a gin and tonic," said Naomi, smiling.

"And I'll have a pint of real ale," said Stan.

"Coming right up," said Horace. He didn't get far before the bartender called over.

"I've got it, I'll bring them over. You sit down, Horace."

First-name terms already, thought Edna. Horace made friends wherever they went. Horace sat in the other armchair. "I'd ask how you're enjoying the tour," he said, "but after today, I'm not sure that would be appropriate."

The couple exchanged a glance before Stan said, "We're enjoying it well enough, it's going to be a great week. There's a lot to look forward to."

"Sad about the professor though, eh?" said Horace, clearly probing.

"Mm," said Stan. "Still, life goes on. We'd rather not talk about it, if that's okay. We want to focus on the bright side."

Edna couldn't believe her ears! From the moment they had joined the tour yesterday until dinner tonight, the Carlisles had behaved as though they were at a funeral rather than on holiday. Now they were all smiles and friendliness. The only thing that had changed was the demise of Professor Miller, along with the amount of alcohol they seemed to have consumed.

"I can't say I took to the professor anyway," she said, hoping it would draw them out. "I hate to speak ill of the dead and all that, but he was a bit too fond of his own voice, as we say up north."

"Now, now, Edna," said Horace. "That's not the way to talk about somebody who's just passed."

"Just speaking the truth," she replied.

"Quite right," said Naomi.

Her husband snapped his head towards her, raising a quizzical eyebrow.

"No, I meant quite right, he was boring," she said. "If we had had to listen to any more of that claptrap this morning, I think we might have packed our bags and gone home."

Now we're getting somewhere, thought Edna. "Had you met him before yesterday?"

Another exchanged glance. "Don't think so," said Stan. "Why do you ask?"

Because you stuck to him like glue, Edna thought, but said, "No reason. I just thought you seemed to know each other, that's all."

The bartender arrived and placed a pint of beer in front of Stan and handed Naomi her gin and tonic. The couple were bleary-eyed. Edna was convinced that, if they went about it the right way, she and Horace would unravel the mystery behind their strange behaviour towards Professor Miller before the night was out.

"What a wonderful place this is," said Horace, clearly happy to play the waiting game. Edna conceded in her head it was the right thing to do at the moment and return to the topic of the professor, later.

"Our room overlooks the sea, and dinner was absolutely delicious," said Naomi, gushing, her speech slurred.

Edna noticed how they held hands, almost as though they were newlyweds. She doubted joining a tour group constituted a honeymoon, but they gave the impression of being very much in love since dropping the 'miseries-of-the-year' impression.

"It's great we're staying here tomorrow night as well," said Horace. "Can't say I'm upset about being in one place for a couple of nights. I don't enjoy swapping and changing beds all the time, and this place is ideal: a good choice by Faith."

"I couldn't agree more," said Naomi. "I love how close it is to the beach and the sea."

"We've been lucky with the weather as well, so far," said Horace.

Edna did an internal eye-roll. Why did the British always feel the need to mention the weather? But then she reminded herself that she often did the same. And Horace was right, it was glorious weather for autumn, although the strong blustery winds made keeping her wigs in place more challenging than usual. The howling wind banging against the windows made the bar even more inviting. But this small talk bored her, so if Horace didn't move the conversation along soon, she would have to.

"Faith is a remarkable woman. She told us she knew you and your friends before this week," said Stan. His speech was less slurred than his wife's but the ruddy cheeks suggested the alcohol was affecting him.

"We've met Faith a few times," said Horace, "In fact, the first time I met Edna, we were on a river cruise and Faith was the guide. At that time, she worked for a large conglomerate."

Edna was pleased he neglected to mention the murder, as that wouldn't have gone down well at the moment. She noticed Marge pass by out of the corner of her eye while taking a sip of whisky. Edna almost jumped up when Marge stumbled close to Casey's table. Casey intervened, and seeing the two women ordering drinks as they settled at the same table, Edna relaxed. Casey and Marge began chatting as though they'd been lifelong friends. *Good old Marge.*

Edna's attention was back at their own table. "When Faith set up with Nick, Horace put business their way to help them get started," she said, hoping they were still on the same subject. Marge was forever telling her to concentrate more, but it was difficult. There always seemed to be something more interesting going on elsewhere, and her hearing problems presented an additional challenge.

Stan raised a quizzical bushy eyebrow.

"I'm retired these days, but I'm still a director of the business I founded – Tyler Avionics. We've always dealt with overseas buyers and other parties interested in avionics parts. My two sons run the business now, but they keep me informed. Faith has been a godsend in the overseas visitor department. She's saved my sons, who don't really enjoy hosting people, countless hours entertaining. She organises trips, and because our visitors travel at all times of year, we've thrown work her way in the offseason. It's a win-win: her business thrives and my sons offload what they hate the most."

"Well, I hope her travel business still thrives after today," said Naomi.

"What do you mean?" asked Edna, seizing the opportunity.

"Well, you know, with the death."

"Though unpleasant, Faith told us after dinner that everybody wants to continue with the trip. It seems nobody's that bothered," Horace said.

"We can't understand why he went so close to the edge in the first place," said Edna.

"Because he lived life on the edge, that's why," said Naomi, before realising what she'd said. She slapped a hand across her mouth.

"So you did know him?" said Edna.

Naomi exhaled the heaviest sigh, glancing at Stan. He nodded. "It can't do any harm now, love," he said.

Naomi's bleary eyes looked as if they were trying to focus on Edna's but failing, so she took another gulp of her drink. "You could say I 'knew' the professor," she made finger air quotes. "We were married for ten horrible years."

Edna had to place the back of a hand under her chin to prevent her jaw from dropping open. *Now this is an unexpected revelation.*

"I take it from what you've just said, and the way he reacted to your presence yesterday, it wasn't an amicable divorce?"

"You take that right," said Stan. "Amicable didn't enter that man's vocabulary."

"He seemed friendly enough to me," said Horace.

"Oh, he could be fine as long as he was the centre of attention and holding the room. But if Miller didn't like someone, well..."

"He's made our lives hell for the past three years," said Naomi.

"So he didn't want a divorce," said Edna. "Why didn't he just get over it? They say women spurned and all that, but men spurned, they are much worse." She knocked back a larger swig of whisky than she meant to. Horace grinned.

"Stan and I met while I was still married to Bodwin; he never got over the rejection or the teasing when some of his students heard about it."

"It wasn't easy for Naomi," said Stan. "She worked on the marriage, but he left her on her own a lot. Whenever he came back from his many research trips, he expected the loyal wife to be sitting in the kitchen, glad her man was home. He was as archaic as the ancient world he inhabited."

So you were the shoulder to cry on, thought Edna but held her peace. Fred wouldn't like it; he got himself in a tizzy over unfaithful spouses.

Naomi interjected. "Bodwin arrived home early from one of his research trips..."

"And well... you know," said Stan.

"I get the idea," said Horace, chuckling. "It wasn't the homecoming he expected."

"It was a shame he found out that way because we'd decided to tell him when he got back anyway," said Naomi.

"Not that he would have taken it any differently if we'd told him and been open with him. He was that sort of man: rejection wasn't in his genes. As I say he lived in a 'pistols at dawn' world. He resented me, and before I knew it, I lost my job."

"What do you mean?" asked Horace.

"Stan worked as a lecturer in the history department. I was the secretary. That's how we met. Bodwin made sure Stan was forced to leave."

"By making your life a misery?" Horace quizzed.

"Oh, he did that all right, but no, he manufactured the theft of some relics the university had borrowed, then he made sure they were found in my office. To avoid a scandal, the university offered me the option of resigning. I argued the toss and told them I hadn't taken the stuff, but they said the evidence spoke for itself. I had to take their offer, but I negotiated an agreement, giving me early retirement. That was the cost of keeping my reputation – and theirs – intact."

"I knew it was Bodwin although he tried to tell me my lover, as he called Stan, was a thief. He believed his little scheme would turn me against Stan, but I handed my notice in and left him," said Naomi.

This is all very enlightening, thought Edna, *and an ideal motive for murder*.

"Was that the last you'd seen of him before yesterday?" Horace asked.

"I'd have left the university gladly if I thought that would be the last of it, but no, Bodwin would never let Naomi be happy. He stalked her."

"Seriously?" Edna felt as if her eyes would pop out if she heard any more about Professor Vindictive.

"Whenever he came back to Cambridge. If I was out with friends, doing shopping, whatever I was doing, he would spring up in my eyeline. It became unbearable." Naomi took another drink.

"Did you report him to the police?" asked Horace.

"We hoped he'd get over it," said Stan, "and just leave us alone, but when we found out he was on this trip as well, it was the last straw. We were going to go to the police as soon as we got home."

"I see," said Horace.

"That must have been awful, but why didn't you cancel the holiday?" Edna quizzed.

"We only found out about it yesterday morning, at breakfast, otherwise we'd have changed the holiday and booked something for another time."

"Are you suggesting that he found out you were coming on this holiday, and then booked himself on it just to harass you? That guy was seriously weird," said Edna.

"We're not suggesting it," said Stan. "We're convinced that's what happened. We wouldn't have known until we got here if Faith hadn't emailed saying that a man by the name of Professor Bodwin Miller had agreed to give talks at each of the historical landmarks we were visiting."

"I'm sure he only did it to frighten us," added Naomi.

"You didn't seem that frightened to me," Edna said, "if you

don't mind me saying, it came across as the opposite."

"You're right. We were shocked more than scared, but we decided after breakfast yesterday, we weren't taking it anymore. We started doing the same to him as he's been doing to us since Naomi left him."

"That explains why you were hanging around so close to him," said Edna. "We noticed you doing that. It seemed to unnerve him."

"Precisely," said Stan.

"And do you think it worked?" asked Horace.

"Well, he threw himself off the cliff, didn't he?" With that, Stan downed the rest of his pint and got to his feet. Naomi followed suit. Edna gawped after the couple teetering out of the bar.

"Well, that was a bombshell if ever I heard one," said Horace, chuckling.

"And a clear motive for murder," said Edna.

"They're going to have stonking headaches in the morning," added Horace.

"Serves themselves right for drinking too much. By the way I like this No.9."

Horace smirked. "Says the lady who doesn't drink too much."

Edna laughed. "Yes, but I can hold my drink."

"I won't remind you of the time we almost had to carry you out of the Wimbledon tennis grounds then." His eyes twinkled. Edna only had a vague recollection of what he was talking about. "I wonder how Marjorie's getting on," Horace added.

"She looks as though she's getting on just fine. How about another No.9?"

Horace chuckled. "Edna Parkinton, you're a hypocrite."

"I only drink whisky when I'm with you lot," said Edna, handing him her empty glass.

THIRTEEN

Marjorie watched Mim fly through the bar and out of the inn as though some imaginary beast was chasing her into the darkness. Casey sat in the far corner of the bar and didn't look up from her phone. Marjorie saw that Horace and Edna were with their targets, and from the way their conversation flowed, they might be making headway.

How to get Casey's eyes away from her screen was now the dilemma facing Marjorie. Interrupting her was unlikely to work and might annoy her. Marjorie moved through the bar slowly, arriving close to Casey's table where she toppled to one side, gripping the edge of the sofa the young woman was sitting on.

It worked! Casey set her phone aside and sprang to Marjorie's aid. "Gosh. Are you all right?"

"I think so, just one of my dizzy spells, that's all."

"Should I ask the hotel to call for a doctor?"

"Oh no, thank you. If I did that every time I had one of these turns, the NHS would have no resources left." *Not that they had any in the first place*, thought Marjorie. "I just need to sit for a moment."

Casey took her arm. "Why don't you sit with me. Lady Marjorie, isn't it?"

"Just Marjorie. That's very kind, but I don't wish to be any trouble. You seem busy." Marjorie indicated the phone's bright screen lying on the sofa like some demanding talisman.

Casey picked it up and thrust it into her handbag. "It's nothing. Please, join me."

"Only if you let me buy you a drink. I see your glass is empty."

Casey hesitated before answering. "Okay, it's a deal."

Marjorie took the armchair next to the comfortable leather sofa. Casey headed over to the bar and was followed back to their table by the bartender. "What can I get you ladies?"

"I'll have a white wine spritzer, please," said Casey, sitting back down on the sofa.

"A brandy for me, please. Put them on my tab," said Marjorie. Casey raised an eyebrow. "My doctor tells me brandy is the best thing for funny turns," she explained.

Casey smiled, her brown eyes bright and friendly, a contrast to the more severe black hair pulled into a tight ponytail. Up close, the earrings decorating her ears sparkled under the light from a standing lamp. Oversized jumpers seemed to be her thing, and jeans. Once the drinks were on the table, Casey's eyes flicked from Marjorie to her handbag. The pull of modern-day technology rivalled drugs in how strong it could be. Marjorie must act quickly.

Lifting her brandy glass and taking a sip, she said as casually as she could. "I think the business at the castle has upset my blood pressure."

A flash of anger crossed Casey's eyes for a brief moment. She took a sip of spritzer but Marjorie could tell she had her attention. "It wasn't the best start to a holiday."

"My friends and I are struggling to comprehend it," said

Marjorie, speaking quickly. "One minute the professor's sharing his vast knowledge, and half an hour later, he's dead. It's difficult to take in."

Casey's brows furrowed and her cheeks reddened. "The policewoman I spoke to said he should have stuck to the paths. Apparently, he's not the first to die at Tintagel Castle; she thinks it's cursed."

Marjorie recalled how Casey and Mim had hurried to the witchcraft museum in Boscastle, making her wonder if they believed in such things. "You don't believe that, do you?"

"Places can be cursed, so can people. Perhaps Professor Miller upset some dark power. When I went to the museum with Mim, we saw effigies the volunteer told us would have been used to harm people centuries ago. I got the impression the professor upset people, so maybe he got what was coming to him."

"That's a little harsh," said Marjorie. "Are you suggesting a dark force was at work, or that his death was something other than an accident?"

"I don't know really. I've been checking the local news channels, and so far, they're reporting his death as an accident. It's been referred to the coroner's office in Truro."

Marjorie imagined that would be routine procedure in a case such as this. "Whatever happened up there, it must have been terrifying for the poor man. I wonder if he was married?"

"He wasn't," Casey answered too quickly.

"Oh, I'm sorry. I didn't realise you knew him."

"I didn't, not personally, but I'm studying for a PhD and was an undergraduate at Cambridge. He had a reputation."

"As a womaniser, you mean?"

"No. I don't know anything about that sort of thing, all I know is he got divorced a few years back."

"What reputation are you referring to?"

"He was arrogant and opinionated. Woe betide anyone who disagreed with him, he hated that." Casey spat the words out with venom. Marjorie's mind went back to something Horace had said about disgruntled students, complaints, and Casey leaving the university at around the same time. Were the two things linked?

"Did you ever disagree with him?"

Casey shook her head, tears threatening to spill. "Not me... a... a friend."

"Someone close to you?"

"Not anymore. The truth of the matter is that if you disagreed with Miller, he made your life hell until you were thrown off the course, or he failed you."

"Surely that's not allowed. Don't they have appeal processes?"

"Yes, but he was always too clever. He gradually wore a student down until he made them feel like they were idiots. Their work then deteriorated, and he had every justification to fail them."

"Is that what happened to your friend?"

Casey nodded. "It was worse for him because he disagreed with the professor in a public lecture theatre. Afterwards, he had a target on his back. He'd been bullied by his father and couldn't take the constant belittling so he ended up leaving. Professor Miller was a vindictive man, some of us complained, and I think maybe the university got wise to him because he stood down. That's why he became a guest lecturer, although he still supervised PhD students, but only those who agreed with his radical views on history."

"I didn't realise one could have radical views on history, I thought history was... well... history."

"It's not as simple as that. There's only so much evidence about things, and the gaps can be coloured, or filled in, by interpretation, especially where ancient history is concerned. Most historians acknowledge it, but Miller thought he knew better. You'd think he was a time traveller from the way he taught his classes. He liked to challenge traditional thinking."

Marjorie didn't think that in itself was a bad thing, but she didn't like the idea of anyone bullying impressionable young students and damaging their confidence before they'd even begun their careers. "Are you a historian yourself?"

"No. I graduated in philosophy, then got a Master's degree and now I'm doing a PhD. My thesis is along philosophical lines, but my ex-boyfriend studied under Professor Miller."

"I get the impression you cared for him deeply," said Marjorie.

"You're very intuitive, Marjorie," said Casey. "You'd make a good white witch. Are you interested in witchcraft?"

Marjorie almost choked on her brandy but recovered enough not to sound flabbergasted when she answered. "I can't say it's a subject I've given much thought to, but obviously you have. Is it part of your philosophical thesis?"

"No, I wasn't interested in it at all until I heard Miller had radical views about its influence on historical legend and mythology. He felt it linked them, especially in Cornwall. At least that's what Mim told me. It was Mim who suggested we visit the Museum of Witchcraft and Magic to view something he had been involved in creating for the museum. You've met Mim, she's an artist. We got on quite well, although she was in a bit of a temper after the museum visit, and now his death seems to have hit her hard. She's hardly spoken a word since the accident."

"You mentioned Mim's desire to see something the professor had created, what was it?"

"The display included ancient stones and tooth-shaped things he reckons were used by soothsayers to predict tidal patterns for smugglers. The professor had donated the finds and added treasure maps."

"Do you think Mim knew the professor?"

"I got the impression they had met in the past, but I don't think she liked him. Perhaps I'm wrong and it was the opposite. Maybe she had a crush on him."

Marjorie frowned. Mim hadn't struck her as a doe-eyed crush type of person, more like an independent and free spirit. Perhaps even manipulative. "What made you think she didn't like him?" asked Marjorie.

"It's hard to say, just a general impression. I think she may have known him more than she let on – she seemed to know a lot about him but she plays things close to her chest. She's slightly eccentric, I'm certain she believes in witchcraft. Maybe that's what's upset her. There was something in a display about projecting bad karma onto others."

"Are you suggesting she believes her thoughts, or your visit, played a role in the professor's death?" Marjorie asked.

"I hadn't thought about it, but maybe that is what she thinks. It would explain her behaviour, and why she's so upset. We were supposed to have dinner together tonight, but she just walked right past our table and took herself into the conservatory."

Perhaps she didn't like the company you were with, thought Marjorie, saying, "Perhaps she needed space after what occurred. We were all shocked by the event. Do the headlines you've read suggest anything other than an accident?" Marjorie checked.

"Reading between the lines, they might. Not that the police believe that. Despite mentioning the place was cursed, the officer I spoke to was agreeing with the accidental death lines. She suggested it would be an open-and-shut case and not to be concerned."

"Did she ask you many questions? I can't say the officer I spoke to asked me very much."

"Just where I was at the time of the accident, did I see anything? That kind of thing. Did you see what happened?"

"I'm afraid not, I was on my way back from a comfort break, and didn't see a thing. I heard a man cry out. I take it you didn't see either?" Marjorie quizzed.

"I saw that woman, Naomi Carlisle – I had dinner with her and her husband – they're okay when you get to know them."

"You were saying . . ."

"Oh yes, I saw her goading him to go close to the edge, which seemed odd. I think she was bored by his dry lecture."

"My friend Frederick found it interesting."

"The content was interesting, his delivery, less so. I'm used to listening to dry lectures, maybe she isn't. Perhaps that's why she tried to liven things up a bit."

"Well, I'm glad he didn't take her advice and go closer to the edge at that time."

"Yes, it's surprising, but then arrogant men do what they want, don't they?"

"I suppose some do," said Marjorie. "Although I wouldn't have thought the professor was a man who would take that kind of risk. Not that I knew him at all."

"He might have thought he knew the area better than he did."

"That's what my friends think." *Or he was lured to his death*, thought Marjorie. "Perhaps something close to where he fell drew his interest, and he tripped over. Do you know where he was?"

"Not far from where he gave the talk, from what I understand."

"Were you with Mim when he fell?"

"No, we'd split up. She wanted to take photos for paintings she's working on. She's putting together a historical exhibition which she wants to display in her gallery next summer. She's seeking fresh inspiration, that's the reason she's on this tour."

Marjorie wanted to ask why Casey was on the tour, but if she was too direct, the girl might clam up. She had to find another way to get the information. "I'm here because my cousin-in-law had it on her bucket list. It made me realise I'd never toured the county myself, something I find amazing at my time of life."

"I suppose you can't see everything in one lifetime," said Casey.

"Indeed not, but I'm sorry I haven't been before because I've fallen in love with the scenery. I knew there was a lot of ancient history, but being up close and personal makes it far more interesting. I'd heard the legend of King Arthur of course, but I didn't know that particular backstory, or of the wizard Merlin's involvement in Uther's obsession with another man's wife."

Marjorie was no closer to discovering Casey's reason for being on the tour. From what she'd said, it didn't fit in with her studies. Something about her manner suggested she was holding back. Could it be something to do with her boyfriend and his relationship to the dead professor?

"What happened to your boyfriend?" Sometimes the direct approach was necessary. She had learned that from Edna, who often seemed able to extract details from people by being forthright.

Casey blinked away tears that threatened to spill from her brown eyes as she studied her drink. "He left Cambridge suffering from depression. Afterwards, he cut off all ties, making it clear he didn't want to keep in touch. It was how he coped with trauma, he'd done it before with his family. I don't know what he's doing now."

"How sad," said Marjorie. "Did you try to keep in touch?"

"Initially, but there didn't seem to be much point. A person can only take so much rejection without falling into despair. I left Cambridge myself and moved to London." Casey drained her wine glass and placed the empty on the table. "It's been nice talking to you, but I think it's time for me to retire. I hope you're feeling better."

"Better? Oh yes, much better, thank you," said Marjorie.

FOURTEEN

Shortly after Casey left, Edna and Horace arrived at Marjorie's table. Marjorie had seen the Carlisles leave around fifteen minutes earlier.

"Here you are, Marjorie, a top-up," said Horace, handing her a glass of brandy.

"Oh, that's wonderful. Thank you."

"Are you all right, Marge? I saw you losing balance, I almost ran over, but then I saw Casey helping you."

"It was an act to get her attention. She was so engrossed in her phone screen, I didn't feel interrupting her was the way to go about things. So I—"

"Improvised." Horace finished for her, tapping his nose.

"Indeed," said Marjorie. "It seemed like a good idea at the time, I feel guilty about it now because Casey was so caring. She didn't have to be."

"At least your ploy worked," said Edna. "Did she tell you anything useful?"

"Before we share our findings, I think we should ask Frederick if he would like to join us." Marjorie glanced over at the bar and noticed the bartender speaking to people sitting on barstools. This table was in the quieter part of the bar where they were less likely to be disturbed or overheard.

Horace tapped a message into his phone. A few moments later it beeped and Horace checked the screen.

"He's on his way down. I'll get him a brandy."

Horace went to the bar and arrived back at the table as Frederick walked in. If Frederick was still upset about the fact somebody had died, and they were investigating again, he didn't show it. His steps were purposeful and when he took his seat, and the brandy from Horace, he smiled warmly.

"Marge was just going to tell us what she found out from that Casey girl," said Edna, showing her usual impatience as Horace and Frederick exchanged pleasantries.

"She's hardly a girl, I would put her in her late twenties," said Frederick.

Edna rolled her eyes, a habit when she was bored.

Marjorie took a sip of brandy and began, "Alas, I didn't discover anything groundbreaking, but I did find out a few things. Casey's ex-boyfriend studied under Professor Miller. She didn't know the professor herself, but her boyfriend seemingly challenged him during a public lecture. Apparently, Professor Miller wasn't a man who took challenge well." Marjorie noticed Horace and Edna exchange a glance.

"Something you've discovered already, judging by that look. Fill us in later, I don't want to lose my thread. From the moment he disputed something the professor said, Casey's ex-boyfriend was intimidated and bullied, something he'd unfortunately experienced before. His work suffered and he became depressed, dropping out of university – or failing – I'm not sure which, and then he left Cambridge... and Casey... behind. They no longer keep in touch. It still hurts, and she's bitter about it."

"What kind of weed dumps his girlfriend because Professor Vindictive makes his life a misery?" Edna shook her head. "These men really need to grow backbones."

"Mental illness is debilitating," Frederick said, "it can ruin lives."

If anyone understood mental illness, it was Frederick. Marjorie and the others were aware of how, as a young man, his former fiancée didn't turn up to the altar, leaving him depressed for years, before he met Flora, the woman he married. He still suffered the occasional low moods.

"I can't understand why a guy would dump a stunning young woman like that," said Horace.

"Trust you to go down that road," said Edna. "You heard Fred. The guy was depressed."

Edna's sudden understanding of depression might have less to do with empathy and more to do with jealousy, but Marjorie believed she meant well. Her cousin-in-law was fond of Horace and would be lost without their friendship.

"Casey said he cut all ties with the people he'd met in Cambridge, including her," Marjorie said.

"Did she say anything else of note?" Horace asked.

"Not really, other than the fact she's been checking the local news and the death has been referred to the coroner. She suggested that, reading between the lines, there might be something more to the tragedy but she didn't elaborate. The police-woman Casey spoke to told her it was being treated as an accident, and mentioned the castle being cursed."

"Oh, my lord!" exclaimed Edna, raising her eyebrows so high they almost reached the low ceiling. "What's the matter with these people? You'd think a police officer would know better."

"Everybody has beliefs, Edna," said Horace, "it doesn't matter what their profession is."

"Well, they should keep their bloomin' beliefs to themselves when they're in a position of authority," said Edna.

Marjorie was inclined to agree with her cousin-in-law on this occasion, although she wouldn't have put it in quite the same way. "That's about it. I didn't discover her reason for being on this tour. She no longer lives in Cambridge, her thesis has nothing to do with history and she's studying philosophy. I believe she could be hiding something, and one can only assume it has everything to do with Professor Miller's treatment of her ex-boyfriend."

"Or she just wanted a holiday and doesn't have any friends," said Edna.

"Are you sure it was the police who mentioned the castle being cursed and not the other way around?" Frederick asked. "We all saw her heading for the museum this morning."

"Initially, she showed an unhealthy interest in witchcraft; she even suggested I might be a white witch."

"That explains a lot," said Edna before her face creased up. Marjorie had to wait until the guffaws and joint snorts shared by Edna and Horace concluded before she could continue.

"It turns out the museum was Mim's idea because the professor had a hand in one of the displays. Apparently Mim was angry following the visit and is unduly upset by the professor's death. She even wondered if Mim had a crush on him."

Edna snorted again. "I can't see how anyone could have a crush on that old fossil."

"I hate to point out, Edna, but we are all older than the late professor was," said Horace.

"Yeah, but we're nowhere near as boring," Edna retorted.

"Casey mentioned the possibility of Mim thinking she might have put a curse on him because there was something about that sort of thing in the museum," said Marjorie. "Or perhaps she spoke to the same police officer that Casey did. Perhaps Mim's impressionable."

Edna huffed but said nothing.

"That's all my news. What about the rest of you?"

"Have you got anything, Fred?" asked Horace.

"Mim's is the most open profile on social media, because of

her business. Although her gallery sells mainly landscapes, some of her art is gothic. She's a member of a Facebook group called 'Unholy Order of Ancient Witchcraft', whatever that means. It's a private group and not one I'll join, even in the interests of this investigation."

"Perhaps Marge should join as their white witch," said Edna.

Ignoring her, Marjorie said, "Some of the works at the gallery reflected that side of her, but I don't see the relevance."

"Perhaps Professor Miller was also into the dark arts," said Horace.

"Now you mention it, Casey's implication that the professor had an alternative view of historical legend and mythology might involve that side of things. She implied his views were radical."

"If you two are done, and you've not forgotten anything else, you'll be amazed at what we found out," said Edna.

"Just one more thing," said Marjorie, ignoring a heavy sigh from Edna. "Casey and Mim weren't together at the time of the professor's death."

"That's interesting," said Horace.

"Mim was scoping landscapes for an exhibition she wants to put on next summer," said Marjorie.

"And what was Casey doing?" asked Frederick, drawing an even louder sigh from Edna.

"She didn't say."

"Okay, Marge. Can I get on and tell you what me and Horace found out?" Edna finished her whisky and placed the glass down hard on the table.

"Please do," said Marjorie.

"You're not going to believe this."

"Try me," said Marjorie.

"Naomi Carlisle is Bodwin Miller's ex-wife."

"That I wouldn't have guessed, but it doesn't appear to have surprised you, Frederick."

"It came up in my research. I was going to tell you, but didn't want to stop Edna in her tracks."

Edna huffed. "Well I bet you didn't find this bit, Mr Clever Clogs. Professor Vindictive caught her and Stan together when he arrived home early from some work thing he was on."

"Actually, I—" Frederick was stopped short by Edna's glare. "Sorry, go ahead."

"Professor Vindictive wouldn't let it go. He wasn't a man to be spurned – or disagreed with – even after they divorced and she married Stan, he stalked her like some lunatic."

"That's dreadful, those sort of things can end badly," said Marjorie.

"Understatement of the year, Marge. He was a nasty piece of work."

"Violent?" asked Marjorie.

"I didn't get that impression," said Horace.

"Domineering and controlling. One of those men who liked to go away and come home to find the dutiful wife waiting for him, according to Stan and Naomi," said Edna. "So everywhere Naomi went, he was there. They are convinced he found out they were on this tour, and that's why he booked it."

"Which also explains their behaviour the morning you and Fred met them," said Horace. "They'd just found out he was on the tour after reading Faith's email about his talks."

"That makes sense now," said Marjorie.

"It also explains why they've been so stressy," said Edna.

"They are relieved the guy's dead," said Horace.

"Why were they hanging around so close to him all the time?" asked Frederick.

"Ah," said Horace, "that was a bit of reverse psychology. They decided they weren't going to stand for it anymore and were giving him a taste of his own medicine."

"It worked," said Marjorie. "We all noticed how perturbed he was by their behaviour."

"And so he should be, horrible man," said Edna. "He got what he deserved."

"Edna!" Horace sounded shocked.

"No, I don't mean the dying bit. Of course I wouldn't wish the man dead. I meant the reverse-stalking thing. He got what he deserved."

"Did they happen to mention where they were when he went over the cliff?" Marjorie asked.

"No," said Horace. "That's a mystery, considering they openly admit stalking him. It's odd they let him out of their sight."

"Unless they didn't let him out of their sight," said Marjorie.

"Maybe they sneaked up behind him and pushed him off the cliff," added Frederick.

Edna's eyes settled on Marjorie's. "Is that what you're thinking, Marge?"

"It's a possibility," she said. "But why admit to stalking him?"

"They denied knowing him at first," said Horace. "It was only after Naomi let something slip that Stan suggested they might as well come clean. Maybe they're doing the reverse-psychology thing again," he continued. "By admitting they were stalking him, they're hoping they can deny killing him so brazenly."

"That's possible," said Marjorie, then noticed Edna urgently motioning with her head and eyes.

Marjorie turned around to see Arthur Denton sitting nearby. As their eyes met, he stood up and headed into the restaurant. Marjorie lowered her voice. "That man has a nasty habit of sneaking up on people. How long was he there?" Marjorie wished they hadn't been quite so loud when sharing what they'd uncovered. Edna, in particular, tended to raise her voice when overexcited.

"I've only just noticed him, Marge. Sorry, he wasn't there when we started. I was so engrossed in telling our story, I can't say when he arrived."

"He's a strange man, that one," said Horace. "Do you have anything on him, Fred?"

"Sorry, I didn't get around to him. It took me a while to find out what I did on the Carlisles."

"How did you find that out?" said Marjorie.

Frederick puffed out his chest, smiling, his grey eyes twinkling. "I searched for his name on Twitter – or X, as it is these days – and found a thread relating to his wife having an affair with a lecturer. The students revelled in it, basically saying similar to Edna, that it was what he deserved. He doesn't appear to have been very popular with anyone in that section of the student fraternity. A few came to his defence, but not many. Some of them called her derogatory names, as you can imagine."

"Quite," said Marjorie.

"So, from the initial thread, it was quite easy because they didn't hold back mentioning names and suchlike. If you ask me, they were mean; after all, he was the one wronged."

Edna nudged Horace. "Told you he wouldn't like it."

"Do you think the professor realised he was being ridiculed on this X thing?" Marjorie asked.

"It was Twitter back then. He doesn't have his own profile on X, so, if he did, he closed it. Maybe he didn't read the stuff, but Stan Carlisle left the university under a cloud."

"Oh yes," said Horace. "Bodwin got Stan the sack. Stan reckons the professor planted items borrowed from the local museum in his office to make it look as if he'd stolen them. To avoid scandal, the university suggested Stan leave. He managed to fight for early retirement and got severance pay."

"Which means the Carlisles have the strongest motive," said Marjorie.

"Yeah, my money's on them," said Edna.

"They are the most obvious, but would the two of them go to such extremes? There would usually be one voice of reason in a couple," Marjorie said. "We still have Casey, who is upset about the injustice done to her boyfriend and who you saw arguing with the professor last night."

"And we have Mim who might have had a crush on him, although why a pretty thing like her—"

"Don't go there again," said Edna. "Sometimes I despair at you, Horace Tyler."

"I'd also like to know more about the omnipresent Arthur Denton," said Frederick.

"Let's finish our drinks and call it a night," said Marjorie. "We've gathered evidence on motive, and thus far, we have three possible suspects."

"You mean the Carlisles and Casey?" asked Frederick.

Marjorie nodded.

"And a loony theory about curses and witchcraft," said Edna.

"Proving anything without the police onside is going to be difficult," said Marjorie. "We have more work to do."

As Marjorie headed to her room after saying goodnight to Edna, her head was churning with possibilities and theories.

FIFTEEN

After breakfast, Marjorie said goodbye to Edna and Horace, who were leaving for the outing to Port Isaac with Faith and several others.

Marjorie and Frederick had their own expedition planned – a stroll along the coastal path west of Trebarwith Strand, where the hotel receptionist, Timothy, promised they would see an abundance of wildlife.

"It's ideal for all walking abilities," he said. "You can do as much or as little as you like, and if you're lucky, you might see some grey seal pups at this time of year."

"Wonderful," said Frederick, his voice excited. He tapped a pocket of his waxed jacket where Marjorie had seen him insert a small pair of binoculars. An SLR camera swung from around his neck and a bulky rucksack rested on his back.

Marjorie's heart warmed as she observed Frederick, his face alight with anticipation. Today promised exhilaration for him – a day filled with walking, birdwatching and photography. Without Edna's ribbing, he would be free to wander at leisure.

"Make sure you wrap up well, though, Lady Marjorie..."

She had tried – and failed – to get the receptionist to drop her title, but at least he'd opted for Lady Marjorie rather than Lady Snellthorpe.

"... The wind will be strong from the north today and there might be a passing shower later."

"Thank you for the warning, Timothy. I've got my coat hanging over a chair ready for action. And you'll be pleased to know, we're both wearing sturdy shoes. If we're not back for afternoon tea, you can send out a search party," she added with a mischievous chuckle.

As they set off, Marjorie unfolded her cane – a trusty support – while clutching her handbag. The cane would help if the wind became too strong, and if she had to stand for long periods while Frederick indulged in his hobbies.

"It's another beautiful day," said Frederick after a quick glance at his mobile to check they were heading in the right direction.

Timothy had warned the path would be uneven in places, and they would have to negotiate a few steep climbs and descents, but both were fit enough to manage as long as they took it slowly. Marjorie giggled.

"What's funny?" Frederick asked, his eyes creasing.

"I was just thinking that while the terrain demands caution, at our age, moving slowly isn't a choice – it's our portion," she quipped, her laughter rich with irony.

Frederick's grin widened. "I've been working on my fitness, even joined a walking group like you recommended. It's been a blessing, although some of their 'rambles' I'd call epic hikes."

"I know what you mean," she said.

"My doctor reduced my blood pressure medication because of the positive effect regular walking has had."

Marjorie couldn't be happier about Frederick taking her advice. Since joining a walking group herself, she felt rejuvenated. She hoped his new routine would bolster both his physical and mental health. "Perhaps I should suggest the same thing to Edna," she said.

Frederick threw his head back, laughing. "I'd love to see you try."

Marjorie worried about Edna's breathless episodes after her hospitalisation, though thankfully they didn't appear to be any worse. They were all relieved the pneumonia she'd battled was unrelated to her cancer, which remained in remission. Marjorie herself had overcome a bout of pneumonia a few years ago but had no long-lasting symptoms.

As they meandered along the rugged path, the scenery grew ever more dramatic. The air was a blend of salty sea and the earthy scent of autumn leaves – invigorating. Flora and hardy grasses lined the path and clung to the cliffs, while the relentless crashing of waves against the rocks filled Marjorie with a deep, almost sacred sense of wholeness. Sometimes, nature's beauty was almost overwhelming.

"Look at the gorse," said Frederick, pointing to clusters of yellow flowering bushes that defied the autumnal reds and oranges. The vivid greens and yellows set against the dark blue expanse of the sea, produced a picturesque contrast.

The rugged stroll had transformed into a horticultural delight. Every so often, Frederick paused to peer through his binoculars, while Marjorie immersed herself in their surroundings. Marjorie's eyes moved to the sandy beach below while Frederick's binoculars were trained on the cliffs. When they stopped, Marjorie too looked at the stratification of the dramatic Cornish cliffs where millennia of geological time showed in the bands of slate and sandstone, their shapes carved by wind and salt spray. All she could hear was gulls' cries competing with the waves. Turning to Frederick, she asked. "What can you see?"

"Nesting sites in the crevices, and there are some unstable ledges high up caused by erosion. There's also a wide variety of gulls – not my speciality. But look up. Those are guillemots. Watch that one."

Marjorie followed Frederick's pointing finger and saw not one, but four guillemots swooping and diving in synchronised grace. After five minutes a chill began to creep over her, so she started walking again. Frederick soon followed her, and as they rounded a bend, one of the steep inclines forced them to slow to a crawl. Marjorie concentrated on every step, rather than the view, until they reached the top and then gasped.

In a secluded cove below, a dozen grey seals lounged among their snowy white pups close to a group of caves. "Now, that's a sight to behold," she said, watching in amazement. "Ralph would have loved this place."

Frederick patted her arm, a flash of shared sorrow in his eyes. "So would Flora."

Wiping away sea spray from his right eye – or was it a tear? – Frederick focussed on the scene below.

"I don't believe I've ever seen them in their natural breeding ground." He removed a large lens from his rucksack, attaching it to his camera and snapping shot after shot.

"It's not uncommon along the northeast coast," said Marjorie, happy to move the conversation on. "Timothy mentioned grey seals are becoming rare across the world. Apparently, the UK has around forty per cent of the world's population."

Frederick put his equipment away and picked up his bag. "I didn't know that. Shall we press on?"

"Yes, please. I'd like to get as far as Tintagel, if possible."

Frederick frowned. "I'm not sure that's feasible, Marjorie. It's an hour's walk on ordinary terrain at a steady pace. At our speed, and on this path, it could take all day."

"Well then, let's venture a little further. I'm feeling rather invigorated."

"As long as you remember we have a return journey." Frederick's new man appeared to be fading fast. Perhaps the rambles he took consisted of short walks. Some of hers were three hours, albeit at a snail's pace with multiple refreshment stops.

"We should have requested a packed lunch," she said.

Frederick patted his bulky rucksack. "Why do you think this thing is so full?"

Marjorie laughed. "I assumed it was all camera equipment. Is it too much to hope there's tea in your bag?"

Frederick shot her a smug smile. "I wouldn't dream of taking Lady Marjorie Snellthorpe for a walk without tea."

"In that case, we'll take a rest in fifteen minutes. That should be about lunchtime."

"Yes milady," Frederick fake-tipped his trilby.

"I'm surprised that hasn't blown away." Marjorie's hood was pulled up and tied tight to keep it in place.

"I've devised an ingenious solution. Not being a fan of beanie hats, I made a strap that I can tighten around my head, and the hat attaches to it with Velcro. It can withstand most weather conditions as long as I don't try to take my hat on and off. Hence the pretend tipping."

Marjorie laughed. With Frederick like this, he was a pleasure to be with.

They continued their walk for another thirty minutes with more stops than Marjorie would have liked as Frederick paused to peer through his binoculars or take photos. Having walked for longer but not further than anticipated since their last conversation they arrived at the foot of a small incline. Marjorie was keen to go over one final hump, but sensed Frederick's hesitation.

"I think we should stop here, Marjorie, and have lunch, then turn back," he said.

Marjorie exhaled. Having enjoyed the walk, but not quite as much as she might have with all the stop-starting, she was about to concede. Just then, voices erupted from over the hill. Heated voices.

Pressing a finger to her lips, Marjorie strained to hear. Frederick stopped unzipping his rucksack. It was impossible to hear clearly with the noise of the waves crashing against the rocks, and the shrieking gulls. The sun dipped behind a gathering cloud formation, casting a cold, ominous shade over them. Marjorie was about to turn away from the murmuring voices when they grew louder.

"I recognise that voice," she said. "It's Mim."

"Do you think she's in trouble?" asked Frederick.

"It sounds like she's giving as good as she's getting, but I can't hear the conversation clearly. Shall we brave one more hill before stopping for lunch?"

Frederick frowned, but relented, hoisting his rucksack back over his shoulder. Marjorie longed for a cup of tea, and with a twinkle in her eye, said, "The things we do to solve a mystery."

They climbed the smaller incline with caution, then emerged over the brow to see a familiar scene. Mim sat on an old paint-stained stool with an easel before her. The indignant woman from the gallery in Bude loomed over her, speaking through gritted teeth. "I'm sorry, but your time is up."

Deciding to make their presence known, Marjorie launched into a loud, jovial conversation with Frederick, aimed at alerting the quarrelling pair. Startled, the older woman recoiled slightly. Leaning in close to Mim, she made a final whispered remark before turning and striding off towards Tintagel.

Mim steadied her easel, as if to signal she resented interruption. Marjorie was determined.

"Good afternoon," she said. "I see you've been making the most of the views and the bright weather. Although, judging by those clouds over there, change is in the air."

"In more ways than one," muttered Frederick from behind.

"Hello," Mim replied, probably none too thrilled at being once again overheard in an argument.

"Didn't we see that woman in Bude? Who is she?" asked Marjorie.

Mim shrugged. "Someone who follows me around."

There's a lot of that as well, thought Marjorie. "She seems rather angry. Are you supposed to paint for her or something?"

Mim snatched at her canvas and started packing her things away. "As you say, the weather's changed. I'm not going to get any more work done today, not with all the interruptions."

Marjorie mused how some people these days could be so rude.

"She's sick," Mim snapped, while packing away and folding up the stool. She threw her things into a makeshift carrier. "You'd better get back – the weather can turn really quickly in these parts, and the high winds can be dangerous."

"As we discovered yesterday," said Frederick. "That was a shocking turn of events, wasn't it?"

Mim hesitated, turning to look at them, as if for the first time. "You mean the professor's accident?"

"Exactly," said Frederick. "Did you know him well?"

"A little. He often visited Cornwall and took an interest in my gallery."

"I didn't realise the professor had an interest in art," said Marjorie, raising an eyebrow.

"The professor had many interests – some of them less respectable than others, if you know what I mean," Mim said.

"Not really," said Frederick. "Are you referring to his interest in the smuggling side of things?"

"He was a dishonest man, that's all I can say. He used people to get what he wanted."

"Did he use you?" asked Marjorie.

"I didn't know him that well, other than the interest he showed in my gallery and that he made promises he had no intention of keeping. You should speak to Casey, she knows more about him than I do, being from Cambridge."

"Did he promise to buy something from your gallery?" Marjorie persisted.

"What? No. Anyway, I must be off – I have more pictures to capture around Tintagel Castle before I head back to the hotel. As I said, you should get off this path before the rain comes."

Marjorie watched Mim struggle with her belongings in her hurried retreat.

"Well, that was strange," said Frederick.

"Most peculiar," said Marjorie. "And she clearly knows that woman far better than she's letting on."

"I got the impression she also knew the professor more than she admits."

"Indeed," said Marjorie. "The more time we spend with this rather odd group of people we're touring with, Frederick, the more convinced I become that none of them are telling the truth. They all appear to have history with Professor Miller."

"I wonder if Faith knows any more about them," said Frederick.

"I doubt it. The booking form only asks the basics – next of kin, insurance, that sort of thing. But after what the Carlisles told Horace and Edna last night, we should ask Faith when Professor Miller booked – before or after them."

"You're right, it might be important," said Frederick.

Marjorie nodded. "It would at least tell us whether he was truly following the Carlisles. We only have their word on that matter, and our observations tell us they were the ones following him."

"Perhaps he left a will that might provide us with more information. These things are often about money."

"Or jealousy," said Marjorie. "Emotions can have a powerful hold over people."

Frederick rubbed his forehead. "As we've discovered in the

past. Now, would you like to have lunch before we turn back, or would you like to head back to the hotel and get warm?"

"I'd like to get back to the hotel, but perhaps we could have a cup of tea. That should make us feel a lot warmer, at least on the inside."

"Good idea," said Frederick, opening his rucksack and removing a large flask. He poured two cups of tea which soon cooled down in the colder temperature.

Marjorie drank from the plastic cup, which was never a favourite, and didn't take much time to savour it as it really was turning chilly. Even though she had a fleece on under her thick coat, she suspected the cold wind would soon overpower her clothing. "I think it's time to go," she said.

Frederick wiped the cups dry with a cloth before replacing everything inside his rucksack. He swung it back over his shoulder and with a spring in his step he headed down the incline again – a warm hotel clearly in his sights.

SIXTEEN

"Good morning." Faith greeted Edna and Horace with a warm smile. "There are just five of you today. Nick will be here soon."

"It looks as though it's going to be a good day for it. I wouldn't want it to rain on our dear Edna's parade." Horace laughed at his own joke.

"Ignore him. I've been excited about visiting a setting where a real television show was filmed – and *Doc Martin*'s one of my favourites. I've watched every single episode. He's so blunt."

Horace chuckled. "Like someone else we know," he said.

"You're going to have a wonderful day."

Edna didn't miss the stress lines visible beneath Faith's foundation. The professor's death the day before must still be uppermost on her mind. Horace climbed aboard the minibus, and Edna squeezed Faith's arm as she passed her.

"Try not to think about it," she said, feeling a hypocrite as she had done nothing but think about it. That was all Marge's fault for embroiling them in her ridiculous habit of treating every death as suspicious. And now, once again, they were all involved.

Edna followed Horace, nudging him as he was about to take

one of the front seats. "There," she said, jerking her head towards the back where Stan and Naomi sat in the aisle opposite Casey.

They might as well do a little digging during the journey, because she didn't want anything to interfere with her celebrity obsession. She would not have her day ruined. Horace got the message and moved further back, shuffling into the seat behind the Carlisles. Edna sat next to him.

"Good morning," said Horace politely. "I hope you enjoyed as good a sleep as I did."

Casey nodded a greeting before shifting from the aisle to the window seat and taking out her phone. *That's her gone then*, thought Edna.

"Not bad at all," said Stan, looking remarkably well, considering how drunk he'd been the night before. Naomi appeared pale and drawn.

Edna and Horace strapped themselves in as Nick boarded. After a preliminary check of her guests, Faith sat down at the front and the journey commenced.

Horace tried his best to engage the Carlisles in conversation but their answers were monosyllabic. Naomi shifted in her seat continuously as though in severe discomfort.

"Are you okay?" Edna leaned over the back of their seat, noticing Naomi wringing her hands.

"I'm fine," she said in a shaky voice.

"She'll be all right," said Stan. "It's the realisation that her torment is over, but he was still her ex, and she loved him once upon a time."

"That was a long time ago," Naomi snapped, sounding more like the person Marge had described meeting on the first day of their holiday.

"But that doesn't mean you don't feel anything, let's be honest," said Stan.

"All I felt for that man was contempt," said Naomi. "I'm not concerned about him, in fact I'm pleased, delighted to be free of him. Everything he did to us over the past few years was unforgivable."

"Can't disagree with you there," said Stan.

"Still, the poor man's dead now," said Horace, "so perhaps we should show a little respect."

"Why?" snapped Naomi.

"No reason, but we've all done things we regret. Who knows, perhaps over the past few days he was regretting making your life a misery."

Edna admired Horace's attempt at reasoning.

"I doubt that." Naomi's cheeks flushed red through her heavy makeup, her voice trembling with barely suppressed rage. "That man's whole purpose in life was to please himself. He didn't give a hoot about anybody else."

Horace had ploughed into a losing battle.

"I was on edge all the time expecting him to pop up at any minute," Naomi continued. "It's been a living hell."

Brought on by your infidelity, thought Edna, although she couldn't excuse Professor Vindictive's behaviour. "What are you most looking forward to today?" she asked, changing the subject before it got any more heated.

"Not a lot, from my point of view," said Stan. "But Naomi enjoyed the programme and it will be interesting to see places that are familiar from the show."

"Now you're talking," said Edna. "I'm really excited about it."

"Well, that's good because we're about to pull in," said Horace as he unclipped his seat belt.

As soon as they got off the minibus, Edna muttered under her breath, "I can't take much more of her. I mean, she might have had a hard time and all that, but I swear she doesn't half feel sorry for herself."

"Well," replied another voice nearby, "she has had a hard

time of it, so I suppose we have to be... a little bit sympathetic," Casey added while still staring at her phone screen.

"Yeah," Edna conceded reluctantly. "I suppose you're right. Although there are two sides to every story."

"You've finally seen that," said Horace. "I didn't think those words would ever come out of your mouth."

She smirked. "Unless, of course, there's not two sides to this story."

"That's my girl," he said with a wink.

Faith spoke to each of them, asking whether they would prefer to tour on their own, or follow the guide she'd hired for a guided tour.

"After sitting close to those two," whispered Edna, "I'd rather go on our own, but..." She paused thoughtfully, adding: "I suppose this guide knows the place better than we do, so let's stick with the group, shall we?"

"Good idea. And I'd quite like to catch a word with Casey, just in case she's got anything else worth adding," said Horace.

"Heaven help us – you're getting more like Marge every day," teased Edna. "Lord deliver me from you amateur sleuths."

"Says the woman who's just as keen as we are, but pretends not to be," Horace replied, a wide grin on his face.

"That's where you're wrong. I don't think I'll ever be as interested in this sort of stuff as you and Marge, but I want to get it over with for less altruistic reasons than you."

They gathered around in their separate pairs, or alone, when it came to Casey. Faith walked over to a woman, presumably their official guide. Edna hopped restlessly from foot to foot, torn between annoyance at having spoken with Naomi and Stan and anticipation at what lay ahead. A day full of potential fun awaited them if only they could enjoy it without distraction.

Edna's eyes wandered around, feeling as though she was on the set of the television series, and even if she hadn't felt that way, the picturesque village would be captivating of itself.

Faith continued chatting to a forty-something woman with wavy red hair. The woman's freckled cheeks reminded Edna of her sister-in-law who had died two years ago. Sadness threatened to engulf her over the guilt she felt at not keeping in touch with her late husband's only sister. The truth was, they had never got on.

"That's our guide, Edna," said Horace. "Are you excited?"

Edna didn't rebuke him for stating the bloomin' obvious as she would normally, all too pleased to have her attention brought back to the present.

"May I introduce you all to our guide for today. This is Lowenna," said Faith, introducing the smiley woman wearing cropped jeans, walking shoes and a puffer coat that stopped mid-thigh. Her brown eyes shone bright.

"Welcome to Port Isaac, or should I say Portwenn," she said in a conspiratorial whisper.

The group chuckled on cue, although Horace asked Edna to explain.

"Portwenn is the fictional village in the series, but it's shot in Port Isaac," she said.

Lowenna spoke in a high lilting voice that cut through the air like a melody. Between that and the salty air, Edna was unsurprised she appeared happy. "If you follow me, we'll start our tour in the village square and then move on to Doc's surgery. We won't be able to go inside because it's actually a working surgery. You can take photos from outside, just be respectful of patients when you do so."

All seven of them followed Lowenna to the village square where scenes from the series jumped out at Edna. She and Horace took photos of the stone buildings before Lowenna pointed out the Old School House where other scenes had been shot. Edna was transported into a different world, imagining herself as an extra on the set. Lowenna shared lots of behind-the-scenes anecdotes from the filming which she'd personally witnessed.

Totally absorbed in her surroundings, it was a little while before Edna noticed Casey had disappeared. She checked over her shoulder to see if she had fallen behind and then looked around in case she had entered one of the small shops. Lowenna had stopped a short distance away from the surgery. Stan and Naomi took photos and asked Faith to take one of the two of them. Edna tugged at Horace's sleeve.

"Where's Casey?"

The wind had given his cheeks a ruddy glow as he replied, "I saw her peel off down a hill, I expect she's gone down to the harbour by herself. She wasn't paying much attention anyway; her eyes are permanently glued to that phone screen of hers."

Edna tutted. "I know what Marge would say about that. As long as she's okay, I don't want another one of us popped off."

Horace grinned. "She'll be fine. I can't imagine anything untoward happening in this quaint little village."

Faith joined them at that moment and explained, "The party is heading for a cliff walk towards Port Gaverne, another place used on location. Are you up to it?"

Horace looked at Edna.

"I don't think so. Why don't Horace and I take a walk down to the harbour, and we'll meet you when you've finished." She had started to feel breathless, something she felt a lot these days, particularly after exertion she wasn't used to. She also wanted to check Casey was okay, despite Horace's reassurance.

"You do that, it's a beautiful place. We shouldn't be too long."

While the Carlisles followed Lowenna with Faith and Nick, both couples holding hands, Edna and Horace retraced their steps to where the path led down to the harbour.

SEVENTEEN

"I didn't want to be with all those love birds anyway," Edna said as they headed along the cobbled streets. At times like this she wondered whether wearing heels was the most sensible thing. Marge would say not, but Edna had always worn heels and didn't want to start looking like some frumpy old woman. It was enough that she carried the extra weight and her hearing was going, she wouldn't let her age define her.

"Like you, Edna, I can't warm to Stan and Naomi, although they were friendly last night. There's something not that nice about them. I feel sorry for her in that she's had a hard time, but—"

"You can only give so much sympathy." Edna finished the sentence for him.

"Yes, that's it," Horace replied. "I feel bad saying it."

"Although her being married to Professor Vindictive goes some way to explaining their behaviour, there are too many moody people on this trip."

Horace opened his mouth as if about to say something.

"Don't you dare, Horace Tyler. I'm nothing like her."

"Quite right," said Horace. "Come along, this is the way

down to the harbour. It's not like you to be worried about someone like Casey Sims. What is it?"

Edna was about to explain how she'd known what it was like to be let down by men before she met her husband when her heel caught on a cobblestone and she almost keeled over. Horace caught her before she landed on the ground.

"That was too close for comfort, Edna. Come with me."

Horace took her elbow and about-turned. Moments later they were in a shoe shop where he insisted on buying her a pair of what he called 'sensible shoes'. Edna conceded because the almost-fall had given her a fright. If Horace hadn't caught her, she could have been hurtling down an incline and ended up badly injured, perhaps even worse. Not that she was going to let him know how scary the moment had been.

"There's nothing wrong with my heels – it was the stupid cobblestones," she complained as they left the shop, her heeled shoes in a shopping bag.

"And because of the stupid – but rather quaint – cobblestones, you have made the right choice," he said, a grin spreading across his face.

They resumed their journey down to the harbour, and as they arrived Edna noticed Casey sitting on a bench which overlooked the boats and the waterside. But Casey wasn't looking at the scenery, or at her phone – a miracle in itself. This time, she was engrossed by the contents of a book in her hand. "She's down there. What's that in her hand?"

"Perhaps she decided to do some reading," Horace said. "She is a student after all."

"Hmm." Edna wasn't convinced that Casey Cellphone would stop looking at her phone to read a book. As they got closer, Edna paused, grabbing Horace's arm. "That's not a novel, or a textbook she's got in her hand. It looks very much like Professor Vindictive's notebook."

"I do believe it is," said Horace, his eyes scrunching into a frown.

Edna approached, glad she wasn't wearing heels or she would have been heard. Sneaking up behind Casey, she snapped, "Where did you get that?"

Casey dropped the book, almost falling off the seat. Her eyes widened in horror when she turned to look at them, her nose ring twitched as her nostrils flared. "You shouldn't sneak up on people like that. Who do you think you are?"

"I asked you a question," said Edna, eyes narrowing, all the empathy from earlier evaporating.

"What are you talking about?" Casey shoved the notebook inside the tote bag sitting on the bench next to her.

"Don't give me that innocent indignation, young woman, I've seen it all before," said Edna. "You were reading Professor Miller's notebook. Now, I'll ask again. Where did you get it?"

Casey knew she was in trouble, Edna could read it by the look on her face, but she remained adamant. "Not that it's any of your business, but I was making notes in *my* notebook. I'm studying for a PhD."

Edna gave an eye-roll. "Are you trying to tell us that Casey Cellphone uses an old-fashioned notebook instead of the latest technology to take notes?"

"So what if I do?" Casey jutted her chin out, clutching the tote bag to her chest.

"We can easily solve this dispute," said Horace. "Why don't you take the notebook out of the bag and show us?"

"Why should I? Who are you to demand anything from me? Why don't you just leave me alone!" Casey's face was red with anger but Edna could see she was wavering as she chewed her bottom lip.

"You either take that notebook out of your bag and prove it's yours, or I'll do it for you."

Casey held her palms up, her hands shaking – with rage, or

fear, Edna couldn't discern. "Okay, okay. You're right. It is his notebook."

"And how did you come by it?" asked Edna. "Was it when you pushed him over the cliff?"

Casey's eyes widened, looking enormous behind the black-rimmed glasses perched on her nose. With her black hair pulled back into a tight ponytail, she reminded Edna of a fierce librarian. "Don't be ridiculous! I didn't push anybody over any cliff. I found it."

"You expect us to believe that?" said Edna, taking a seat on the bench next to her. Horace sat the other side.

"I'm telling the truth. I found it. I heard a loud shout not too far from me around the time he went over the cliff, so I ran to see what was happening. When I got close, I heard a scuffling sound – as if somebody tripped. But I don't know whether that was the professor falling, or whether it came afterwards, it's all a blur. That's when I found his book just lying on the ground. So I picked it up and put it in my bag thinking I would give it back to the professor when I saw him."

"Oh yeah, sure – after he went flying down a cliffside! Don't take us for fools," said Edna, not sure what to believe.

"I didn't know it was the professor, in fact, I didn't know anyone had gone over the edge at that point."

"I realised, and I was a lot further away than you say you were," said Edna, incredulous.

"Look! I took the book – that's all I did. He fell over the side of the cliff and I put it in my tote bag because I wanted to go through and see if he documented any of his academic misconduct."

"So now you did know it was him?" Edna's eyes locked on Casey's.

Casey still hugged the tote bag tight, staring at the boats but her eyes seemed glazed over. "It was wrong of me to take it, but I couldn't have helped even if I'd wanted to. Someone had clearly had a tragic accident, I wasn't thinking. The notebook was too big a temptation. I had to know what it contained."

"And why would he document misconduct in his notebook?" asked Horace.

"I don't know. Some people do that sort of thing. Isn't it like killers keeping trophies from their victims? Perhaps he liked to brag about the people whose lives he'd ruined."

"Such as your ex-boyfriend," said Edna, softening.

"Your friend told you that, I suppose. Yes, like my ex. I wondered if the professor had written anything I could use to discredit him."

"Even after he was dead," said Horace. "That's a bit mean, isn't it?"

"I've already told you, I wasn't certain he was dead, was I? I wasn't convinced I recognised the voice. Yes, I heard a man cry out and a loud thump as he must have hit the ground, but that's all. For all I knew it could have been him I heard scurrying away, dropping his notebook in a hurry."

"So now you heard someone scurrying away?" said Edna with a huge sigh.

"I told you, I thought I heard something. Once I knew he was dead, I assumed it was the professor falling but I didn't know that at the time."

"Or you pushed him," said Edna, raising a quizzical eyebrow at Horace, wondering what he was thinking.

"Look, I didn't push him, all right." Casey's voice had raised in pitch, almost squeaking.

"Did you also help yourself to the professor's briefcase?" asked Horace.

"No! Why would I? I'm not a thief," snapped Casey.

"And yet here you are in possession of a dead man's notebook," said Edna. "I'm sure you'll forgive me if I don't believe a word that comes out of your mouth."

"Believe what you like. I did not take any briefcase because I didn't even know one was missing," replied Casey.

"Someone removed it from the minibus when we checked in at the inn," said Horace.

"Who would want to do that?" Casey asked.

"Who indeed?" said Edna sarcastically.

"I'm telling you it wasn't me." Casey shifted in her seat, looking more and more uncomfortable. "All I did was look for evidence of misconduct."

"What did you find?" asked Edna.

"A load of drawings and pictures of ancient statues, creatures and stuff, along with treasure maps – at least that's what they are labelled as. I think he might have been a treasure hunter; there's list after list of pieces and prices – things he'd donated to museums for rewards. Also, a list of items for sale from what I could gather. There's an auction coming up of an ancient find. He worked with someone who followed his directions and found things for him. From what I can make out, he declared some of his finds as ancient treasures to help his" – Casey used her fingers to form air quotes around the term – "'expert' standing while keeping others and selling them on to private collectors."

"Does he say who this person he worked with is?" asked Horace.

"No. It could be one of his students. Some were in awe of him – not everybody disliked his ways."

"Okay. So here's what's going to happen," said Edna. "You're going to hand over that notebook to Faith and she will give it to the police. Don't leave the country, because they are going to want to speak to you."

Casey exhaled. "That's fine. I was going to do that anyway, once I'd read it, although I would have done it anonymously, or said I found it somewhere else."

"Says the woman we're supposed to believe," said Edna, her voice dripping with sarcasm.

"I was hoping to find something I could use against him, that's all."

"The man's dead," said Edna, her sympathy returning. "Take my advice and leave it. You know what they say about vengeance."

"That's easy for you to say; he didn't ruin your life. I'd met my life partner and that man ruined him, and in turn broke my heart. I have no qualms ruining his reputation even after he's dead. It'll probably be ruined anyway, because I'm sure some of the things the notebook reveals aren't legal. It won't take long for people to dig up the dirt on him."

"Aren't you studying philosophy?" asked Horace.

"Yes, so what?"

"Well, isn't that all about the greater good? Surely it can't be of any benefit to drag a man's name through the mud after he's dead?"

"I think it would be of great benefit: it will heal the many. The people whose lives he damaged."

"She's got a point," said Edna, recognising that some men needed exposing. Then she eyed Casey again. "But you're still going to give that book to Faith as soon as she arrives down here and tell her where you found it."

"I'd rather do it at the end of the tour, I don't want to spoil everybody's day."

Edna was about to argue, but Horace intervened.

"She's quite right, Edna. We don't want to ruin everybody's outing – including yours – and it won't do any harm to wait."

"Fine," Edna said, sighing. Horace was right, as he so often was, and he was one of the few men since her Dennis died who she trusted.

"Why don't we go grab a nice scone or something in a café?"

"Now you're talking," said Edna.

"We'll see you later," she said to Casey. "Don't do anything stupid."

As soon as they were out of earshot, Horace said, "Do you believe her?"

"Not a word," said Edna. "She hated the man, she'd have no regrets pushing him over the edge for the greater good, as she calls it, and healing the many. She's lucky I didn't point out that if her ex really loved her, he wouldn't have dumped her."

"You're all heart," said Horace with a grimace.

"I'm only telling the truth. He left her broken-hearted." A memory of Edna's first love who had given her up because his parents told him she wasn't good enough surfaced out of nowhere. They'd got no right to judge her but Edna realised in that moment that sometimes she judged people quickly as a protective mechanism. Perhaps she should study psychology.

Horace dragged her from her musings. "We'll discuss it with Marjorie later on, and Faith, once she knows about the book. I expect she's already reported the stolen briefcase."

"Yeah, well let's hope PC Plod is interested, otherwise we might have to go down to the *Doc Martin*'s false police station and get one of them involved."

"Ha ha," said Horace, snorting. "Come on let's feed you before you get grouchier than you are."

EIGHTEEN

When Marjorie answered her door, she found Edna moving from foot to foot, her eyes sparkling, and exuding barely contained excitement. She said she and Horace had important information. Marjorie had been asleep, but didn't hesitate in agreeing they should dine after the others to discuss the case in private.

The corridors of the seaside inn were quiet, with the distant murmur of guests making their way to dinner when Marjorie entered the bar. The evening light cast long shadows through the windows overlooking the Cornish coastline. If they didn't have a suspicious death to solve, it would be picture-perfect. She walked with purposeful strides, spotting Horace, as usual, buying drinks.

He stood at the counter, his tall frame stooping, partly with age, partly through leaning with one elbow on the bar. As he usually did, he wore a tailored suit, although his jacket was hanging over a backed barstool. He gestured at the bartender, no doubt sharing one of his endless supply of anecdotes. A pot of coffee and two mugs sat in front of him – she suspected the second was for Edna, who hadn't yet emerged downstairs.

Marjorie joined Horace but insisted on paying for hers and Frederick's drinks. The bartender, a young man wearing a black waistcoat, had attentive eyes. He smiled at Marjorie.

"Can we have two pots of tea brought through to that quiet table in reception?" she asked him, pointing towards the less populated area where they could speak more freely.

"Of course," he replied. "You take a seat and I'll bring them over."

Marjorie thanked him and made her way to the reception area, adjusting her cardigan around her shoulders. The temperature had dropped since the showers of the afternoon and the building, though charming, had draughts.

Horace followed a few moments later with a tray holding the coffee pot, mugs and a jug of milk, his movements careful so as not to drop anything.

They were soon joined by Edna, who bustled in with Frederick trailing behind her. Edna wore a bright floral dress and had opted to be a blonde this evening. Frederick, as always, wore a fresh checked shirt with clashing tie, all part of his individuality. The bartender brought a tray of tea with biscuits and a bowl of nuts, the china clinking softly as he placed it on the table.

They waited for the bartender to leave, his footsteps receding as he entered the bar. A group of people, dressed for a night out, passed through reception towards the entrance, laughing and climbing into a taxi. The receptionist – a young woman Marjorie hadn't seen before, with long wavy hair and a professional smile – moved into a side office after answering the phone, leaving them free to talk without being overheard.

"Would you mind having a quick look around to make sure Arthur Denton isn't within hearing distance?" Marjorie said to Horace, her voice just above a whisper. She wasn't going to be caught out again by the writer, who had the annoying habit of being close by when least expected.

Horace nodded, rising from his seat with surprising agility for a man in his eighties. He disappeared around the corner, his footsteps fading before returning.

"He's not in the restaurant," Horace said, settling back in his chair. "The barman said he went out for a walk."

"Good. At least that way, we'll see him when he comes back inside," said Marjorie, pouring herself a cup of tea. The porcelain teapot was decorated with a bright floral pattern, steam gently rising from its spout. "Frederick and I have news but we're not certain it's relevant..."

As she spoke, Edna fidgeted in her chair as if about to burst, her fingers squeezing against the armrest, her coffee untouched. The blonde wig was perfectly coiffed, and she wore a heavy layer of makeup. But she was a pressure cooker about to blow.

"... but I know Edna and Horace have something important to share. So let's start with them. Shall I pour for you?" She checked with Frederick, who nodded, his bald head shining in the light as it moved. His calm presented a balance to Edna's frenetic movements.

Given permission to speak, Edna set off like a steam train, gurgling out revelations, hardly pausing for breath. Her words tumbled over one another and were incomprehensible, apart from the culmination that she and Horace had caught Casey Sims with Professor Miller's missing notebook. Edna's eyes were wide, her false eyelashes flicked up and down, and as she gestured animatedly, she almost knocked over her coffee mug.

It took a while for Marjorie to process the latest revelation. "I had the feeling she was hiding something last night but I thought it more to do with her ex-boyfriend, not this." The tea's warmth spread from the cup to her fingers, a comforting sensation.

"Yeah, Marge, but don't you see it has everything to do with her ex." Edna leaned forward so eagerly she almost tipped out of her chair.

Horace caught the back of it. "Steady on, old girl."

Not to be stopped, Edna continued. "She hates the professor so much that even if she's telling the truth when she says she found the notebook, she's determined to do him damage even now."

Marjorie set her teacup down with a gentle clink. "I'm sorry, I must have missed that part," she said, trying to piece together Edna's disjointed account. The reception area's brighter lighting highlighted Edna's frustrated face. It could be difficult to keep up with Edna at the best of times, but just now, it was almost impossible. "Please could you start from the beginning."

Edna huffed, her chest expanding under her dress, but Horace laid a calming hand on her forearm. "You drink that and I'll fill in the gaps," he said in his measured voice.

"Okay but I don't think I'm the only one who doesn't listen around here," Edna replied, sulkily picking up her coffee mug. She took a defiant sip, leaving a smudge of bright pink lipstick on the rim.

At least I don't need hearing aids but refuse to wear them, thought Marjorie, waiting for Horace to take over the story. The thought brought a private smile to her lips as she reached for a shortbread biscuit.

"Edna was worried about Casey leaving the tour of Port Isaac," Horace began, his voice clear, "and when the others headed on a hill walk to Port Gaverne, we agreed to meet them at the harbour. I knew that's where Casey would be because I saw her heading that way."

Edna gave a short laugh, the sound sharp in the quiet space. "He always knows where the young women are." Her eyes narrowed, a hint of jealousy flashing across her features before disappearing behind a sip of coffee.

"On the way, Edna nearly fell over—"

"They don't need to hear about that," Edna protested, her

cheeks colouring beneath her blusher. She set her mug down with more force than necessary, the liquid sloshing dangerously close to the rim.

"Oh yes we do," said Marjorie with a chuckle, feeling the mirth afforded by a brief respite from the serious conversation.

"She got a heel stuck in the cobblestone pavement," Horace explained, his lips twitching at the corners. "It was quite precarious actually."

Marjorie sighed, picturing Edna teetering on the uneven stones in her impractical footwear. "One of these days you're going to have a nasty accident." Her concern was genuine.

"Yeah, well we nipped into a little shoe shop and Horace bought me a pair of flat shoes, so can we get on with the story now?" Edna retorted, flashing a glare across the table. "And you can wipe that smirk off your face, Fred."

Marjorie had also noticed Frederick's amusement – not that he would have found it funny if Edna had fallen. She came to his rescue before Edna took another bite out of him. "I notice you're not wearing the new shoes this evening."

Edna huffed, slurping back a mouthful of coffee. "I'm going to need something stronger if we don't get to the point." She glanced towards the bar.

Horace stopped laughing and proceeded, his expression serious once more. "Edna spied Casey first and noticed what she was reading. We were able to get close without her realising because... well... without the noise from the heels."

"Can we please get to the point," said Edna, although even she had to smile at the story.

"Anyway, Edna challenged Casey, who hid the notebook in her bag, denying having it. When Edna pressed her..."

Marjorie could imagine how that went but concentrated on what Horace was saying. Edna's method of 'pressing' people for information was legendary among their group.

"... she eventually admitted it was the professor's but said she found it. She denies having anything to do with Bodwin's accident or even seeing him. Her story is that she heard the same thing the rest of us did – a man crying out before falling, except she was closer."

"Plus, she reckons she heard a scuffle," said Edna.

Frederick leaned forward. "What sort of scuffle?"

Horace took a sip of coffee before answering, his expression thoughtful. "If she's to be believed, it could have been the professor tripping over before going over the edge or something else."

"Except, it was that sound that drew her attention to the notebook," added Edna.

"If she's to be believed," Horace reiterated, his tone suggesting he too had reservations.

"Did she tell you what was in the notebook?" Frederick asked, practical as ever.

"He kept meticulous records of ancient finds and drew pictures of them and treasure maps. Casey believes he could have been declaring some and selling other pieces on the side," Horace said, his voice dropping lower, though nobody was close enough to overhear.

"I doubt any of that's relevant," Edna added with a dismissive wave of her hand that nearly upset the nut bowl. "It's Casey we should be focussing on."

"Faith's in the manager's office speaking to the police, according to the bartender," said Horace. "So Casey must have done what she had to and owned up."

Marjorie felt the more clues they unravelled, the more complex this case became. It was like being stuck in a maze with no way through. She absently poured another cup of tea.

"You said you and Fred had something to share," Horace prompted after a few moments of silence.

Marjorie set down the teapot and exchanged a glance with Frederick. "Only that we came across Mim having an argument with the same woman we witnessed her arguing with in Bude."

Edna's eyes bulged as she looked at Marjorie, her heavy lashes widening with them. "Not another stalker?"

"It's hard to say. Mim wasn't in the mood for talking, she couldn't wait to be gone from us, actually. All she would say is that the woman follows her around." Marjorie recalled Mim's flustered state as she disappeared with her bundle of supplies.

"But what about that 'your time's up' comment?" said Frederick, his quiet voice firm. "In light of recent events, I think we should mention it to the police once Faith's finished talking to them."

"That sounds ominous," said Horace, rubbing his chin thoughtfully. "But it could mean anything. It might mean she's not going to wait any longer for a commission or something."

"True," said Marjorie, considering the alternative explanation. "And more likely." She didn't want to jump to conclusions either way; it was easy to misinterpret fragments of overheard conversations.

"Perhaps I should have a word with Mim," said Horace, squaring his shoulders.

"Not a good idea," said Edna, eyes pleading with Marjorie's. Marjorie suspected it wasn't jealousy alone causing Edna's fear. She herself had noticed the bohemian-styled woman flirting with him.

They weren't able to discuss the matter any further as a number of people spilled into reception from the bar after dinner. The quiet corner they'd claimed filled up with boisterous guests.

Marjorie glanced at her watch, a delicate gold timepiece that had been a gift from her late husband, Ralph. "Let's eat and discuss it again after dinner," she suggested, gathering her cardigan around her shoulders.

While Edna and Frederick moved towards the restaurant, Marjorie took the opportunity to speak with Horace.

"I hope you don't mind me asking, but I've noticed your soft spot for Mim. She reminds you of someone, doesn't she?"

Horace's usual jovial expression changed. "I met a young woman who was spirited and artistic like Mim early on in my career. I was too busy building my business and didn't realise I loved her until she died in a car accident." His eyes glistened under the lighting. "One of life's regrets, I suppose."

Marjorie squeezed his arm, "We all have those but don't make the mistake of trying to make reparation by proxy."

"I won't, Marjorie. But don't you sometimes long to break free of an ageing body and be young again?"

"Frequently," she said, "but I'm also enjoying my latter years with three wonderful friends."

Horace smiled, holding out his arm for her. "Me too."

As they headed into the restaurant, Marjorie caught Fredrick's eye. Neither she nor he had discounted Mim from this mess.

NINETEEN

After another wonderful dinner, the four friends returned to the same quiet table in reception now that the earlier crowds had cleared. Outside, a full moon shrouded the surrounding cliffs in nighttime mystery. The sound of waves battering against the rocks with the incoming tide brought Marjorie much pleasure. She would have liked to sit in front of the wood-burning fire in the bar, but didn't want anyone hearing their conversation.

"The case as far as I see it," said Marjorie, her left hand cupping the base of her brandy glass, "has thrown up just how many people disliked Bodwin Miller. With the latest evidence we have to assume that Casey Sims is a strong contender for killing him." Her eyes surveyed her friends. Although in her eighties, her mind remained as sharp as the brooch pinned to her cardigan – except Edna might dispute that fact.

"My money's on her," said Edna with characteristic bluntness, her rouged cheeks flushing deeper, either from her conviction, or as a result of the whisky she supped. "Although Stan and Naomi were a bit weird again today."

Frederick's head shot up, the wrinkles on his forehead deepening. "You didn't mention that before," he said, setting his glass down with a soft clink on the polished table.

Horace reached for his whisky, swirling the amber liquid. His brown-tinted eyebrows twitched slightly as he spoke. "Sorry, we were too busy telling you about Casey. They weren't as friendly as they were last night, but I put it down to Naomi having a hangover."

The telephone rang in reception and the receptionist took the call. A bartender moved across the room, collecting glasses from nearby tables, each showing that life went on.

"I'm still not sure about the Carlisles," said Marjorie, her voice lower as a couple wandered past, arm in arm. "They might have been friendly last night, but the fact remains, they have a very strong motive."

"As does Casey," Edna said, pouting. Her lipstick smudged at the corner of her mouth. As if aware, she rifled in her handbag for her compact mirror and dabbed away the smudge, continuing, "I think she pushed Professor Vile over the edge and then stole his notebook because she was determined to get revenge for being dumped."

Frederick sighed, pinching the bridge of his nose. "I'd hardly say he dumped her when he was depressed."

"I agree with Fred, Edna. It's quite clear the poor chap had some sort of mental breakdown," said Horace, his tone sympathetic.

"But you know what I mean, love spurned is a strong motive for taking revenge." Edna's voice rose a few decibels before she caught herself and glanced around the room. In a more normal tone, she said, "Casey blames Professor Vile for the relationship breakdown, that's a strong enough motive, isn't it?"

A newspaper on a nearby table swayed as the entrance to the hotel opened, sending a draught through the room.

Frederick rubbed his forehead and scrunched his face. "I thought he was Professor Vindictive."

"I reserve the right to change it to whatever's appropriate," said Edna.

"Well, what about Mim Butterfield? Twice we've seen her having a row with a mystery woman. I'd like to know what that's all about," Frederick said.

"Or we could stick to the facts," said Edna, her tone impatient. "Now we're on one case, I don't particularly want to know the ins and outs of a silly artist and her fallouts."

"Neither do I," said Frederick, his voice steady despite Edna's dismissiveness. "But what if it's relevant to the case? We know she has a dark side and a lot of anger. Marjorie recognised it in her art when we visited her gallery."

Marjorie nodded, recalling the violent brushstrokes and sombre palettes that had characterised some of Mim's works — scenes of coastal beauty rendered with an underlying current of menace.

"Just because she's interested in the dark arts and is moody, doesn't mean she goes around popping people off," said Edna, rolling her eyes. The bangles on her wrist jingled as she gestured.

Horace cupped his glass thoughtfully, saying. "I agree there's a difference between exhibiting darkness through art and actually killing people. Plus, we don't have a motive, but I take your point, Fred. At this stage, we can't exclude anybody. However, Casey is now the strongest contender, caught red-handed with the professor's notebook."

The notebook in question was now in the hands of the police. With no sign of Faith, Nick or Casey, Marjorie assumed they were still answering questions.

"Which she denied at first," said Edna. Her voice was triumphant as if she had already extracted a confession.

Marjorie took a moment to gather her thoughts, savouring the last sip of brandy. It warmed her throat as it went down. "I have to agree with Horace and Edna. You said Casey was cagey about the notebook, and Edna had to apply pressure to force her into admitting it."

"It's all right, Marge, I wasn't going to thump her," Edna sounded defensive. "I haven't thumped anyone since I was in the school playground. Although I've met many people I wouldn't mind punching." Edna burst out laughing, joined by Horace. There followed a joint snorting session.

Marjorie waited patiently for the laughter to subside, her own lips curling upwards in amusement. Frederick, on the other hand, remained serious, his attention fixed on his brandy.

Once they were paying attention again, Marjorie said, "Let's just consider everybody again. We have Casey who took the professor's notebook, but we don't know for certain whether she took it after pushing him off the cliff, or whether she found it like she said."

Marjorie once again had to block out the image of the late professor's broken body lying on the rocks where he'd landed.

"My money's on her," said Edna, adjusting her position in the chair, which was a trifle small for her ample frame. "I just want to point that out."

"As you've already done," muttered Frederick, the veins in his temple visibly throbbing.

"Then we have Stan and Naomi Carlisle," Marjorie continued. "They have strong motive and admit to stalking the professor, claiming they were getting their own back for his stalking them in Cambridge. Let's also bear in mind their animosity towards Professor Miller was obvious from the start."

"And we don't know yet, that he stalked them," said Frederick. "It could have been the other way around, and they were harassing him. That's what it looked like to me."

"Indeed," said Marjorie ignoring a harrumph of disapproval from Edna.

"Why would they suddenly stop following him and decide

they weren't playing that following game any longer?" said Frederick, leaning forward to set his empty glass on the table.

"This is a murky business," said Horace.

"Except, if the Carlisles did it," said Edna, "they were complicit. Which, in my opinion, makes it less likely because most murderers work alone."

"There have been some infamous partnerships, but, on the whole, I agree with Edna," said Marjorie.

"So what you're saying," said Frederick, his logical mind seeking clarity, "is that if either one of them wanted to murder Professor Miller, one would have stopped the other."

"Yeah, that's sort of what I'm saying," said Edna. "I can't see it being them even if they were ecstatic about him being dead – but who wouldn't be in their situation?"

"Stan implied today that Naomi still cared about Bodwin," Horace said.

Frederick shot an eyebrow up. "Seriously?"

"That's what I thought too," said Edna.

"Naomi refuted it," said Horace. "If it wasn't a hangover, she seemed down over something. Whether it was the professor's death or guilt over the relief her nightmare was over is hard to say."

A momentary silence descended as they each contemplated what they had discussed. The pieces were coming together but the final picture remained fragmented.

"Did I tell you what a great time we had?" said Edna, her flighty attention span shifting. "I've never been on a real TV set before – not that it was the real set, but it was a real setting."

Edna diverted their attention away from the discussion for ten minutes, sharing details about the *Doc Martin* television programme, and various episodes she'd enjoyed. Her hands moved as she used gestures to describe scenes, her voice rising with every story.

Frederick rolled his eyes on a couple of occasions but

seemed to concentrate on his own thoughts. It was always best to let Edna get these things out of her system before trying to return to a serious conversation. Edna's enthusiasm was both endearing and exhausting.

Outside the hotel windows, the waves continued their rocking and rolling. Occasional lights from torches as people walked on the beach came into view.

Once Edna finished, she looked at them expectantly.

Marjorie steered the conversation back. "To recap: we have three main contenders and Mim Butterfield, who doesn't seem a likely candidate, but who may be hiding something. Frederick and I believe she knew the professor more than she lets on. I too would like to get to the bottom of the argumentative woman she keeps meeting, if only to exclude her from our enquiries, as the police would say."

Edna rolled her eyes. "If you say so, Marge."

"My offer stands to have a word with her, we seem to get on," said Horace.

"No, you bloomin' won't," said Edna. "She'll end up charming you and you'll find out nothing."

"You have a very low opinion of me," said Horace, placing his hand on his heart, feigning hurt. The performance was undermined by the twinkle in his eye.

"Only when it comes to women," said Edna sharply, but with an undercurrent of affection. "We don't know why she has taken such a liking to you."

"Why shouldn't she?" Horace said, straightening in his chair.

"She has made a beeline for you," Frederick added, his tone matter-of-fact.

"Maybe that's because I'm amicable." He shot Edna an accusatory glance. "Unlike some people."

"I'd also like to know why she has she been cosying up to you," Frederick persisted.

"Oh, don't start, Fred," said Horace, his tone shifting from defensive to conspiratorial. "We men need to stick together, especially when we're being browbeaten."

"I'd hardly call you browbeaten, Horace Tyler," Edna replied, her hand reaching out to pat his arm. "You love every minute of it."

"Nevertheless," he continued, "you're not acknowledging that my charm works occasionally – and that some people can genuinely like me."

"Why don't we park Mim and concentrate on the others," Marjorie said, although she'd like to know why Mim had left a barely thriving gallery to join this tour.

"I liked one of her paintings," said Frederick, "It was of the south coast of Cornwall – a sunset over a cove with a cliff in the background."

"Doh! We weren't talking about art," said Edna, exasperation on her face.

"Sorry," said Frederick, blinking. "My mind wandered back to the gallery."

"Okay, anyone else on our list?" Horace asked.

"Arthur Denton," said Marjorie. "A man who rarely speaks but is always hanging around."

"Well, he's a writer, isn't he?" said Edna. "We can exclude him. He's got no motive."

"None that we know of, but I'm sure he has a Cambridge link," said Marjorie. The writer's sneaky presence disturbed her.

Horace looked at them, saying, "I caught hold of him last night after we split up and got a book title out of him so I ordered one. It's being delivered here, in fact, it's probably waiting for me at reception. I'll see if I can find any clues in it."

"Good idea," said Marjorie. "There's nothing more revealing than what a person writes in their fiction, I expect it'll tell us lots about the real Arthur Denton."

"And it might not," cautioned Edna dismissively.

Marjorie's head ached. At times like this she felt it would be better to just leave things to the police and let them go round and round in circles. It was stressful trying to rule strangers out of a murder. "I'd hoped Faith would have put in an appearance tonight, but she's obviously still tied up with the police. Our next step must be to speak to Faith and Nick."

"Well then," Horace chimed in cheerfully, draining the last of his whisky, "I suggest we have another nightcap and wait for her to appear."

"My turn," said Frederick, standing with a slight grimace. "Ouch, my knees are sore after our walk."

"I'll nip over and see if my book's arrived. None of our chief suspects are around at present," Horace said.

Edna added matter-of-factly, "I saw Mim heading outside again."

Marjorie found it interesting that Edna kept tabs on Mim's movements, but not on any of the others.

A small brandy wouldn't go amiss before retiring for the night, she decided, but if Faith didn't appear soon, their conversation would have to wait until morning. The case, like an early-morning fog, grew more opaque with every clue.

TWENTY

Edna and friends had moved into the bar, where Frederick bought them drinks. Horace was in possession of his novel and placed it on the table. They chatted amiably about Cornwall and the next few days while they drank their nightcaps.

It was getting late and Edna's patience was waning. "Where the heck's Faith?"

"If you mean your tour guide, she's in the manager's office, talking to a detective," offered the bartender who was clearing tables. He lifted his head. "Here they come now."

All four heads swivelled in unison to see who the officer was that Faith had been speaking to. "I don't recognise him," said Marjorie.

"Me neither," said Edna.

They were sitting at the table Marge had occupied with Casey the night before. Marge checked over her shoulder.

"Denton's not there," said Edna. "I saw him pacing the beach when I looked out just now. At least, it looked like him from the silhouette under the moonlight." She had been making certain Mim wasn't heading back inside, determined to keep her away from Horace.

For once Marge was wrong about her motives. Edna suspected Mim was after Horace's money, and she would protect him at all costs, even if it meant the others believing she was jealous.

"That's a relief," said Marge. "I don't want him listening in to any more of our conversations."

Edna still hoped it was case closed after discovering Casey with the professor's notebook. Hopefully the detective heading their way with Faith had arrested the girl, and they could get on with their holiday. Marge wasn't convinced about Casey, despite the evidence pointing to her, but she wasn't always right even if the others thought she was. Edna conceded that Stan and Naomi had the strongest motive but they just didn't strike her as the types who would plot a murder – unless it was a spur of the moment thing. If they were guilty, they wouldn't have told her and Horace about Miller's stalking and their pathetic game of tit for tat.

When Faith arrived at their table, she gestured to the wiry man standing with her. "This is Detective Inspector Penrose. I've told him about you four and how Edna and Horace persuaded Casey to hand over the professor's notebook."

The man gazing down at them was tall, at around six feet, his dark brown hair was greying at the temples, and his deep-set hazel eyes considered each of them in turn, before settling on Marge. "You must be Lady Marjorie Snellthorpe," he said in a matter-of-fact way.

"Marjorie, please. How do you do?" Marge replied.

The inspector's eyes moved to Edna. "Edna Parkinton, I presume?"

"You're well informed, Inspector," said Edna shooting a look at Faith.

"I'm Horace Tyler and this is Fred Mackworth," said Horace. "Can we get you a drink, Inspector Penrose?"

"No thanks. I'm just leaving, but Ms Weathers wanted me

to meet you as you were the ones who discovered the young lady with the notebook." The inspector looked to be in his late forties, Edna thought, and seemed in a rush to get away from them. "Thank you for your assistance," he added reluctantly before turning on his heel and racing towards the exit.

"A man of few words," remarked Marge.

"He's a little on the direct side," said Faith. Her lids looked heavy.

"You look tired, Faith. Can I get you a drink?" said Horace.

"A tonic water would be nice," she replied, "if you don't mind."

"Anyone else?" asked Horace. As they'd waited a long time and had already finished their drinks, no-one appeared keen to have more alcohol.

"I'll join Faith with a tonic water," said Marge. "Apparently it's good for cramps, which I occasionally suffer from."

"Nothing for me, thanks." Fred waved a dismissive hand.

"Me neither," said Edna. "If I have anything else to drink, I'll be up all night."

"Okay, two tonic waters coming up," said Horace.

Faith took a seat on the edge of the sofa.

"Where's Nick?" asked Marge.

"He's going over the itinerary for tomorrow," said Faith. "The meeting with DI Penrose took longer than expected, so I let him go up while I waited for the DI to finish with Casey."

Horace returned with the tonic waters and set them down on the table. Edna could wait no longer.

"Are you going to tell us what happened? Did he arrest Casey?"

"There's not a lot to tell." Faith sighed. "As I said, DI Penrose interviewed Casey alone, and he's satisfied with her explanation. He's not going to charge her and doesn't seem too interested in the contents of the notebook. Although he will pass it to another team to see what they make of the late professor's dealings. Investigating a dead man's shenanigans aren't a priority, is what he said."

"Is that it?" said Marge. "He's still going along with the accident theory?"

Faith nodded. "Yes, he says they are convinced Bodwin fell over the cliff."

"Casey?" asked Edna.

Faith shrugged as she took a thirsty drink from her glass. "As I said, he believes the professor must have dropped it or left it behind deliberately by way of a confession."

"How ridiculous!" said Marge. "What kind of theory is that?"

"It's as good a one as any of ours, Marge," said Edna, although she didn't believe it for a minute. "If the police are satisfied, perhaps we should accept it and leave it at that."

"Perhaps we should," said Frederick, clearly as keen as Edna was to put this whole fiasco behind them.

"What did the diligent inspector have to say about the briefcase?" asked Marge, unusually sarcastic.

Faith returned the glass to the table with a heavy sigh; she'd obviously had a long evening. "No luck there, I'm afraid. Casey invited the inspector to look in her room. I accompanied him at that point, and there was no sign of any briefcase. Inspector Penrose suggests it could have been an opportunistic theft."

"How convenient," said Marge, a steely gaze in her eyes.

"Look, Marge, it doesn't seem as if there's anything else to find," said Edna.

"So that's it, you're prepared to accept this ridiculous notion that Casey found the notebook that Professor Miller never parted with, then hid it, and that the briefcase was taken by some random stranger," said Marge.

Faith yawned. "Sorry I haven't been able to help, but I'd better head upstairs. I'll see you all in the morning. Thank you for the tonic water, Horace."

"My pleasure," said Horace, who had barely said a word until Faith left, then he eyed Marge.

"You're not convinced, are you?"

"Not in the slightest," said Marge, to which Edna's heart sank into her stomach. So much for it all being over and case closed.

"Well, if you're right, Marge, and someone killed Professor Vile," she said, "it has to be Casey. She's lying through her teeth and DI Plod just isn't interested."

"That may well be true," said Marjorie. "The fact remains, a man's life has been taken and the person responsible remains free. It isn't right. What we know is that people may have had every reason to dislike him, but nobody had the right to take the law into their own hands. And as we don't have the death penalty in this country, it's not even the law they've taken into their own hands: it's murder. And for that reason, I'm determined to put an end to their scheme."

Edna exhaled the breath she had been holding while Marge delivered her convincing speech. "It feels like we're back to square one because all we seem to be doing is going round and round in circles and getting nowhere," she said.

"Not nowhere exactly," said Horace. "Come on, Edna, we've got three strong contenders. We have to keep digging and prodding, and hope that one of them, or all of them, makes an error of judgement and confesses. Or we make it so they are left with no alternative. Casey may have won round one, but we're not beaten yet."

Marge straightened up. "It's time we became more challenging. We've been nice enough thus far and have gathered a lot of information, but I suggest we need to dispense with the softly-softly approach and get these people talking. Somebody knows something, and one of them may have seen something, even if they don't consider it important. We have to find that person." Marge was on a roll, and there was no stopping her now. "I suggest that from tomorrow, Horace, you and Edna speak to the Carlisles again, preferably separating them so their stories can be challenged without one being able to back the other up."

"We can do that," said Horace with a grin.

"I'll have a word with Casey," Marge added, "and I believe that Frederick and I should tackle Mim and find out what she's all about, while getting to the bottom of these arguments. I suspect she's the one Professor Miller mentions in his notebook."

"What person?" Edna felt confused.

"Remember," Horace replied, "Casey said that the professor was working with someone local, collecting treasure."

Edna had a vague recollection of the earlier conversation but sometimes things got so confusing she couldn't keep up.

"Yes," said Marge. "And we know that after Mim visited that museum she left angry. We should telephone the museum and pay due diligence in relation to what that was all about. Failing that," Marge continued, "if we think it's worth the effort, one of us can take a taxi back to Boscastle and find out what upset her, because clearly something did."

Edna didn't dare argue with Marge when she was in this type of mood. Her intelligent blue eyes were set, determined, and there was no stopping her now.

"Well, if we're going all guns blazing," Edna said, "I might have a word with this Arthur Denton chap and ask him exactly what he's listening out for all the time."

"Good idea," said Marge. "Now we have a plan, but I'm tired; it's been a long day, and an even longer evening. Annoying and totally unproductive in terms of what the police are going to do."

"So it's down to us," said Horace. "The awesome foursome."

Edna shot him a disdainful look. "You and your awesome foursome, this isn't a spaghetti western," she snapped, hating how Horace thought these things were a game. "You need to go to bed."

"Quite right," he said, nodding, and chuckling at the same time. "We'll get on with it tomorrow."

So much for my bucket-list holiday, thought Edna.

TWENTY-ONE

The next morning, Marjorie woke tired after the exertions and excitement of the day and evening before. She'd found it difficult to sleep with her mind focussed on the frustrating police conclusion, despite Edna and Horace's discovery. Relieved morning had come, she moved her legs over the side of the bed and stood to stretch them.

Before retiring the night before, she had looked out of the window and watched Mim pacing under the moonlight. As Edna had seen her leave the inn hours before, Marjorie wondered if the arguments with the mystery woman were playing on her mind. Marjorie had studied Mim for a little while but wasn't too concerned for her safety as there were a number of people taking late-night strolls. In the end, she had closed the curtains and retired.

Marjorie mulled over everything they had found out about their tour companions. It was clear that Stan and Naomi Carlisle had the strongest motive for killing the professor – if indeed he was killed, she reminded herself. And having placed themselves so close to the dead man they were the ones that seemed the most likely. It was odd how most of the tour party had Professor Miller in their sights, and yet none were around when he actually toppled over the edge of a cliff. This meant that one or more of them was lying, and highly probable that someone knew who killed him.

Whatever had happened in the end, there had been evil intent from the start, but she couldn't work out who did what, when, and whether people other than the Carlisles and Casey had enough of a motive to commit murder. She reasoned that the most unlikely was Mim, but sometimes the least obvious became the most obvious when all was revealed. *If only Ralph were here. He was always my sounding board*, she thought. Although Ralph would be horrified at how she and her friends had become amateur sleuths.

"This won't do," she muttered. "Time to get up."

Marjorie washed and dressed, then opened the curtains. She saw Frederick heading out for a morning stroll. He had told her that, in addition to his ramblers group, a morning walk was a new habit to help him keep in shape. Marjorie recalled how embarrassed he'd been a couple of Christmases ago when he and Horace had needed to assist someone from her garden and he'd barely managed. That must have spurred him on to work on his fitness, having let himself go after his wife died.

Like the evenings, the mornings were becoming darker as the clocks didn't go back from British Summer Time until the end of the month, but it was light enough. One could never tire of the view of the rocks and the beach below. Marjorie watched a golden retriever dashing in and out of the sea while its owner threw a ball into the waves – the dog swam enthusiastically to retrieve it, returning triumphantly to its owner, in order to do the same thing over again.

Her eyes moved to Frederick, who stooped to take his shoes and socks off before starting along the cove beach. Marjorie almost wished she'd dressed earlier and joined him. Her husband had loved beach walks almost as much as he'd loved fishing. She hoped Frederick's knees, which had been aching the night before, would stand up to the uneven surface. Marjorie recalled feigning a totter to catch Casey's attention the other night, which made her chuckle softly.

She looked back at the retriever and its owner until the dog disappeared behind a rock. The picture-postcard scene was transformed instantly into one of chaos. The dog ran back and forth in frantic circles, its bark changing pitch. The retriever kept running towards something, backing away, and then approaching again. People began running towards the sound and Marjorie opened her window in growing horror as the dog's owner stumbled backwards, his hands flying to his mouth.

He shouted urgently, "Come here, Indy! Come away," all the while pulling the canine back from the rock.

Marjorie noticed feet poking from the edge as the people gathered around. Someone shouted, "Call an ambulance!"

Frederick came into view, and then disappeared behind the rock only to reappear with a hand clasped tight over his mouth. Two men pulled the person who the dog had found into view. Unmistakable streaks of wild red hair stood out as the sun emerged.

Marjorie had seen enough. Quickly slipping into her walking shoes, she grabbed her coat and left her room. She banged on Edna's door in passing but didn't wait for her to answer before heading downstairs. By the time she arrived at the scene, Frederick was working as self-appointed crowd controller, telling people to stand back while two people attended Mim Butterfield.

"Marjorie, you won't believe what's happened," he said, breathless.

"I saw from my window," she replied. "Who are those people?" Marjorie gestured to the man and woman wrapping Mim in a silver blanket.

"One's a doctor staying at the inn, the other's her husband. I heard them mention hypothermia and the husband collected that blanket from the inn. They've cut away her wet clothes and have been treating her since they got here. An ambulance should be here soon. The doctor says there's a pulse, but it's weak. She must have been out here all night." Frederick took his eyes off Marjorie for a moment, spreading his arms and shouting in frustration. "Please stand back! We're waiting for the emergency services! Unless you're a medic, please stand back!"

In situations like this, Frederick sounded so much more confident than he usually did. Marjorie saw blue flashing lights approaching the inn and paramedics hurried across the sand towards the scene, their bags swinging over their shoulders, carrying a stretcher between them. Out of the other eye, she noticed Edna and Horace racing at her, not quite as quickly as the paramedics, but not bad considering their ages.

"What happened? Did you bang on my door?" said Edna. Having stopped walking, her breathing sounded laboured.

"Yes, I'm sorry, I didn't want to wait. I'd seen what was happening from my window and felt you should know."

"Have you heard of texting?"

"I didn't—"

"Oh, don't tell me, you didn't have your phone on you! Of course you didn't. And even if you had, it wouldn't have been charged."

"Edna, calm down," said Horace. "Now's not the time for reproach. Let's hope this poor woman survives."

It appeared that the doctor's efforts were successful; as she moved Mim onto her side, Marjorie heard her say something reassuring to her husband. Others from the tour party arrived, including Faith and Nick. Poor Faith's eyes were on stalks, clearly unable to believe what was happening. Again.

"Can anyone tell me what happened here?" Marjorie turned around to see DI Penrose from the evening before, his hair barely combed, and wearing the same clothes. He seemed a lot more concerned than he had done last night. "Never mind. Don't answer! Wait there and don't move!" He pointed at the four of them angrily. Next, he stumbled across the sand, his squeaky shoes not made for the beach. He spoke to the doctor and then the paramedics before barking orders at two uniformed officers. "Get these people out of here. I want to talk to everybody in that tour group – and I mean everybody!" he shouted.

"Methinks the inspector isn't a morning person," said Horace with a smirk.

Edna smoothed her blonde wig, which was a little lopsided. "Yeah, well I can understand that."

DI Penrose caught up with them as they were making their way back to the inn. "Follow me, please." The sentence might have included a 'please', but there was no doubting it was a command not a request.

Marjorie, accompanied by Edna, Horace and Frederick, followed the inspector while the ambulance crew hurriedly loaded Mim onto a stretcher and overtook them. A few minutes later, they climbed into the ambulance along with the doctor and drove away with lights flashing and sirens blaring. Marjorie shot an empathetic smile at the doctor's husband. "Thank goodness your wife was here."

He nodded. "I don't think the poor woman would have survived if she hadn't been."

Marjorie watched the tired-looking man hurry inside.

"What was the silly woman doing, going swimming in the sea in autumn?" Edna asked.

"I doubt she went swimming of her own volition," said Marjorie. "This is attempted murder – and if that woman doesn't survive..."

Edna's face paled more than usual. Obviously, her rude awakening hadn't given her time to apply makeup. She looked wan in the morning light.

As they moved towards the entrance, Inspector Penrose had disappeared from view. Marjorie heard Faith gathering the rest of party and urging them to eat.

"Please go inside for breakfast, our travel plans are delayed for now. The police would like to speak to everyone."

"I don't see why we should be interviewed," complained Stan Carlisle.

"Me neither, nor miss out on our morning's trip. At this rate, we'll need a refund," Naomi added.

Edna snapped her head to the side, giving Naomi a look that would turn oil to concrete.

"People shouldn't go into these dangerous waters – there's a lot of rocks about," said a guest who wasn't in their party, heading in out of the cold.

"I don't believe Mim would have gone swimming," said Casey, appearing behind them.

"Let's not jump to conclusions," Faith interjected in her caring way. "We don't know if she was in the sea at all, yet. She was found behind some rocks. All will be revealed, I'm sure, but thank goodness she's alive."

"Will she survive?" Casey asked, looking around nervously.

"It's not certain," replied Faith, shaking her head side to side. "The doctor who attended says it's touch and go. She's accompanying the paramedics to the hospital."

Marjorie felt the familiar weight of responsibility settling on her shoulders. Today, she was determined they would expose a killer, come what may.

TWENTY-TWO

"The inspector asked me to request you four wait here," said Timothy when Marjorie and her friends arrived in reception. It was abundantly clear from the bellowing coming from the manager's office that Detective Inspector Penrose wasn't a patient man and he certainly wasn't having a good day. When he emerged from the room, his face was puce.

"Right. All four of you are here, I see," he said, motioning for them to follow. Marjorie and the others did as expected and followed him inside. The manager's office was spacious enough for one or two people, but a little cramped for five. They shuffled around to fit and Timothy kindly brought in three extra seats so they ended up sitting in a row as if summoned to see the headmaster. Penrose made no effort to ensure they were comfortable, which they weren't, instead plonking himself behind the manager's desk, showing no qualms about taking over the office.

"Thank you, Timothy," Marjorie called to the retreating receptionist's back.

Penrose ran a hand through his hair making it look more

windswept. His deep-set eyes scanned them. "What happened?"

"How are we supposed to know?" said Edna. "I'm not long up."

"What about you?" Penrose looked at Marjorie.

"All I saw was Miriam or Mim – she prefers to be known by that name – Butterfield strolling along the beach late last night. There were other people around, and she seemed safe to me, so I didn't think any more of it. I went to bed."

Penrose gestured a rolling motion with his hand, she assumed he wanted her to move along.

"When I woke this morning and looked out of the window, I saw a man throwing sticks for his dog, a golden retriever."

Penrose couldn't disguise a heavy sigh as he squeezed the bridge of his nose like Frederick tended to when stressed.

"Then," continued Marjorie, "I saw the dog run behind a large rock and start barking, its owner pulled it away. The tide was receding, you see. When two men moved the woman into the open, I saw the bright red streaks of hair spreading on the wet sand; I knew it was Mim, the artist."

"And why do you think she'd want to do herself in?"

"You tell me, Inspector! I don't imagine she did want to do herself in, as you so put it. And I would appreciate it if you took us more seriously." Marjorie was tired of being treated like an idiot.

He held his hand up in submission. "Okay, okay, I get what you're saying. Believe it or not, I have been taking this whole thing seriously. We had an anonymous tip-off late last night confirming erm... my suspicions..." He couldn't maintain eye contact and she knew he was lying.

The arrogance of the man! He'd had no suspicions whatsoever when he left the night before.

"... confirming my suspicions that Professor Miller's death wasn't an accident."

"And this anonymous tip-off? Where did that come from?" said Edna.

The inspector couldn't resist rolling his eyes. "The clue is in the word 'anonymous', Mrs Parkinton."

"All right. You don't need to be shirty with me." Edna was also clearly losing patience, having been woken early and not having eaten. Marjorie felt he should beware an angry Edna, who finished: "If it weren't for us, you wouldn't know anything at all!"

"I'm not sure I know anything anyway, other than the fact I have a suspicious death on my hands – and a possible attempted murder."

"You knew all along Mim was attacked," said Marjorie, picking up on his words immediately.

"It would appear so, from what the doctor and attending paramedics told me. The bruises to her neck were most likely sustained by being held under the water, although rocks can cause damage. But we don't believe her injuries came from the rocks. The doctor suspects someone left her for dead and that she somehow made it out of the water before collapsing behind those rocks. She's suffering from hypothermia. I'll know more when she's been examined at the hospital. For now, all efforts are on keeping her alive."

"The anonymous tip-off you received, Inspector. Was it from a woman?" asked Marjorie.

"That's very perceptive of you, Lady Snellthorpe. Yes, it was."

"And you believe it was Mim Butterfield?"

"I'm keeping all options open at the minute but, as you know, we have an anonymous tip-off followed by a woman almost drowning shortly afterwards."

"I hear you, Inspector. So, assuming it was Mim Butterfield, what did the tipster have to say?"

"You may not quite understand this, Lady Snellthorpe, but

this is my interview. You are my witnesses. I ask the questions, you answer them, and then *I* investigate."

"Which is why you didn't want to tell us anything last night, even though you were in possession of this tip-off," Marjorie said.

"As a matter of fact, I wasn't in possession of it. I received the call when I got back to the office. It was late. Way past my, and possibly your, bedtime. That's when I heard about it and that's when I realised that my erm... theory was correct."

He was clearly sticking to his *theory* point, even though Marjorie and the others knew otherwise. But at least she'd gleaned more information.

"I don't think there's anything else we can tell you, Inspector," said Frederick. "I was out for a walk this morning and I saw the dog thing happen too. Two men pulled Mim away from the rock, and then the doctor arrived. We were lucky someone who knew exactly what to do was staying at the inn, or it could have been a very different outcome."

"Yes, and twice as lucky for us the doctor is a forensic medical examiner from London," said the inspector.

"I wondered how she came up with the clear attempted-murder theory," said Marjorie, not adding, *and why you took her findings seriously.*

"If that's everything?" Penrose made to stand up, but Marjorie urged the others to remain in place.

"We can tell you nothing more about what happened to Mim, but please allow us to enlighten you on our theories so far," said Marjorie.

Penrose flopped back down in the chair, rubbing his head. "If you could make it quick. I have work to do."

"We didn't believe the professor's death was an accident from the start, but as your officers didn't seem too interested, we've gathered some information by ourselves."

The inspector frowned but let her continue.

"Most of the people in our tour party have something to hide, but there are a few people higher on the suspect list. With regards to Mim, I suggest you begin by investigating the strange woman who has been arguing with her ever since we arrived in Cornwall."

"And this strange woman is?"

"I'm afraid Mim wouldn't tell us, but Frederick and I have twice witnessed the pair having heated arguments. First, at Mim's gallery in Bude, and yesterday on the coastal path."

"I see, but you don't have the name of this woman?"

"Sadly, no. Nor do we know what they were arguing about."

"Mim wouldn't tell us who she was," said Frederick. "She could be anyone – a disgruntled customer, even – but the important thing is that she told Mim her time was up. In the light of this morning, that could be important."

"Did you see this woman anywhere near the professor?"

"No, we didn't," said Marjorie.

"Okay, we'll look into it." Penrose shifted in his seat again.

"We do have other suspects," said Marjorie, determined he wouldn't dismiss them until he'd heard what they had to say.

The inspector couldn't resist an eye-roll as he waved a hand for her to continue.

"You already know about Casey Sims and the notebook. And I expect, from your investigation, you're aware that Naomi Carlisle is the professor's ex-wife."

The cough and splutter suggested that the inspector wasn't aware, and that he hadn't started investigating. He'd only just begun to take any of this seriously, and they were right to continue their investigation.

"Carry on!" he snapped, clearly not one to admit to any errors on his part.

"Naomi and Stan – her current husband – had an affair," said Edna, "while Naomi was still married to Professor Vile – that's Miller to you – and he didn't take rejection well when she left him. They divorced. Naomi married Stan, but she says her ex stalked them constantly and wouldn't give them any peace."

"Of course, we only have the Carlisles' word for the alleged stalking," said Marjorie, proud that she had picked up some police terminology. "And what we witnessed suggested the opposite: that they were doing the stalking."

"How so?"

"After we arrived in Bude, they stuck to him like glue," said Edna. "She said it was because they'd decided to turn the tables on him, to see how he liked being followed all the time."

"And you believe her story?" asked the Inspector.

"Not in the slightest," said Frederick.

"I do," said Edna. "Professor Vile was a nasty piece of work, if you ask me."

For the first time Marjorie noticed an upturn at the corner of the inspector's lips. Perhaps he found Edna's blunt way of speaking amusing. Having witnessed his manner so far, they were two of a kind.

"Thank you. Now, I suggest you get on with your day and I'll get on with interviewing people – starting with Mr and Mrs Carlisle, as they are persons of interest in relation to the professor's death."

"But why would they attack Mim?" Marjorie quizzed.

"That's a matter for us. Perhaps you'd like to leave things to the police now, Lady Snellthorpe. I'm sure we'll have answers in due course. In the meantime, thank you for your assistance with our enquiries. You're free to go." This time he did stand up, opening the door to usher them out.

TWENTY-THREE

"Does anybody mind if I grab a shower and put my face on before we eat breakfast?" Edna said. "I'm starving, but all this activity is too much for me before a wash."

"That's an excellent idea," said Marjorie. "I'd quite like to make a phone call. Shall we meet in an hour?"

"Sounds good to me," said Frederick. "I'd like to take a shower as well. My feet are covered in sand and my trousers are wet."

Marjorie returned to her room and removed her mobile phone from a drawer. After plugging it in to charge – Edna had been quite right about its uncharged state – she made a telephone call. Having found out as much as she could from her first call, she followed it up with a second.

Her friends were already settled in the restaurant when Marjorie arrived. They ordered food and looked around to check no-one would overhear them. She hadn't seen Arthur Denton at all and he appeared to have missed the dramatic event earlier.

The restaurant was almost empty as most guests had left for outings. Marjorie had seen all but the Carlisles and Arthur

Denton waiting to be interviewed or interrogated by Inspector Penrose.

She chuckled at the thought. "I feel sorry for the others having to come under the inspector's not-so-delightful charm."

"I wonder how he got that job," Edna said. "His team must hate him."

"He's certainly brusque, and pig-headed," said Horace.

Marjorie finished the fruit plate she'd chosen for breakfast. "Sadly, I am of the same opinion. He wasn't going to admit to being wrong in not investigating Professor Miller's death, was he?"

"I agree, Marge. It's still going to be down to us to find out what happened. Who were you phoning, by the way?" Edna was speaking in between mouthfuls of sausage from a full fried breakfast.

Marjorie poured herself a second cup of tea before answering. "I was making enquiries about the woman Mim had her falling-outs with."

"Well, please tell us before I choke on my bacon." Edna had indeed moved on to the plentiful rashers of bacon on her plate, putting far too much in her mouth at once.

"Aha. The mystery woman is her stepmother."

Frederick stared in astonishment. "I would not have guessed that. There's not that big an age difference. I'd say Mim's late forties and the woman around sixty."

"Yes, well, I telephoned the gallery and spoke to the friendly young lady named Ginny who Frederick and I met when we visited on our first day. She's managing it for Mim while she's away. Poor girl sounded devastated by what had happened. Mim's stepmother had already told her about it. Ginny gets on well with her employer and is a mine of information."

"What did she have to say about the stepmother?" Edna

asked. Having managed to consume her bacon, she now placed her knife and fork down on the plate and refilled her coffee cup.

Marjorie took another sip of tea. "Mim and her stepmother don't get on."

"As if we hadn't gathered that," said Frederick.

"Quite," said Marjorie. "Although they don't get on, Mim's late father didn't have much money. The stepmother, Geraldine, has plenty of money, according to Ginny. Mim's father persuaded Geraldine to lend her the money to open the gallery, which she did, on condition Mim paid it back. As you can gather, since Mim's father passed away, she has reneged on the deal and hasn't been paying the agreed monthly instalments."

"Hence the 'your time is up' comment," said Frederick.

"Geraldine has been trying to get Mim to take responsibility for the loan, but both she and the gallery have fallen into financial difficulty. I'm not sure the gallery was ever a success. Ginny believes it was more of a passion project for Mim than a business, and it hasn't turned a profit. According to Geraldine, Mim has no financial nous."

Horace was all sympathy. "Fancy being left in that predicament after losing her father."

"Oh, trust you! The girl's an irresponsible idiot, if you ask me," said Edna, her reaction quite the opposite.

"Irresponsible or ignorant, perhaps," said Marjorie, wondering if that was the reason Mim had been cosying up to Horace in the first place. "However, she doesn't deserve to be in the position she's in now. Geraldine, as the next of kin, is with her at the Royal Cornwall Hospital in Truro."

"If Mim survives, they might be able to settle their differences," said Horace, ever the optimist.

"If, being the operative word," said Marjorie. "By all accounts it might not be good news. But I'm not sure how much of that is hearsay and how much is fact."

"At least that mystery is solved," said Frederick. "I assume Geraldine has an alibi for the time of the attack?"

"She was in Bude at a meeting with business colleagues and stayed the night with, erm... her boyfriend."

"Blimey! She didn't waste much time. When did Butterworth Senior pass away?" Horace asked.

"Six months ago, though the gallery had been struggling for a few years. According to Ginny, the combination of her father's declining health, reduced tourism during the pandemic, and rising rents had been slowly strangling the business. Several shops in the area didn't survive and their closure meant reduced footfall. Mim's father had been too proud to admit to the extent of the financial crisis, using more of Geraldine's money to cover Mim's basic operating costs without telling either what he was doing. His death was the hammer blow to an already precarious situation, and Mim found herself not only grieving but discovering debts she didn't know existed. Her stepmother was angry that her money had been invested in a failing venture and, according to Ginny, their marriage was already on the rocks, which was another reason Geraldine wanted her money back."

"So we can exclude Lady Chatterley for Mim and Mim for Professor Vile then," said Edna.

Frederick looked horrified, but Horace chortled at Edna's name-changes. "You really have a way with words."

This led to another joint laughter and snorting session.

Frederick muttered, "I don't see what's so funny. And if this Geraldine woman was seeing her boyfriend before her husband died, I don't blame Mim for not wanting to pay her back."

Once Horace and Edna's attention was refocussed, Horace said, "The important thing now is that Mim must have seen or suspected something relating to Professor Miller's so-called fall, and blowing the whistle led to her being attacked."

"Ginny had heard about what happened to the professor but didn't know any more than that, so couldn't help on that score. She did, however, confirm that Mim knew Miller and he had recruited her to do some work for him, promising to pay her. Alas, Mim recently realised she was waiting for a big payday that was never coming."

"He used her," said Horace. "I'm liking our dead professor less and less."

"Yeah, Marge, why do we care?"

"Because not only has someone taken his life, but they have now attacked an innocent – albeit gullible – woman. I suggest we move from here; the staff would like to clear away." Marjorie noticed a couple of waiters hovering.

Having finished breakfast and drained tea and coffee pots, the four moved into the familiar bar. The bar itself was closed, and the room empty, so they sat close to the wood-burning fire. Once settled, Marjorie told them what else she'd discovered.

"The latest item Mim gathered for Professor Miller is to be auctioned any day now."

"How on earth do you know that?" asked Edna.

"After Ginny confirmed Mim had been working for him, I remembered how everyone said she was angry after the museum visit in Boscastle. I telephoned the museum and asked to speak to the curator."

"Using your title, I suppose," said Edna.

"It comes in handy sometimes. Anyway, I discovered why Mim was so upset after leaving the museum the other day."

"Don't keep us in suspense, Marge."

"Her latest discoveries included a few ancient pieces of gold coinage, and the professor was clever enough to pay her a percentage of the reward, but he told her that the biggest piece, a gold statuette, was a fake and worthless. However, when she visited the museum to view the pieces she had found that he'd arranged to go on display, she happened to pick up a leaflet. It isn't the museum auctioning the item – and he's lucky they didn't pick up on it and report it – but they often display leaflets for auctions in case they, or their visitors, wish to buy something."

"Why didn't the museum know it was part of his stash?" Horace asked.

"The seller wished to remain anonymous."

"No surprise there," said Edna.

"It turns out the item Mim found is immensely valuable, and even the usual reward, let alone a profit from undeclared treasure, would have gone a long way towards releasing Mim from her stepmother's debt."

"If she had any intention of paying her," said Frederick. "People do lead complicated lives, don't they."

"Some do," said Marjorie. "So Mim was being cheated out of a lot of money."

"No wonder she was so angry," said Edna.

"If she wasn't in hospital, she would go to the top of our suspect list, but I guess we can rule her out." Horace sounded pleased, once more showing how Mim had managed to manipulate him.

"If the same person who killed Miller tried to kill Mim, it might just be that her crime is one of being gullible, and possibly covering up for a killer, at least initially," said Marjorie.

"Do you think she tried to extort money from the person, or persons?" asked Frederick.

"It's a possibility. She's behind on rent because Geraldine won't pay any more."

"Or it could be she was so angry with Miller that she dragged her feet before her conscience got the better of her," said Horace.

"So we're back to Casey or the Carlisles then?" said Edna.

"We still have Arthur Denton," said Marjorie. "I don't think we should rule him out just yet. Remember, he was out on the beach last night."

"But I'll say this yet again: Casey Sims stole the professor's notebook!"

Marjorie suspected Edna still saw Naomi Carlisle as another one of the professor's victims and would find it difficult to believe she had anything to do with his death.

"But she didn't steal his briefcase," said Frederick.

"We don't know that," said Edna. "She might have hidden it before letting the police search her room – she had plenty of time."

"Speaking of rooms" – Marjorie lowered her voice – "I wonder if we should look in Mim's. Unlike Casey, she didn't seem quite as attached to her phone. She might be the type of girl who would leave it in her room when taking a walk along a beach. We have a limited window of opportunity while Inspector Penrose is busy."

"I don't feel comfortable with that sort of thing. How do you suggest we do it, anyway?" said Frederick.

"We ask Timothy for the key."

"Oh yeah, and he's going cough up a key so we can go rooting around a guest's room," said Edna.

"He might, if we play it right," said Marjorie, thinking. "What I suggest we do is tell him that I've spoken to Ginny who's caretaking Mim's gallery, and she's worried because Mim has an important meeting which obviously she can no longer attend. Then I tell him that Ginny asked me to retrieve Mim's telephone and take it to her stepmother at the hospital."

"Explaining that Mrs Butterworth doesn't want to leave Mim's side in her current condition," said Horace.

"You can be really devious when you want to be, Marge," said Edna.

"This is bordering on obstruction," said Frederick. "Which is a crime."

"But we'll be helping the inspector. After all, Mim's room won't be his top priority. Let's face it, he doesn't appear to be the most diligent man, especially since he's discovered Naomi is Professor Miller's ex-wife."

"Devious but brilliant," said Horace. "I vote we do what Marjorie's suggested – it sounds like a way forward to me."

Frederick rubbed his head hard. "You're all mad."

Ignoring Frederick, Edna made to stand up. "Let's get on with it then."

"Actually, Edna, I was wondering if you would do something else. If you look behind you, Arthur Denton has arrived in reception and is sitting with a face like thunder. Do you think you could distract him? We don't want him knowing what we're up to, especially as we know how good he is at listening to other people's conversations. You might also find out what he is up to?"

"All right, I'll work my charm. At least I've got my makeup on now and my favourite wig." She patted the red wig she had donned before joining them for breakfast, then stood up and headed towards her quarry.

TWENTY-FOUR

While Marge and the others stayed put, Edna strode into reception and sat herself in the chair opposite Arthur Denton. For once, he wasn't taking notes. In fact, with his knee bouncing up and down as though on a string, Edna suspected he was agitated or angry – perhaps even frightened. She gazed into his eyes and realised it was the latter.

"Mind if I sit down?"

"I'd rather be alone," he said.

Edna was angry about people being hurt, both physically and emotionally, and she was determined to give Marge and the others time to do what they needed to do. She sat down. "Tough. We don't always get what we want. I'd rather not have had my holiday going down the pan, but here we are. It is what it is. Besides, I want to have a chat with you."

"Me?" His eyes widened. "Why?"

Edna took advantage of throwing him off guard. "I want you to know you don't fool me. Your unhealthy interest in everyone's business ever since we got here has been noted. Particularly your interest in the late Professor Miller."

He opened his mouth to say something, but she carried on.

"If I didn't know better, I'd think you were behind what happened to that poor woman now lying in a hospital bed fighting for her life. Is that enough for starters?"

He sank into his chair, taken aback. "How could you think for one minute that I'd be involved in anything like that?"

Edna shrugged. "Perhaps you decided it was time to act out your crime fantasies, instead of writing about them."

"They are not fantasies, and that's a ridiculous thing to suggest," he said.

"Well then," she pressed, "why don't you enlighten me? What was your interest in the professor, and why were you out on the beach last night at the same time as Mim?"

"I had no interest in the professor, and I don't know what leads you to believe otherwise."

Edna inhaled sharply in an effort to control herself. "Oh, just the way you hung about listening in to his every conversation. If there's anyone who has behaved suspiciously over the past few days, it's YOU!"

"That's absurd. I've done nothing wrong, and I shall tell the police as much if they ever get around to interviewing me."

"Yeah," Edna shot back defiantly. "And I'll tell them how you were hanging around the professor the whole time. If you're so innocent, why don't you just tell me what you were up to?"

"What's it got to do with you?" He glared at her.

"I'll tell you what it has to do with me. I'm here on my bucket-list holiday, and it's being ruined by people being knocked off, and the sight of Mim being taken away on a stretcher this morning has made me angry. That's my interest, so what's yours?"

"All right, all right. Look," Arthur stammered defensively, "I went for a walk last night and I saw Mim, but we didn't speak. We both had things on our minds. She was talking on the phone, but I didn't hear what she was saying..."

Oh dear, poor Marge isn't going to find a phone, thought Edna.

"... I can assure you she was still out walking when I came indoors. I ate a late dinner before going to bed."

"What about Professor Miller?" she asked.

"I didn't hurt him either," Arthur insisted. "I wouldn't hurt anybody in real life. My stories come from my imagination, they are not steeped in some sick desire to kill people. I don't go around murdering people just so I've got a good story to tell."

"Come on then," Edna urged, growing impatient. "You still haven't told me why you were following the professor."

"I wasn't following him as such," Arthur protested. "I just wanted to make sure that he wasn't going to tarnish my reputation!"

Edna wondered if she'd missed something – whether her hearing was playing up again. "And what made you think he had any interest in you or your reputation?"

"Well..." He hesitated before saying, "Not me as such. My great-great-grandfather was a smuggler and his ancestors were all smugglers."

"You've gotta be kidding me," said Edna, incredulous. What was it about Cornwall and its smuggling?

"I'm not kidding. They were smugglers and I didn't want any of our names, or my family name, tarnished."

Edna felt she'd heard it all now. What did it matter what his great-great-grandfather did? Her father had been a gambling addict and a womaniser who'd deprived her of her inheritance, but that didn't define her. Or did it? Was that another reason why she judged people so harshly? She shook the thought from her head, refocussing on Arthur Denton. "What made you think he was going to do that? And how important is it to you to protect your family's name?"

"Look, maybe you think it's petty, but my family's reputation is everything to me. We've spent generations becoming respectable. My great-grandfather died in poverty trying to go legitimate, and my grandfather worked his fingers to the bone to give us a clean name. Professor Bodwin Miller was a self-interested treasure hunter. His real interest was in making money and being known as the world's leading expert. I wasn't going to let some treasure-hunting academic drag us back into the gutter. It was fine when he stuck to ancient settlements, but once he started digging deeper into smuggling rings and uncovered treasure maps, he was like King Midas. He wanted to track down pieces that have been hidden for years."

"I can believe it," said Edna. "His notebook was full of treasure maps. Casey Sims found it."

"Is that what happened to it? It wasn't in—"

"Ah, so you were the one who stole his briefcase!" Perhaps they needed to consider Arthur Denton as a serious suspect.

"As you know so much, maybe you're the criminal."

"Look, mate, I just want to get this fiasco over with so that I can get on with my holiday. So let's hear the rest of it."

"There isn't much to tell. I took the briefcase in the hope of finding the notebook and the maps; had I managed to lay my hands on it, I would have torn out any pages relating to my family history, but somebody else got there first. Did Casey kill him?"

Edna thought for a moment before answering. "The jury's out on that one. We don't know. But if you're not guilty – which you still could be – it narrows the field, doesn't it?"

Arthur seemed more self-assured as he stared at Edna. "Surely, if she was in possession of the notebook, she's the one who killed the ridiculous man."

"Just because he found out about your family history doesn't mean he was ridiculous," said Edna, trying to be reasonable even though she didn't have a high opinion of the dead man herself.

"His theories were inept. Nobody in sensible academic circles believed a word he said."

"And how would you know that?" Edna asked.

"I studied history at Cambridge and knew him when he started out. He was arrogant then, and the more accolades they bestowed upon him, the more arrogant he became. He'd always had an interest in Cornwall – and yes, he was quite brilliant in some areas – but he wouldn't let the past lie. If anyone's a fantasist, it was him."

Edna considered what Arthur was saying. "Because of his interest in ancient treasure?"

"Precisely."

"So what would you have done if you'd found this notebook?"

"I told you: I'd have torn pages out and he'd have had to start all over again. But I hoped he would lose interest, because I heard he'd found a valuable piece which he was about to sell."

"He didn't strike me as the sort of man to leave anything alone. Particularly not his ex-wife." Edna still felt sorry for the rather obnoxious Naomi, even though she didn't like her.

"What do you mean?" asked Arthur.

"I thought you studied at Cambridge, surely you knew the man was married?"

"That was decades ago, how would I know?"

"Did you know he often visited Cornwall?" Edna persisted.

"Of course I did. And he tricked Mim."

"Did she tell you that?"

Arthur Denton's face reddened.

"You did speak to her last night, didn't you?"

Edna could tell he was about to clam up unless she tried a different tactic. "Were you following him? Did you see them together?"

"As a matter of fact, yes. That's what I've been doing. I hang around in the background as a non-existent writer who nobody takes any notice of. I listened and I followed him and discovered he was using her to find treasure for him. I kept an eye on her too and discovered her gallery was in debt, which is obviously why he was able to manipulate her into working for him. I knew she'd found a valuable piece. I had a quiet chat with her at Boscastle once she separated from the younger woman with all the earrings."

"Casey."

"Yes, the one who you claim has Bodwin's notebook. And the rest, as they say, is history."

"Literally," said Edna. "First, he's dead. Now Mim's fighting for her life. So the people who had access to your ancestors' maps or treasure or whatever you want to call it, have disappeared in a matter of days."

Arthur leaned forward, his eyes intense. "Look, I'm not sorry that Professor Miller is out of the way, but I wouldn't have killed him. That's not how I go about things."

"But you would have stolen from him?"

"As you already know I took the briefcase, I see no point in denying that."

"Was there anything useful in the briefcase?" Edna wondered if it might add to what they'd found in the contents of the notebook.

Arthur Denton shook his head. "I don't think so, but I was so angry his notebook wasn't there, I didn't really go through the rest of the briefcase. And I was worried it might be found after I heard Faith tell you the briefcase had been stolen."

"You just overheard that, did you?"

"I've admitted to everything I've done, but I will not admit to killing people or trying to drown people. Perhaps she got depressed about her debts and decided to end it all?"

"You'll find out soon enough when you're interviewed by Inspector Penrose in there. That's not what the police think," said Edna.

Sweat dripped on Denton's upper lip, his eyes widened. "I'm telling you the truth. I wouldn't have killed him even if he'd done what I dreaded most. The worst I would have done was slow him down and hope to deflect his interest."

Edna looked up to see the Carlisles pass by, moaning to each other, and Inspector Penrose entering reception. His eyes narrowed as he stared at her.

"Yes, Mrs Parkinton?"

She met his gaze with determination not to let him intimidate her. "I'm allowed to speak to fellow travellers, aren't I?"

"Not in the middle of a murder investigation, you're not. Now please leave until I've spoken to everybody concerned."

"Yeah, how's that going then?" Edna's voice dripped sarcasm.

"Wouldn't you like to know?" he said. "Now, if you'd be so kind as to leave us..."

"Okay, I'm going. See you later, Arthur – we might need to talk again."

TWENTY-FIVE

The trio entered Mim's room quickly. Marjorie quelled her unease at the duplicity she'd employed to gain access. The folded easel she and Frederick had seen Mim using leaned against the wall, along with a large sketch pad.

Horace checked every surface. "There's no phone, Marjorie." He lifted the lead of a phone charger, still plugged into the wall.

"She must have taken it with her. We should leave," said Frederick, who had made it clear he didn't wish to be there.

"Not so fast, Fred. Now we're here, we might as well have a quick look around," said Horace. "Perhaps she wrote things down." Horace rubbed his hands together as if raring to go..

Apart from the charger, the easel and sketchpad, and a pair of brightly coloured dungarees hanging over the back of the chair, the room was identical to Marjorie's.

"She didn't strike me as the notebook type, but she might have sketched what she saw," said Frederick reluctantly.

"Let's do a quick search and see what we find. You never know, she might have sketched our killer," said Marjorie with a nervous chuckle.

"Wishful thinking," said Horace. "Edna's doing a good job down there with Arthur Denton, isn't she?" he continued admiringly. "He seemed totally absorbed."

"Shell-shocked, more like," said Marjorie. "I wonder what she said to get him to open up."

"Whatever it was, it worked," said Horace.

"Shall we get a move on, and then we'd better get out of here. I can tell Timothy that Mim must have had her phone with her. In a way, it's a good thing because we don't have to lie to him."

"We've already lied to him," said Frederick, his voice sounding shaky, "telling him we're on a mission for a step-mother we've never spoken to."

It was I who lied, thought Marjorie, but understood Frederick's reticence. "We passed the time of day with her."

"You mean she glared at us. Twice," said Frederick with a grim laugh. "I'd hardly call that passing the time of day."

Frederick could be infuriatingly self-righteous at times, and right now Marjorie felt on edge enough without him sending her on a guilt trip. "I expect she's feeling repentant about her behaviour now her stepdaughter's fighting for her life."

"Don't you believe it," said Horace. "Some people's hearts are glacial."

Marjorie wondered why Frederick and Horace were procrastinating over the room search. The latter had seemed enthusiastic when they came in. "I expect you're right. But I really believe we should do what we're here to do. Spread out" – Marjorie headed towards the bedside table – "and start checking drawers. I hope when people go through my belongings someday, there might be a little something to cheer them up," said Marjorie.

"And I hope when they're going through mine, they find nothing," said Frederick. "Because I don't want to leave behind a whole load of clutter for my kids to sort through.

When my parents died, it was a nightmare trying to clear the house."

"I think we're forgetting this is just a hotel room, and Mim's not dead," said Marjorie, opening another drawer. She almost wished she had tasked Frederick with keeping Arthur Denton occupied, although he wouldn't have had anywhere near the success Edna had. Exasperated, she looked at her two friends. "I don't think we're going to find anything here. As you suggested, Frederick, Mim may not have made notes. I expect that, unless the person who tried to drown her has her phone, it's lying on the seabed."

"We know Arthur Denton was on the beach last night," said Horace.

"I hope Edna has found out what he was up to, because the inspector's not going to give us any information. I'd love to know what the tip-off entailed."

"Can we go now?" said Frederick. "I really don't like searching somebody's room without their permission."

Not that you've done any searching at all, thought Marjorie. "We do have permission," she said, sounding almost as belligerent as Frederick.

"No, we don't. We are here under false pretences, and if DI Penrose turns up, we are in deep trouble."

Marjorie sighed. Frederick was right. They shouldn't be going through the belongings of somebody they hardly knew, no matter how good the intention. The desire to find out what had happened waned. Horace continued opening drawers but Frederick stood at the door.

"Perhaps it is time to leave," said Marjorie, looking at Frederick. "I'll let Timothy know we found nothing."

"I wonder when the police are going to let us carry on with our travels," said Horace, still moving clothes around. "As much as I like this place, I'd still like to see the other parts of Cornwall Edna's looking forward to."

"Perhaps Faith will have more news. Are you ready?" Having done nothing but pace for ages, Horace was now vigorously rifling through the chest of drawers.

"I hope Mim survives," said Horace. "Such a good-looking girl."

"Don't let Edna hear you say that, Horace. She'll say you're only thinking about looks."

"I don't see why a man can't appreciate a woman's looks. When did that become a crime?"

"Come on, Horace, it's time to go." said Frederick. "I'm really not comfortable being in this room."

"Wait a minute."

"What is it?" asked Marjorie.

Horace kneeled by the bottom drawer, removing what looked like a diary from beneath a pile of neatly folded bright t-shirts. "Now we're talking," he said. "Even I don't have the audacity to read a woman's diary." He handed it to Marjorie. "You'd better see if there's anything of significance."

Frederick's eyes darted between the diary and the door. "Make it quick."

Marjorie started leafing through the pages of the diary. "I'll start from the day before yesterday.

"Anything?' asked Horace.

"She's writing about Boscastle... the museum visit... she's furious about being lied to." Marjorie's eyes scanned the text. "The pen stroke here is deep and heavy – angry. I'm not a handwriting expert, but I would interpret it as ira—"

"Graphologist," said Frederick.

"Pardon?" Horace asked.

"A handwriting expert is a graphologist. What about after the professor died?" Frederick asked.

"Here – she mentions the accident, calls it justice being served. She felt guilty for not caring..." Marjorie paused, her finger tracing a line. "She's written something later."

"What?" Frederick asked.

"Wait." Marjorie's voice dropped. "Listen to this: 'While walking, I remembered seeing something after Bodwin went over the edge.' She's rushed back to write it down while it's fresh."

"Does she say what she saw?" Horace asked.

Horace and Frederick had lost all sense of hesitancy over reading a woman's diary and were leaning so close she could smell aftershave and feel breathing on her neck.

Marjorie read slowly: "I saw her and him coming from the spot where Bodwin had fallen.'"

The three friends exchanged glances. Frederick's eyes widened. "Her and him: the Carlisles, then."

"It's odd phrasing," said Marjorie.

"What are you thinking?" he asked.

"I'm not sure yet. It's all a bit jumbled after that. I think that was the last entry; most likely she went out again after writing that and called the police."

Marjorie stared at the final paragraph, unable to take her eyes off it.

"It was the Carlisles," said Horace. "We were right all along. I knew those two couldn't be trusted."

"It's damning, isn't it? But still not enough evidence. All she says is she saw the two people. It doesn't mention seeing them killing him."

"Nevertheless," said Frederick, "it narrows it down. Now put that back and let's get out of here."

"We need to give it to Inspector Penrose," said Horace, whose moral compass must have kicked in.

"If you think I'm going to confess to that inspector down there that we've rooted around in this woman's room and not only found but read her diary, you've got another think coming." Frederick's face was so red, Marjorie feared his doctor might need to increase his blood pressure pills again. "No way!

I suggest we leave it on top of the bedside table, and suggest the inspector looks in Mim's room for clues."

Horace slapped Frederick on the back. "Great idea. Let's do that." He took the diary from Marjorie and placed it on top of Mim's bedside table.

"Wait," said Frederick as they prepared to leave. He returned to the diary. "We need to make sure it looks like she left it out naturally." He carefully repositioned the book, as if Mim had been writing in it and set it aside.

"Good thinking," said Marjorie, always impressed by his attention to detail.

Frederick held up a hand as they reached for the door. "Fingerprints," he said, producing a handkerchief from his pocket. He carefully went around the room wiping the drawer handles and anywhere they had touched before wiping the door handle and opening it to check the corridor was clear.

"I never would have thought of that," Horace admitted.

Frederick straightened his shoulders as if to say – quite rightly – his careful and methodical nature was valuable rather than just cautious. He nodded, indicating the corridor was clear.

They slipped out quietly and Horace pulled the door closed. They made it three steps along the corridor when they heard footsteps and Stan Carlisle's voice complaining about being questioned.

There wasn't time to unlock Mim's door and the footsteps were nearing the top of the stairs.

"There," said Frederick pushing them into a narrow housekeeping alcove where they squeezed behind a laundry cart just as the Carlisles entered the corridor.

They held their breath as the footsteps came nearer.

"Hold on a minute." Stan stopped just outside their hiding spot. They were so close Marjorie could hear them breathing.

"Got it," Stan said finally, and they proceeded to their own room. They heard the click of the door opening and closing.

"Now," Frederick whispered, and they crept out of the alcove, moving quietly towards the stairs.

"That was close," said Marjorie, whose heart was still pounding. "Thank you, Frederick."

"Anytime," he said with a slight smirk.

TWENTY-SIX

When Marjorie, Frederick and Horace arrived downstairs it was almost lunchtime, and Faith was nowhere in sight, nor were any of the others from their party. With no inkling as to when they might get on with the next part of their journey, Marjorie hoped the new information would speed things along.

Scanning the bar, Marjorie saw Edna sitting on a barstool. "There you are, I didn't know whether to come up or not. I thought we could have hot drinks in the conservatory as it's empty."

"Will it be warm enough?" Frederick asked.

The bartender answered for him. "It's like an oven in there as long as the sun's shining. And it is today. I'll bring you pots of tea and coffee."

"Thank you," said Marjorie, before speaking to Horace. "I'll join you after I've returned this to Timothy."

Horace tapped his nose as he tended to do when sharing a secret. "Righto."

Marjorie slowly wandered into the reception, looking around to make certain no-one was watching her. She needn't have worried. Word must have got around about the inspector's presence; the place was empty. Marjorie strolled over to the desk.

"I'm sorry, Timothy, it was a waste of time." She handed back the key. "Thank you for your help but Mim must have taken her phone with her to the beach. I'll let her stepmother know, although I doubt there's anything she can do about it. It will be ruined by now."

"Okay, Lady Marjorie. It was good of you to try." He turned and hung the key back in its place.

"Has Inspector Penrose finished his interviews?"

"Yes, thank God. He's been upsetting all our guests. A very glum author has just left."

"Arthur Denton." *So much for his secrecy*, thought Marjorie.

"That's the one. He's just stormed out saying to let the guide know he's gone for a walk."

"Speaking of our guide, have you seen Faith or Nick?"

"Not recently, but the good news, for you anyway, is that she's asked us to prepare her bill, so you must be checking out today. I'll miss you all, it's been fun having so many interesting people to stay."

"That's good of you to say so," said Marjorie, imagining the manager might be of a different opinion.

"Don't let on I told you, I expect she wants to tell you herself."

"Your secret's safe with me. Is the inspector still in your manager's office?"

Timothy rolled his eyes, nodding.

"I might just have a quick word with him."

"Rather you than me."

Marjorie smiled before knocking on the manager's door.

"COME IN." The yell reverberated through reception causing Timothy to clap a hand to his mouth.

"Be careful," he mouthed.

Inspector Penrose's mood seemed no better than it had been

earlier. That was until he looked up to see her. Then he smirked. "Oh, it's you. You'll be pleased to hear, Lady Snellthorpe, that the real police have done their job, and we're about to make an arrest."

"The Carlisles?" she quizzed.

He exhaled an exasperated breath. "You'd like it to be them, wouldn't you? From what I hear, you don't like them."

"I've said no such thing," she said, a little sharper than intended. Penrose really was a most infuriating man.

"For your information, it's none of your business who it is. Now, please let me get on with my job, unless you've got anything to add to your story."

"I'm not sure I like the way you say 'story' as if I make things up, Inspector." But then a guilty pang hit her, having just made up a whole raft of things in order to persuade Timothy to let them inside somebody's room. "Have you checked Mim's phone?" she asked, moving onto safer ground.

"Erm. No. I assume it fell in the sea when someone tried to drown her." He rubbed a hand through his hair, flustered.

"One shouldn't assume things, especially when one is a police inspector doing his job." Realising she needed to row back before she aggravated the annoying DI, Marjorie added, "She was walking along the beach and may have planned to paddle in the sea. Not everyone takes their phone everywhere. And Mim Butterfield would be more likely to carry a sketch pad than a phone."

"Well, I..."

"I just thought you'd want to check, if only to find out whether she was the person who called you."

"She was. We've traced the call and the number." He waved a dismissive hand.

"Nevertheless, she might have left clues on her phone, taken photos, or written something down," Marjorie persisted. "Don't you think you should check her room?"

The inspector sighed heavily. "As I said, Lady Snellthorpe, leave these matters to the police. We're not incompetent and we're not clumsy: we're methodical. Just because I said we hadn't looked in her room yet, doesn't mean we weren't going to. In fact, it's the next thing on my list."

Of course it was. Not, thought Marjorie, but with battle won, she said, "In that case, I won't trouble you any further, Inspector, and I'm glad you've found your..." she waited for him to say man or woman but he didn't respond.

Instead, he clamped his lips tight, folding his arms before grinning. "You don't think I'm going to fall for that trick, do you? Rest assured you'll find out soon enough. You and your party are free to go. I've informed Ms Weathers. I expect you'll all be checking out later today, so goodbye." The wretched man turned his back on her like a spoiled child.

"I expect we will. Thank you so much for your time. It's been a pleasure meeting you."

He harrumphed.

Marjorie left him to his thoughts, which most likely weren't the same as hers. She could only hope they changed when he found the diary.

TWENTY-SEVEN

Marjorie left Inspector Penrose's makeshift interview room with a satisfaction that warmed her more than the promise of tea. She caught Timothy's exaggerated grimace directed at the closed door and grinned.

After passing through the reception area of the old stone inn, the soft murmur of conversations greeted her as she made her way through the bar. People chatted with drinks in hand while waiting for the restaurant to open for lunch.

The conservatory was adorned with tall windows offering panoramic views of the cove below. On any other day, she would have been eager to stroll along the beach. Instead, she made her way towards her friends.

They had secured a corner table. Two trays sat before them: a delicate, though large china teapot on one and a coffee pot on the other. Along with a plate of shortbread biscuits which – judging by the sprinkling of crumbs across Edna's ample chest – had already been sampled.

"Here she is, our own Miss Marple," Horace announced, his face crinkling into a smile.

"Stop your teasing," Marjorie chided, though pleased by the comparison. She settled into a wicker chair, arranging her cardigan around her shoulders to protect them from any draughts.

Frederick poured her a cup of Earl Grey tea, ensuring he added milk first, just as she preferred. His attentiveness touched her. Their friendship had blossomed over the past few years and at times like this, it showed. "Thank you," she said, lifting the cup. His thoughtfulness made her willing to forgive him his petulance during their reconnaissance mission in Mim's room. Frederick had never embraced their amateur sleuthing with the enthusiasm she and Horace shared.

"I've just come from speaking to our warm and welcoming DI," she said, leaning forward slightly.

The others grinned but listened.

Marjorie lowered her voice though there was no-one nearby. "He is, or was, about to make an arrest."

"The Carlisles." Horace clapped his hands in satisfaction. "We've just filled Edna in on what we found in the diary."

"I knew it was them, although yesterday I was convinced it was Casey." Brushing biscuit crumbs from her floral blouse, Edna rushed on: "Anyway, I'm glad they've got them."

Marjorie shook her head as she lifted the cup to her mouth. The pleasant scent wafted upwards. "Actually, I'm almost certain it isn't the Carlisles he's intending to arrest. He's being his belligerent self and wouldn't say who it is but was smug when I mentioned the Carlisles, which makes me think it's not them. We'll find out soon because he says we're free to go. Which means there will be at least one more person missing from our party when we leave."

"It must be Casey, then," said Edna, reaching for another biscuit. "We can finally get on with our holiday. I've been looking forward to it for months, and whoever he arrests, it's a good outcome even if we didn't help him."

The sea breeze rattled the glass panes, and Marjorie glanced out at the blue sky with a few scattered clouds on the horizon. The weather on the north Cornwall coast could change in an instant, a lot like the direction of their investigation.

"I think we gave him a fair amount," said Marjorie, with pride. "He wouldn't be anywhere without us, and I've just nudged him in the direction of Mim's room. So let's hope he stops his nonsense and arrests the right people. He's so erratic, I wouldn't be surprised if he was about to arrest Timothy."

Horace chortled, his shoulders moving up and down, as did Edna. Frederick merely raised an eyebrow, his expression one of mild amusement.

"How did you convince him to check Mim's room?" Frederick asked.

Marjorie took a welcome sip of tea before answering, relishing the comforting warmth as it reached the back of her throat. A group of seagulls wheeled overhead, their cries muffled by the glass but still audible.

"It wasn't hard; I played to his ego. As we've discovered, he's not one who wishes to lose face. I suggested he look for her phone, since not every woman takes their phone out. It hadn't occurred to him, of course, but he wasn't going to admit it. He had the gall to say it was the next thing on his list, so he'll do it now." She recalled the inspector's tight-lipped, haughty expression: one of a man knowing he'd been outmanoeuvred but not prepared to back down.

"What did Arthur Denton have to say for himself, Edna?" she asked, moving the conversation away from Inspector Penrose.

Edna's face brightened at being the centre of attention. "Can you believe he reckons he was worried about his ancestral reputation? His ancestors were smugglers, so he'd been following Miller to make sure he wasn't going to ruin their – and by association his – reputation."

Marjorie's brow furrowed as she took a sip of tea. "How odd."

"He also admitted to stealing the briefcase but said he didn't find anything because it was the notebook he was after. He was furious that was missing. I told him who had the notebook and challenged him on what he would have done to get it. He denied intending to harm Professor Vile and said he was just trying to slow him down. All Denton said he intended to do was tear the relevant pages out. He knew about the auction, and how Miller used Mim. He hoped the sale would put an end to Miller's treasure-hunting research."

"I see," said Marjorie, mulling it over. "He was a long shot, but I'm not convinced by that story."

"Whatever the real reason, he's only guilty of being annoying," said Edna, reaching for yet another biscuit.

Marjorie watched as sea spray hit the rocks below. The wind was getting up. "I would have almost liked it to have been him because I don't like people who sneak around," she said, thinking of Denton's unwelcome presence and evasive eyes.

"As opposed to what we've been doing," said Frederick, with a wry smile.

"There's only so much forgiveness one can receive for a cup of tea," said Marjorie, chuckling.

Edna puffed out her chest. "Yeah, well, I didn't sneak up on him. I went in for the jugular and challenged him. It's the only way to deal with blokes like that."

"Hear, hear, Edna," said Horace, raising his coffee cup in salutation. "With the case solved it's too early for a whisky so let's enjoy our tea and coffee while we wait for an update from Faith."

"I'm just glad to have it all over with," said Edna, dusting sugar from her fingers before removing her compact to reapply lipstick.

"So am I," said Frederick. "I hate this sort of thing."

"Yes," said Marjorie, placing her cup down on the saucer, where it landed with a delicate clink.

"Oh no, she's got that look on her face again," said Edna.

"What look? This is my face."

"You don't fool me. It's that 'I'm not convinced the inspector's going to arrest the right person' look."

Marjorie touched her cheek and in a teasing tone replied, "I didn't know I possessed such a look. I'm happy to enjoy my tea and put the whole thing behind us." She hoped she sounded more convincing than she felt, because she didn't trust Inspector Penrose to reach the right conclusion. However, she hoped he would follow the evidence, now that she'd pointed him in the right direction.

The clouds on the horizon grew darker, creating shadows in the conservatory much like Marjorie's unease. The weather was moving in along with the wind lifting the spray.

"How about we celebrate with cake?" Edna suggested.

"Edna, it's almost lunchtime," said Marjorie, checking her wristwatch.

"Okay, I'll go without, as long as I'm allowed dessert after lunch. I like the food in this place. Who knows where we'll be staying tonight, it might be the pits."

If you'd read the itinerary you would know, Marjorie thought, but said, "Faith won't have booked anywhere remotely like you've just described. Drink your coffee."

She gazed outside as raindrops began to fall against the windows. Something niggled in the back of her mind, some detail or connection she'd overlooked. The pieces were all mingling into one – Miller's treasure hunts, his death, Mim's almost-drowning, the crucial diary, Arthur Denton's ancestral concerns, the Carlisles' behaviour, Casey's anger – but the piece that pulled the case together eluded her.

The rain grew heavier, streaming down the windows, distorting the view outside. Meanwhile, Penrose was about to make an arrest. And somewhere in the recesses of Marjorie's mind, a connection was waiting to be made. If only it would come to her.

TWENTY-EIGHT

Just as they were about to go in to lunch, and Marjorie was having a quiet conversation with Horace about Edna and her hearing aids, all hell broke loose. Raised voices boomed from the bar. Marjorie and friends hurried to see what was happening. Arthur Denton was being pinned to the ground by two police officers.

He was yelling and protesting innocence while one of the officers forced his hands behind his back. She managed to cuff his wrists.

"Get off me, you idiots! What are you doing?"

Marjorie looked on in total confusion.

"Keep hold of him, will you," the female officer said as she spoke into her radio, calling for assistance.

"Well, this isn't what I expected," said Horace.

"I'm telling you: I'm innocent. Get off me!" Arthur Denton kicked his legs, striking one of the officers on the shin.

Detective Inspector Penrose appeared, his face as dark as thunder. "Mr Denton. You have already been cautioned and are under arrest for the murder of Professor Miller, and the attempted murder of Miriam Butterfield. I'm now adding resisting arrest and assaulting a police officer to those charges. I suggest you calm down and come with us."

Denton wasn't listening, he continued to struggle and managed to get to his feet, shaking off the police officers, and even with his hands manacled behind his back, he surged like a wild thing. A table went flying as he tried to run.

Guests stood aside but found safe positions from which to watch. As the commotion grew louder, two more police officers burst into the bar and another barred the hotel exit.

"Mr Denton, calm down or we will have to use a taser," shouted Penrose.

Denton's eyes were wild, darting around in every direction until they settled on Edna and Marjorie.

"Tell these idiots it wasn't me."

Marjorie didn't quite know what to say. She was as confused as he was.

"These people have got nothing to do with it," said Penrose, glaring at Marjorie and her friends. "This is your final warning, Denton. Come with us, or I will instruct an officer to taser you." One of the officers who had come in last held what looked like a gun in his hand, aiming it at the author.

Denton stopped struggling, standing still. His shoulders sagged, looking less like a wild beast and more like one trapped and accepting its fate. Fear filled his eyes. And once more he looked at Marjorie.

"I didn't do what they're saying. You must believe me. It wasn't me. I'm telling you, it wasn't me. This is not right."

The officers took his arms and roughly escorted him from the hotel. As a surge of guests followed, so did Marjorie and friends. They watched as he was pushed inside a police car, both prisoner and captors now drenched as the rain was falling in torrents.

As the crowd scattered, Penrose stopped and turned to look

at the four friends. "I told you, Lady Snellthorpe, that we would make our arrest today. I hope you are satisfied."

"Did you look for the phone?"

"It wasn't in her room, as I knew it wouldn't be. We found a diary but it has no significance."

Marjorie squeezed Edna's arm to stop her saying whatever she was about to say.

"Are you certain you have the right man, Inspector?" Marjorie held his gaze.

"Enjoy the rest of your holiday, Lady Snellthorpe." With that, he turned on his heel, pulled the collar of his mac up and raced out of the hotel, climbing into a waiting car.

"Well I never!" said Edna. "As Horace said, that was unexpected. Arthur Denton wasn't the one I was thinking would be arrested today."

"Me neither," said Marjorie, deeply concerned. "I'd like to know what they've discovered that we haven't. Oh, look, here's Faith, perhaps she can tell us."

Faith appeared in the reception area just as the police cars disappeared into the distance.

"Oh my goodness. I'm so pleased I've caught you." Faith waited for the final few guests to disperse. Having witnessed the most exciting thing that might happen during their holiday, they filed into the restaurant for lunch and, no doubt, a gossip.

Faith was breathless, her face pale as she looked at them.

"Why did they arrest him?" Marjorie asked.

"One of the officers – a young woman who likes to chat – told me that Arthur Denton had been trying to trace a gold statuette. It was... how do I say this... loot, smuggled by his ancestors. He discovered that Professor Miller had obtained the relic via Mim. It's due to be auctioned off. As you can imagine, Arthur was livid but wouldn't put in a claim of ownership."

"We heard about the smuggling bit," said Edna. "He said was protecting his family reputation."

"Oh, is that why he wouldn't admit to it? I don't think he could have claimed it anyway."

"He couldn't," said Frederick, "and neither could Professor Miller sell it. At least, not legally."

All eyes were on Frederick, who flushed red. "I looked it up. If smuggler's loot is found and is considered treasure – which no doubt this statuette would be – it belongs to the Crown. I was going to tell you all but we erm... got distracted."

"Interesting," said Faith. "So Professor Miller had no right to put it up for auction in the first place. Nevertheless, according to the officer I spoke to, the statuette was Denton's family's most prized treasure, and the most valuable. According to the police, if it had been sold it would have set him up for life."

"Does he not make enough money from writing?" Horace asked.

"I'm not sure about his financial situation, but according to the police he was desperate to get his hands on this statuette. It was very underhanded the way Mim and Professor Miller went after it. He told Mim the statue was brass and worthless. Once she found out it was gold and that it was going up for auction overseas, she was furious."

"We knew a lot of this, apart from Denton wanting the statuette for himself. Denton must have cornered her during the trip to Tintagel Castle," said Marjorie.

"Yes. She confessed to being angry after the visit to the museum, which is when she discovered the statue was going on sale. And that's when, the police think, he determined to have it out with Professor Miller. They believe Denton and Bodwin argued, and he pushed the professor over the edge of the cliff."

"But why attack Mim?" asked Edna.

"To keep her quiet, I suppose," said Frederick. "If she confessed to Denton about the statue thing and was starting to put things together, perhaps he was scared of being found out."

"Okay, I see that – to a point," said Marjorie. "But something doesn't sit right with me about the whole thing. Why would he deny it so vehemently? We saw his reaction."

"Yeah, but we also saw his strength," said Edna. "I wouldn't want to be on the other end of that temper."

"Edna makes a good point. I've been reading his first book and there's a lot of violence in it," said Horace.

"It looked more like a terrified anger to me. I think he even frightened himself," said Marjorie.

"I'll take your word for that," said Faith. "I missed that part."

"Why did Mim mention seeing her and him in her diary?" Marjorie went on.

"I'm afraid you've lost me," said Faith.

"Long story," said Frederick, frowning.

Marjorie continued, "We assume she's referring to the Carlisles."

"But she doesn't name them," said Horace, "so it could be a separate her and him, like Casey – because we know she was in the vicinity, since she picked up the notebook – and Denton."

"All this is too much for my tired brain," said Edna. "You know what, I think I'm going to put my hearing aids in. I can't hear what's going on half the time."

"Hallelujah!" said Marjorie, exchanging a glance with Horace.

"Good for you, Edna," said Horace.

They waited while Edna removed two tiny cases from her handbag and fitted her hearing aids. This took longer than expected because of a few failed attempts, and when she did get it right, Horace had to find out how to switch them on for her.

"There you are. You're going to be a part of every conversation now," said Horace with an enthusiastic grin.

"Don't you believe it," said Edna. "I can still manage selective hearing."

"Of that, I have no doubt," said Marjorie. "Now, back to the Arthur Denton situation; there's still a missing link I can't join. I think we need to eat, perhaps I'll be able to concentrate afterwards."

"Okay. Now the good news," said Faith. "We will be checking out this afternoon. And will move on to Newquay. I'd better find Nick and the others. Enjoy your lunch."

TWENTY-NINE

After checking in to the hotel in Newquay, Marjorie was pleased to have some time to herself. Once again she had a room overlooking the sea, and she sat in an armchair by the window to enjoy the view.

Faith had chosen top-class hotels in beautiful spots for the holiday, but Marjorie had a problem. Although they had moved locations, she couldn't move on; she was more convinced than ever that the investigation was not yet concluded. There was still a lingering something just out of reach, in the back of her mind, that she felt was key.

Looking out at the beach, Marjorie felt she'd never tire of watching seagulls diving in and out of the sea. Children played happily and people walked their dogs. She thought of Edna as she watched a couple eating fish and chips while strolling along the seafront. Just then, for no reason at all, the clarity that had evaded her pinged in her brain. The final piece of the jigsaw clicked into place. All she had to do now was prove it.

Marjorie spent the next hour on the telephone. Each call added evidence to support her theory. The most difficult call was the one with Inspector Penrose, who initially dismissed what she was telling him. It took time and a lot of patience to convince him that she could back up what she was saying. All they needed now was the confession.

Marjorie hurried downstairs and into the hotel lobby where she had agreed to meet the others. "We need to delay our planned walk," she said. "DI Penrose is on his way over."

"What the heck for?" Edna moaned.

Marjorie looked around, lowering her voice. "Because I know who did it."

Edna rolled her eyes before widening them. "Seriously, Marge. Must we go through all this again?"

"I promise, this is the last time, Edna. Let me explain..." The four friends moved into a quiet corner where she explained what she'd been doing, and about the revealing telephone conversations. But, she pointed out, they still had to prove it, and the only way to do that was to meet with the killer.

As the foursome entered a quiet lounge overlooking the sea, they found the Carlisles and Casey relaxing around a table, although they weren't speaking. As usual, Casey was tapping and staring at her phone. Naomi flicked through a fashion magazine and Stan read a newspaper.

"I'm pleased we've found you," said Marjorie. "It saves us having to gather everyone together when Detective Inspector Penrose arrives."

"What are you talking about?" asked Casey.

"The inspector is coming to arrest the real killer," Marjorie said.

Stan stared at her as if she'd gone mad. "He's already arrested that Denton chap."

"Yes, but I'm afraid he arrested the wrong man. You've probably read about such things," she continued. "I expect it will turn out that Arthur Denton was helping the police with their enquiries – that's what they usually say when they get it wrong."

Casey looked up at Edna and Horace. "What's she talking about?"

"She believes the real killer is here," said Edna.

Casey, Naomi and Stan gawped at each other. "That's ridiculous," said Naomi, throwing her magazine across the table. "We don't have to listen to any more of this nonsense. Let's go, Stan."

"Here's the inspector now," said Horace. "I suggest you wait for him."

Inspector Penrose entered the room, appearing less angry than he had done on their previous meetings. They all sat down while the inspector pulled up a stool for himself.

"What's this all about, Inspector?" asked Stan, his voice rising in decibels.

Their attention shifted when they saw Mim enter the room, being pushed in a wheelchair by the less-angry stepmother.

Marjorie was delighted to see her, as was Horace, whose eyes sparkled. Casey went over to hug her. "Thank God you're okay," she said.

"Thanks," Mim said. She looked pale but determined.

"I suggest we all sit back down and get this over with," said Penrose. His mood might have improved, but his manner hadn't. A man of few words who liked to get on with things.

Naomi looked uncomfortable but accepted her fate while Casey returned to her seat. Geraldine sat next to Mim, who remained in her wheelchair.

"I'll let Lady Snellthorpe begin," Penrose said.

Marjorie eyed the gathered crowd. "First of all, Mim, I need to apologise and confess that we read your diary while you were in the hospital."

Casey shot Marjorie a look of outrage as if it had been her diary they had read. Had they done so, it would most likely be filled with anger about her lost love, so Marjorie could understand it. "We noticed you wrote in it the night before you were attacked and mentioned seeing 'her and him' shortly after Professor Miller's death. That's when you phoned the police to tip them off that the professor's death may not have been an accident."

"We know all this," said Naomi. "Why drag it all up again? I so want to forget about it and be rid of that man for good."

"You are rid of him for good, aren't you?" said Penrose.

"I don't mean it like that," said Naomi.

"Well, perhaps the sooner people be quiet and listen to what Lady Snellthorpe has to say, the sooner you can get on with your holiday. Some of you, anyway." Penrose glared around as if daring anyone to speak again.

"Quite," said Marjorie. "As I said, Mim, I'm so sorry we read your diary, but it was the mention of seeing her and him that made me think. I wondered why you didn't mention seeing them if you meant the Carlisles—"

"Because we had nothing to do with it."

Penrose shot Stan a look that would melt a furnace, so he shut up and Marjorie carried on.

"I think you were referring to seeing Casey."

Mim nodded. "Sorry, I saw you coming away from where Bodwin fell."

"I've already told them: I found the notebook on the ground. I didn't push him over, his death had nothing to do with me," snapped Casey.

Following another glare from Inspector Penrose, this time aimed at Casey, Marjorie went on. "And I don't believe the gentleman you saw was Arthur Denton. I believe it was Stan Carlisle."

Mim nodded again.

Naomi's head shot up, her eyes flashing. "Stan would never—"

"I was with Naomi," Stan interrupted.

Naomi's head shot to the left, staring at her husband in disbelief. "When?"

"When Miller went over, you know I was with you."

"Do you know that?" asked Marjorie, fixing her gaze on Naomi, who appeared confused, and frightened.

"Of course she does," snapped Stan. "We were together the whole time. You all saw us, we were always together."

"Is it true?" Marjorie asked Naomi again. "And think carefully before you answer, because Professor Miller wasn't the only victim. Mim almost died too. In fact, let me help you here. This afternoon I telephoned the inn where we stayed and managed to speak to the night receptionist who was on duty last night. He saw a man go out at around midnight."

Stan's face went puce as he glowered at Marjorie.

"The man wore a ski mask, so he couldn't be certain who it was."

"Stan doesn't own a ski mask," Naomi said, but her voice had lost some of its conviction. She looked at her husband. "You don't, do you?"

Stan looked at the inspector. "It's obvious, isn't it? It must have been Denton."

"Naomi," Marjorie said gently but firmly. "The receptionist couldn't work out who it was until the man came back from his walk. Although he still wore the mask, he was so wet, he left a trail of water through the reception area. Being conscientious, the night receptionist didn't want to risk any guests slipping. He cleaned and dried the floor in reception. Concerned the sandy water would damage the carpets, he then filled a bucket with soapy water and towels and treated the marks all the way upstairs."

Stan's fists were clenched, his face darkening. "You interfering old..." He half-rose from his chair before Horace shifted forward, ready to intervene. The inspector tensed, one hand moving towards his radio. "The marks stopped outside of your room." Marjorie looked at Naomi, who stared in horror at her husband.

"So I went for a walk. I didn't see anyone in reception otherwise I'd have told him where I was going."

"Doh!" Edna slapped her forehead with the back of her hand. "You went for a walk wearing a ski mask. Do you think we're stupid?"

Stan's voice rose. "It was cold and the wind was blowing. I don't have to listen to this." He stood abruptly, towering over the seated group. Marjorie leaned back as his shadow fell across her. "You think you're so clever, don't you? Meddling in things that don't concern you."

"Sit down, Mr Carlisle," Penrose commanded, his hand now clearly on his radio.

"Or what?" Stan's eyes were wild, darting towards the exit.

"Stan," Naomi pleaded, pressing her fingers to her temples. "This is insane. Stan, tell them you didn't go out."

Her voice seemingly calmed him, as he flopped into a chair.

"Did you know your husband left the room?" Marjorie asked Naomi.

Naomi shook her head. "I take sleeping tablets. I've had to ever since Bodwin started the stalking business. I struggle to sleep without them."

"Okay, so I went for a walk. That doesn't mean I attacked anyone. Did you see who attacked you?" He stared at Mim, his eyes just visible beneath the bushy eyebrows.

Mim shook her head. "No, I didn't see them."

"We have discovered you were in the close proximity of a man we deem to have been murdered and a woman who someone tried to drown. That's enough for me so far," said Penrose. "All we need to confirm now, is where you really were at the time of Professor Miller's death."

"I'm telling you I was with my wife." Stan's eyes pleaded with Naomi.

She shook her head, unable to make eye contact with her husband. Instead, she looked at Marjorie. "We had a row. He wanted to carry on stalking Bodwin, but I'd had enough of it all. I wanted to forget about him and try to make the most of our holiday. Stan wouldn't leave it alone, so I went for a walk. He told me he was near the castle the whole time until he heard the cry. When I joined him, we went together to see what had happened."

"I suggest to you," Marjorie said to Stan, "that, being angry after the argument with your wife, you decided to confront Professor Miller. You argued and you shoved him over the cliff. You also took his notebook, but heard somebody coming, and dropped it before running away."

"What a load of rubbish! How can you pay attention to this rambling old codger?"

Penrose stared him down. "Don't worry Mr Carlisle, if your fingerprints and DNA are found on the professor's notebook, along with Casey's here, that will add to our growing body of evidence. Nobody else has touched the notebook apart from the professor himself."

"He might have showed me his notebook."

"You'd have had no reason to look at it, Mr Carlisle, and the two of you weren't exactly on friendly terms. Why don't you admit what you did and be done with it?" Penrose pressed.

Naomi's voice broke. She looked at Stan with growing horror. "Please, for heaven's sake, Stan. Tell the truth. I can't take this anymore."

"I'm telling the truth," Stan said desperately. "I was with you."

Naomi closed her eyes, tears pushing their way out. When she opened them, the fight had gone. "No," she whispered. "No, you weren't. What have you done?"

Stan's face softened before hardening again. "I didn't mean to kill him, all right? I just wanted to have it out with him." He looked at Penrose, his voice rising. "I was angry after our row. Why wouldn't I be? I was so fed up with him stalking my wife and making our lives hell. We felt under threat the whole time and I—" His voice cracked. "I just wanted him to stop."

He looked at Penrose, then away. "I asked him to stop. You know what he did? He laughed. Laughed!" Stan's face reddened. "Called me a no-good wife-stealer, said Naomi would eventually come back to him." Stan's hands clenched into fists. "He was patting his notebook the whole time, smirking like he had something hidden. I thought he might have written notes about us, or had photos, or—"

"So you took it," Penrose prompted.

"I snatched it. When he tried to get it back, I put my hand out to stop him, but the rocks were wet from the sea spray and he—" Stan's voice broke completely. "He lost his footing and fell backwards. It happened so fast." Stan put his head in his hands before looking again at his wife. "It was an accident. I didn't mean to kill him."

"If you had been honest from the start, we might have believed you, but you did mean to kill Mim," said Marjorie.

"Why would you do that?" Naomi asked.

"I knew she'd seen me. And when I saw how upset she was after his death, I knew it was only a matter of time before she'd tell the police. She was going to tell them, Naomi. She was going to ruin our marriage. I did it for us."

Naomi stared at him in disbelief. "And what do you think you've just done? I wanted to be free. I thought we were, but not at any cost. You lied to me."

The room fell silent as realisation dawned. His gaze settled on Marjorie. "If you'd just minded your own business—"

Stan's hands clenched and unclenched. For a moment, Marjorie saw the violence that had pushed a man off a cliff, that had held a woman underwater. The same hands were mere feet away from her.

Penrose's voice cut through the tension. "The incident at Tintagel Castle would have most likely been judged as manslaughter," he said. "But your attempt on Miss Butterworth's life was planned and intentional. Stan Carlisle, I'm arresting you for the attempted murder of Miriam Butterfield, and for the murder of Professor Miller. I'll leave it to the prosecution service to decide what charge that ends up being."

Penrose followed procedure, explaining Stan's rights, before summoning uniformed officers with a wave of the hand.

"Naomi, I'm sorry. I'm so sorry."

She couldn't look at him.

Stan Carlisle left the room with the two police officers, his head bowed. Naomi rushed after them, clinging to her husband. "I love you, Stan. I still love you."

The room remained thick with tension after Stan's departure. Marjorie realised her hands were shaking.

"Are you all right?" Frederick asked.

"That man..." Edna patted Marjorie on the shoulder. "Thank God the inspector was here."

Mim, Geraldine and Casey looked shellshocked. Marjorie and friends decided to leave them.

Inspector Penrose accompanied them from the lounge. "It appears I misjudged you four. Thank you for your help. I expect Arthur Denton will also be very grateful. He claims he was going to declare the statuette as Crown treasure but, after Miller's death, he didn't dare mention it because he thought it would incriminate him."

"Which it would have," said Edna.

Inspector Penrose continued. "He doesn't need money, he's a millionaire and has made a fortune from his books."

"I was going to tell you all that," said Frederick. "I've been looking him up."

Edna rolled her eyes.

"Anyway. Thanks, but I don't want to see you lot again. Is that clear?"

"Are you suggesting we're banned from Cornwall, Inspector?" Marjorie asked, chuckling.

Penrose produced a huge grin. "Not quite, but if you do come back, stay out of my sight."

THIRTY

As the four friends strolled along Newquay's beach in the early evening, the rain had long since cleared. The temperature had dropped but was still in double figures. Marjorie wore sturdy shoes, a full-length coat and a scarf to shelter her neck from the wind. Edna was wearing the sensible shoes she and Horace had chosen when they visited Port Isaac, although, not feeling the cold as much as Marjorie did, she wore a light Regatta jacket with a hood. Frederick and Horace wore overcoats and Frederick's hat remained firmly in place thanks to his ingenious solution of a Velcro band, which Marjorie hadn't shared with Edna, who might make fun of him.

The orange light of the setting sun was visible on the cliffs, blinking every so often on the sea in the distance as if saying goodnight. Edna was delighted they had agreed to fulfil her wish of outdoor fish and chips. After delaying their earlier walk to wrap up the investigation, Marjorie had succumbed to Edna's whim. Her cousin-in-law chattered like an excited schoolgirl and had been bouncing up and down ever since they bought their fish suppers. Her joy, Marjorie imagined, was as much about having the crime solved and being able to 'crack on with our holiday', as she put it, as it was about fish and chips on the beach.

They moved away from the firm sand to a path and found a comfortable bench. As Marjorie unwrapped the traditional white wrapping paper, she inwardly admitted that the aroma of fish and chips mixed with sea salt was a delight.

Horace offered a warning. "Watch out for marauding gulls. They have no fear in these places and will have your chips out of your hands as quick as a pickpocket snatches a wallet."

"We'll be okay," said Frederick, "they're more interested in those two fishing boats coming in with the day's catch."

Marjorie watched the gulls trying their luck with the boats but the fish were well packed. They gave up and started diving for any fish disturbed by the boats' movements instead. "Such clever creatures," she remarked.

"Maybe, but they can be a real nuisance," said Horace. "Scared the life out of my grandkids when they were younger."

Marjorie tucked into her fish just in case the gulls decided to head their way; she was enjoying the experience. It had been years since she had done anything as simple as this. She and Ralph had often enjoyed a fish supper before an evening stroll when they stayed at any British seaside resort. Perhaps that's why she had been reluctant to repeat the experience with others. She looked up to see Faith and Nick, hand-in-hand, heading their way. The couple stopped when they reached them.

"Well, well, well," said Nick. "I never thought I'd see Lady Marjorie with a tray of fish and chips outside of a restaurant."

"She's joining the plebs for a bit," said Edna, still munching on a mouthful of chips.

"This isn't a new experience for the aristocracy, you know, nor is it the first time I've enjoyed fish and chips by the beach."

Edna stared, wide-eyed. "You made out it was the lowest of the low."

"I did nothing of the sort. I just didn't see the point of wasting money when dinner's already been paid for. If you must know, it was something Ralph and I did together."

"Oh, I see," said Edna without sarcasm. She, Frederick and Horace all knew what it was to have loved and lost. "Although it's hard to imagine you with your fingers covered in grease."

"Hardly that. It wasn't the Dark Ages, they did have wooden forks in those days."

"Like the one you're using now?" said Nick, clearly amused.

"No, it was one of those two-pronged things. We would stab at the chips and hope for the best. Fish was always the more challenging to eat. But it was more about the setting, creating atmospheric memories and enjoying each other's company."

"Like now," said Edna. "I haven't enjoyed myself this much in a long time." Having finished her meal, she scrunched the paper over the tray.

"Indeed," said Marjorie, realising that sometimes the simplest things could bring the most pleasure.

Faith looked at them admiringly. "I still can't believe you guys. You've managed to catch a killer again, and yet you take it all in your stride. I would never have guessed it was Stan Carlisle. How did you work it out?"

"It was all Marjorie this time," said Horace.

"Not all," said Marjorie, before Edna went into a sulk. "If Edna and Horace hadn't caught Casey with the professor's notebook and Edna hadn't found out how important Arthur Denton's ancestry was to him, we wouldn't have made any further enquiries. And if Frederick hadn't agreed to an impromptu foray in Mim's room, we wouldn't have found her diary. That was important. What bothered me about Mim's entry was her reference to seeing her and him. If she had been referring to the Carlisles, she'd have written 'them'. 'They' being a couple. Most couples are referred to as a unit, separating the pronouns like that didn't make sense. I couldn't believe it was

Arthur Denton, although I did feel there was more to his story than he let on. And apart from when he was listening in to conversations and trying to find out what Professor Miller was up to, he was always writing. We now know his Miller interest related to the gold statuette. We're a team, you see."

"Yep," said Horace, wiping his hands on a handkerchief. "We work well together."

"You won't be surprised to hear Naomi's returned to Cambridge. I can't help feeling sorry for her."

"Some women choose the wrong blokes," said Edna.

Nick put a protective arm around Faith as if shielding her from her past choices. "And Mim will make a full recovery," he said. "Thanks to you lot."

"More thanks to that doctor on the beach," said Frederick.

"Casey and Mim are happy to continue the tour even with our diminished numbers. Arthur Denton is on his way back, having been released without charge," said Faith. "He asked me to thank you but I expect he'll want to do it personally when he arrives."

"If he doesn't choke on his words I might owe him an apology as well," said Edna. "I gave him a hard time about his ancestry. But, if you ask me, he's still a strange one."

"Not as strange as a bunch of fogeys in their eighties insisting on playing amateur detective," muttered Frederick, as he too scrunched the remains of his chip paper into a ball.

"There is one thing I've been meaning to ask," said Marjorie. "For clarification. Did Professor Miller book onto the tour before or after the Carlisles?"

"After," said Faith.

"So he was the Professor Vile the Carlisles said he was," said Edna. "I'm with Faith, it's a shame for Naomi. She suffered at his hands for years and still doesn't get the happy ending she deserves."

"Which is Stan's doing," said Marjorie. "He should have

taken his wife's advice. And attacking Mim in that way was unforgivable, in my opinion."

"We're just happy it's all over," said Faith. "I'd like to go back to what we're good at. And on that note, we hope you four will continue the tour," said Faith.

"Wouldn't miss it for the world," said Horace.

"Wonderful. In that case we'll leave you to your evening. After lunch tomorrow we're heading for Perranporth. Edna will be pleased to know its location was the inspiration behind *Poldark*. The author Winston Graham lived there."

"There was a lot of smuggling in that programme," said Nick, winking.

"I've had enough of smuggling to last a lifetime," said Edna. "My interest now lies in scenery, rock pools, and beaches."

Faith and Nick walked on, laughing as they did so.

"Speaking of rock pools, there might be just enough light to see a few before we head back to the hotel," said Frederick.

"You've got to be kidding me," said Edna.

"Now, now, Edna," said Horace. "We've done your thing, so let's do Fred's. By the way, gang: where's our next trip going to be?"

"I think we should wait and see," said Marjorie with a grin. "It's been an eventful few days, but there's still a lot of Cornwall to explore before this one ends."

"As long as we don't find any more bodies," said Frederick. "I'm running out of blood pressure medication."

"We do seem to attract adventure wherever we go," said Marjorie.

"Adventure?" Edna snorted. "Is that what we're calling it now? This time it's been a murder, a near-drowning, and me having to wear sensible bloomin' shoes."

"Don't forget you finally got to wear your hearing aids," said Horace with a chortle. "That's a miracle in itself."

"Yeah well, I can hear you too clearly. I might take them out again."

Don't you dare, thought Marjorie, but kept the thought to herself.

"Well," said Frederick, "at least us travelling together is never boring."

"Now that's a surprising conclusion, coming from you," said Edna. "Did I just hear Frederick Mackworth admit he enjoys our 'adventures'?"

"I said it's not boring," Frederick protested, but he was smiling.

"That's practically an admission you're joining the amateur detective society, Fred," said Horace, which set him and Edna off in one of their joint snorting sessions.

Marjorie watched her three friends with deep affection. "I think we make rather a good team," she said, smiling.

"The awesome foursome strikes again," said Horace once he stopped laughing.

"Oh, for heaven's sake," said Frederick, but he was still grinning.

A LETTER FROM THE AUTHOR

Thank you for reading *Murder on a Bus Tour*. I hope you enjoyed Lady Marjorie and friends' latest outing.

If you want to hear about all my new releases with Storm Publishing, sign up here:

www.stormpublishing.co/dawn-brookes

And if you want to keep in touch about all my books, and receive a free novella, sign up here:

www.dawnbrookespublishing.com/subscribe

If you enjoyed this book and could spare a few moments to leave a review that would be hugely appreciated. Even a short review can make all the difference in encouraging a reader to discover my books for the first time. Thank you so much.

The Lady Marjorie Snellthorpe Mystery series follows a spirited quartet of octogenarians who prove that age is no barrier to sleuthing. Led by Lady Marjorie, they bring decades of life experience and distinct social backgrounds to the world of crime-solving.

United by their sharp minds and a shared love for justice, they navigate their differences with humour and heart. Though they may not always agree, when it comes to solving murders, they're an unstoppable force.

I created this series to celebrate the wisdom, humour, and

resilience that come with age, showing that even in their golden years, these four are far from done with adventure.

Thanks again for being part of this amazing journey with me and I hope you'll stay in touch – I have so many more stories and ideas to entertain you with.

Dawn Brookes

facebook.com/dawnbrookespublishing

tiktok.com/@dawnbrookesauthor

youtube.com/dawnbrookespublishing

bookbub.com/authors/dawn-brookes

ACKNOWLEDGEMENTS

As always, thank you to my best friends Sue and Ruth for their early reads and suggestions. They have been with me since I reinvented myself as a writer in 2016 and never seem to mind when I spend our holidays looking for murder scenes.

I'm extremely thankful to my loyal band of readers and reviewers who make the writing worthwhile.

I'd like to thank Naomi Knox from Storm for her edits and suggestions which have gone a long way to making the final version a polished and satisfying read. Thank you to the rest of the editing team at Storm Publishing who bring the whole thing together and ready for publication.

Thank you to cover designer Emily Courdelle for another wonderful cover.

A huge thanks to everyone else at Storm who work so hard to bring books to life, and who have believed in me and the Lady Marjorie Snellthorpe series and were happy to commit to putting the books in the hands of more readers.

Thanks to my family and immediate circle of friends who are so patient with me when I'm absorbed in my fictional world and for your continued support in all my endeavours.